THR3E

By Twyla Turner

©Copyright Twyla Turner
Cover Art: Africa Studio/Shutterstock.com

This book is a work of fiction. Names, characters, businesses, places, events and incidents are either the product of the author's imagination or used in a fictitious manner. Any resemblances to actual persons, living or dead, or actual events is purely coincidental.

To my family and friends for your continued support and encouragement. And to my readers- your reviews, excitement for my stories and spreading the word about them; means more to me than you'll ever know.

Other Books by Twyla Turner

The Struck Series
Star-Struck
Awe-Struck

Damaged Souls Series
Scarred
Open Wounds – Coming Soon

Table of Contents:

Chapter 1
Chapter 2
Chapter 3
Chapter 4
Chapter 5
Chapter 6
Chapter 7
Chapter 8
Chapter 9
Chapter 10
Chapter 11
Chapter 12
Chapter 13
Chapter 14
Chapter 15
Chapter 16
Chapter 17
Acknowledgements
About the Author
Connect with Me

Chapter 1

"YES! Amber, I passed! I passed! I passed my clinicals! I'm officially an RN!" Simone screamed as she shut her laptop and jumped off of her bed after checking her final grades online.

Simone ran into her roommate and best friend's room and leapt onto the bed Amber was currently occupying, jumping up and down. Her heavy braid that contained her thick jet black wavy hair smacked her back every time she came down from a huge bounce. And her large black horn-rimmed glasses slid down her nose, making her look more like an elementary school teacher or librarian than a fresh out of nursing school, RN.

"Oof, you're killing me Simone!" Amber grunted as each bounce jarred her once relaxed body. "I don't think I've seen this much enthusiasm out of you since...well, ever." Amber tried to hide her smile.

"Oh, come on. Jump with me. I need to celebrate." Simone pouted.

"Well jumping on a bed like a seven year old is not the way to celebrate a grown up accomplishment. We should go have some drinks. Get wasted!" Amber jumped up at the idea, starting to jump with Simone. Simone knew that if there was any reason to drink Amber would get excited.

"Eh, I don't know about that. I'm fine celebrating right here, with maybe a movie and some popcorn." Simone plopped down on the bed out of breath and panting. *I really should start working out. Whew!*

"Aw come on, Simone! You never go out. And I mean *never* go out. This is a huge moment for you. We should really celebrate it, like any normal person would. Especially before you go off to the wilds of Alaska to find your mother's tribe, leaving me all alone." Amber pouted her naturally full red lips at Simone.

"Oh you're meeting me up there in about a week after your interview, so stop pouting." Simone said, not falling for Amber's ploy. "So how about we get some champagne and just drink here? I'd be willing to do that." Simone bargained.

"How are you *ever* going to lose your virginity, if you don't get out there to meet anyone?" Amber said rolling her eyes in exasperation.

"Even if I did go out, no guys would be interested anyway. I'm a nerd and fat. No guys ever pay attention to me, and I'm okay with that. I'm too busy with my career right now to focus on anything else." Simone defended.

"Simone Dyani Staton! You are not a nerd and you are *not* fat! You just like to read and study more than most people and you have curves to die for. I'm a stick-figure, and I hate it. No boobs, no ass, no hips…a fucking carpenter's dream…straight and flat as a board." Amber said as she twisted and turned to look at her tall lean five-foot-nine frame.

"Oh yeah, then the world must be full of carpenters, because guys are constantly falling all over themselves to talk to you. Oh and not to mention the yearly flyers you get from the random people that pass them out for try-outs for *America's Next Top Model*." Simone smiled at Amber knowingly. The redhead was gorgeous and she knew it. Luckily for Simone she wasn't a stuck up bitch about it.

"Shut up! I do not get one a year!" Amber blushed.

"Ha! I know you save them in your nightstand, on the off chance that you'll finally give in and really try-out." Simone knew she had her.

"Fine! I get a lot of them…and maybe just maybe, I keep them. But that still doesn't change the fact that you need to meet someone. Hell, you don't have to date them. Just have a booty-call and pop that damn cherry already! You just turned twenty-nine for Christ's sake! That shit ain't normal! Plus, there's nothing like a guy that can lay some good pipe." Amber said as she pulled on a pair of jeans over her slender hips. They were perfectly distressed and holey, which she'd done herself. Amber was a brilliant designer and seamstress. And had an interview for a seamstress position for an up and coming fashion house based out of Seattle.

"Gross, Amber! Besides you can't miss what you've never had. I'm okay with being a spinster or old-maid. So love doesn't come easily for me. Well, studying does. Understanding biology and science does. Getting my career in order does. I can live with that." Simone said with a conviction that she wasn't so sure she truly felt.

She thought that it would be nice to have someone. To be kissed passionately. For a man to look at her and fall head-over-heels. But that's not the way her life worked. It never had, and she'd become mildly content with the way things had turned out. Mainly focusing on her career, since that was all she had.

Her dad, Carl Staton had died in the Gulf War when she was a little girl. And her mother Halona died of a brain aneurysm when Simone was eighteen, a few months before she was to leave for college. Her mother's death had shocked and devastated her, and college was put to the wayside. Though her mother had been an RN, being a single parent, she hadn't saved up a lot of money. So Simone had to fend for herself for the next four years, working multiple jobs to take care of herself. When she was finally ready, when her heartbreak had subsided enough to focus again on school, at twenty-three she went back to school, luckily everything was paid for because of her half Native American heritage.

Simone's mother had been full Tanana tribe, one of the numerous tribes of Alaska. And Black-American made up her other half on her father's side. Both of her parents had been only children, so there were no aunts or uncles to go to. And her mother's tribe hadn't been pleased that Halona had left the reservation and they basically disowned her. So Simone had no one until she met Amber her freshman year at Washington State University.

Amber and her family took Simone in and treated her like one of their own. Being four years younger than Simone, Amber was like a little sister to her. Simone kept Amber on the straight and narrow, which Amber's parents loved her for. And Amber infused life and impulsiveness (well as impulsive as Simone ever got) into her life.

Simone was going to miss Amber for the first week of her trip to Alaska, to find her mother's tribe and family. They had been pretty much inseparable since they met. So she was nervous to head up there on her own, but she had been planning and saving for this trip for several years and had to be brave enough until Amber could meet up with her later. Having no family made her yearn to find her mother's tribe.

"Okay. So how about this? We can at least go to my parents' house to celebrate you passing nursing school. We could grab a bottle of champagne on the way. I'll call them and my brother and sister to let them know. How about that?" Amber asked before adding, "Plus, they all want to see you before you go on your trip. Come on…you know you want to." Amber coaxed, as she dragged Simone out the front door.

Chapter 2

Sunday afternoon, Jackson Cole pulled up to The Drake Lodge & Sled Tours, owned by his best and oldest friend and housemate, Xander Drake. Jackson also owned his own company, J.C. Lumber in Fairbanks, Alaska. But this week he was going to take a few days off to help Xander, who was short staffed this week because of a flu outbreak. And Xander had a young woman coming in from Washington. She was coming into town for a few weeks to find, meet and learn about the Tanana Tribe in the surrounding area.

Xander was taking out time for the girl's first week here to show her the ropes of working with the dogsleds and show her the area. And Xander preferred to go out with more than one guide, but needed what was left of his staff to assist his other guests that were steadily coming in for the Northern Lights, which was at its busiest right now after the holidays. So Jackson had volunteered to help him as a secondary guide for the girl, since he also had plenty of experience with the dogsleds.

Jackson got out of his pickup truck and slammed the door. It was noon and still dark, being that time of year. The lack of sun in the winter and too much sun in the summer got under the skin of many from the lower forty-eight, but it was all he'd known his thirty-two years. He hoped this girl could adjust to it, because he wasn't in the mood to tolerate a bunch of bitching and moaning.

As Jackson walked into the lodge, Xander looked up from talking to the front desk rep. "Hey, Jax! You here to grab some lunch?" Xander said before walking over and clapping his friend on the back.

"Yeah. And to bring you a couple fifths of whiskey from the house, just in case this girl is a brat. You know how the girls from the lower forty-eight can be." Jackson raised one eyebrow as he pulled the bottles from the inside pockets of his coat, just thinking about the pampered girls. Life in Alaska could be rough, and took a lot of backbone.

"Aw come on dude! We haven't even met her yet. We don't know for sure how she'll be. And having a fresh face around here wouldn't hurt either." Xander waggled his brows at Jackson.

Jackson shook his head at his friend. "A one track mind."

"Hey man, we haven't been with anyone in months. The last was Tracy. And she turned out to be one mean manipulative cheating bitch." Xander shuddered.

They had always had an unusual relationship. Early on, they had realized that they more often than not had the same taste in women. And instead of fighting over them, they just chose to share them. The arrangement worked out well if the girl in question was okay with it. It wasn't the strangest thing in the world in Alaska, considering the ratio of men to women. It was slim pickings, so they worked with what they got.

Jackson knew that it had been a while since they had been with anyone, but he was getting tired of things going nowhere with the women they dated. He wasn't sure if Xander was ready for anything serious, considering his free spirit, but Jackson was ready. And the fact that he knew every single woman in a hundred mile radius only made him more depressed. He wanted none of them and whenever women from the lower forty-eight came to town they rarely stayed. So the prospects for his future, *their* future, looked bleak.

Tires crunching through the hard packed snow brought Jackson out of his reverie.

"That must be her. Mike went to pick her up from the airport. Oh and by the way, her name is Simone Staton." Xander said as he started to make his way to the door.

Jackson followed him to the landing at the top of the stairs in front of the lodge. He could make out two people with bags making their way to the stairs. As Simone came into the soft lamp light Jackson caught his breath and sensed Xander's reaction as well. She was bundled up like an Eskimo, not used to the cold of an Alaskan winter, but living his whole life there Jackson could see beauty even wrapped in a hat, scarf and puffy down coat.

She had beautiful downturned dark brown eyes, which could only be described as permanent bedroom eyes. She had a straight nose, broad high cheekbones and extra full lips and a wide mouth, that begged to be kissed. And her skin was a rich smooth toasted caramel color with tones of red underneath. Jackson wasn't sure what her exact nationality was, but he knew from experience that Native American was in there somewhere without having been told beforehand, with those exotic looks.

"Hello." She spoke in a soft shy voice, looking anywhere but at him or Xander for that matter.

"Hello. Simone, right?" Jackson reached out to shake her hand and shivered at the contact, when she took his hand.

"Yes." Her voice quivered.

"I'm Jackson Cole and this is Xander Drake, the owner of the lodge." Jackson nudged Xander to bring him out of his stupor.

"Uh...oh, sorry. Hi, I'm Xander. It's nice to meet you, Simone." Xander finally remembering his manners, reached out to shake her hand as well. He took a little longer than was polite to release her hand.

"Here, let's get inside before you freeze to death. I'm sure you're not used to this frigid weather." Jackson stepped aside to let her in.

"Thanks." She said softly.

Hmm...she's a quiet one.

Once inside Xander offered to take her coat, hat and scarf as Mike took her bags to her room. As she shrugged off her coat, unwrapped her scarf and took off her hat, she revealed more of her body, enclosed in a fitted flannel shirt and boot-cut jeans that hugged her hips, ass and thighs. Jackson had to swallow several times from the saliva that had pooled in his mouth.

She had an ass that made a man want to weep. Solid thighs, large hips, a waist that curved in dramatically in comparison to her lower half and perfect perky full little breasts. It was an hourglass shape, if the hourglass's bottom half was quite a bit bigger. A body made for a man to hold on to, to gain leverage as he slammed into her again and again.

Jackson shook his head trying to get himself together, because things were getting a little uncomfortable in his jeans. He looked over at Xander, who was also staring and fidgeting. Simone just looked around the lobby of the lodge or the floor, anywhere but at them. Jackson realized that their silence and staring were making her uncomfortable.

"Uh, this is a really beautiful lodge." Simone said softly, pushing up her glasses and tugging nervously on her long braid, as she bravely tried to look at them from under her long lashes.

Jackson knew that most girls did that kind of move to be coy and seductive. This girl didn't have a seductive bone in her body, but it nearly brought him to his knees regardless.

"Thank you. I had it built about five years ago, when I got tired of working for this chump." Xander piped in, finally finding his normally talkative and flirtatious personality. "But for once Jackson will work for me this week." He jabbed Jackson in the ribs with his elbow.

"Don't get used to it, Xan. And if you try to boss me around even once this week, you're gonna find your ass tied to the back of my sled, being dragged across Fairbanks." Jackson punched Xander in the arm.

Simone bit down on her lips to keep from laughing. "What will you be doing this week Jackson?" She said as she stared at his chin.

Wow! This girl can't even make eye contact. God would I love to bring her out of her shell. Hmm...maybe by the end of her trip. Jackson mentally rubbed his hands together with glee.

"He'll be coming along with us on your first dogsled tour. So you'll have the both of us. I like having two guides on a novice run, one in the front and the other taking up the rear." Xander said barely containing his smile.

Jackson picked up on the double entendre and mentally shook his head. *Real subtle, Xander.*

"Oh. Um...okay." Simone said looking down at the floor.

"Let's show you around and get you settled. I'm sure you're tired from your trip and would like to get a little rest before we set out tomorrow." Jackson said, taking over the dominant leader roll, as usual.

"Yes. Thank you."

~~~

OH MY GOD! Simone thought as she walked into her room after the tour Xander and Jackson took her on. Simone had never been around such rugged gorgeous men in her life. She'd had absolutely no idea what to do with herself or where to look, because if she looked, she'd never stop staring.

Jackson was all serious, dominant manly man. He was a giant. Simone figured he was somewhere around six-foot-five, considering he stood about a foot taller than her average five-foot-five height. And he was built with solid muscle. Chopping wood must do a body good. If there was any sun this time of year, the span of his shoulders alone would block out the light. His hair was unruly curls of chestnut that curled around his ears and collar of his red and black flannel, and flopped on his forehead, giving him a slightly boyish look. From the quick glances she was able to make when she felt brave enough, she saw that he had piercing gray eyes, a firm mouth, his bottom lip was plumper than the top and a square jawline that was so chiseled you could crack walnuts on it. The sexy five o'clock shadow came together with the overall look to make him appear like he'd just walked off of *GQ's* Lumberjack Edition.

Xander was beautiful. Like what you'd think the archangel Gabriel would look like. He was also tall, not quite as tall as Jackson, but close. He was also a little more lean than his burly friend, like a swimmer, but no less formidable. And his features were light, like his flirty personality. His wheat blond hair was mostly straight, but waved just a little at the ends, to make him look like a shaggy surfer. He had hazel eyes that bordered on green, with crazy full kissable lips and dangerously sexy dimples that made the heart melt.

They were emphatically the most beautiful men Simone had ever had the pleasure of being in the company of. And she had no earthly idea how she was going to spend the next few days with them, let alone the next couple of weeks. Staying at the lodge, she'd be sure to see Xander all of the time, but if Jackson was his best friend, it was pretty likely that she'd run into him a lot as well.

Simone shook her head, trying to get the image of the two sexy men out of her mind. It wasn't as if they'd ever be interested in her anyway. And even if they were, she'd have no idea which one to pick. She was equally attracted to both. *Maybe I could have both. Wouldn't Amber just love that! Keep dreaming Simone.* Simone sighed as she started to unpack her things and preparing a duffle bag for the two day excursion that started in the morning.

She hadn't even had sex with one man, and now she was thinking of two. She thought she must be out of her mind. She had no idea what to even do with the two big men. What she needed to focus on was her research on her family. Studying was what she knew, what she built her life around. Sex and men weren't subjects she knew very well. And who would be interested in her pear-shaped body anyway? Her massive ass, hips and thighs and bookish ways didn't inspire too many sonnets.

As she finished unpacking her luggage and reorganizing her duffle bag, Simone looked around the beautiful modern rustic room. Xander had given her a suite since she was going to be there for a while. It had a little kitchenette, living room and bedroom. The room was decorated in earthy colors and the focal point was a huge king size bed that sat in front of a beautiful fireplace. *I really don't need* that *much bed. But I might as well take advantage while I can.* Simone flopped back on the big bed, thinking that she could get used to it after sleeping on a full-size bed for years in her apartment with Amber. Her mind wandered back to the men she'd be spending a couple of days with…alone. Her stomach flip-flopped at the thought. She had never in her life spent that much time with any man, let alone two. *This should be interesting…and terrifying.*

~~~

Xander sat with Jackson, both having a few beers before lunch. Xander's mind kept going back to the wide hips, round ass and thick thighs of their new guest.

"So…what do you think about Simone?" Xander asked Jackson before taking a sip of his beer.

"I was waiting to see how long it would take you to bring up the subject of your new guest. It actually took you longer than I thought." Jackson smiled at his friend.

"Aw, come on man! You know you couldn't keep your eyes off her either." Xander defended.

"No I couldn't. She's beautiful…but also very shy. I'm not sure she'd be able to handle the kind of relationship we're looking for." Jackson considered.

"We don't know that yet. Maybe we can get her out of her shell. We'll have a couple days alone with her." Xander said, mentally rubbing his hands together.

"Be careful, Xander. You push too hard and she'll run. Plus, she's only here for a couple of weeks. And she may not even stay, and I'm so tired of these relationships not going anywhere." Jackson warned.

"Oh stop being a Debbie Downer. We haven't gotten laid in months, and even then it was mediocre. I need some pus-"

"Hey, Simone!" Jackson cut off Xander before he could finish his crude sentence, when Simone walked into the dining room of the lodge. "Ready for lunch?"

"Yes, thank you." Simone responded shyly.

"Come sit with us. Can I get you a beer?" Xander stood up and pulled out a chair, thankful for Jackson's interruption.

"Uh, I'm not much of a drinker." Simone said as she sat in the chair Xander pulled out for her.

"That's okay. We've got anything you want. Soda, tea, water, juice…anything." Xander suggested.

"You know what? I think I will have a beer." Simone said taking a deep breath, obviously wanting to loosen up.

Xander quickly strode into the kitchen to get her a beer. He hoped that it would relax her enough to make her a little more comfortable around them. Then maybe they could feel her out, see if she might be attracted to both of them as well and would be open to a relationship with both of them.

He grabbed a beer and hightailed it back out to the dining room, not wanting to miss out on the initial bonding it took to get one woman to take on two men. But when he came out of the kitchen all was quiet at their table. Simone's head was down looking at her hands and Jackson was just staring at her silently, like a predator observing his prey.

Xander shook his head. *And Jackson thinks I'd scare her away. His creepy serial killer stare will probably do more damage. Jesus, Charles Manson, lighten up!*

"Here ya go, Simone. Unfortunately we don't have any light beer. But if you sip it, it should be fine." Xander said handing her the ice cold brew.

"Thank you." Simone said softly as Xander sat down on the other side of her.

Simone looked at the men on either side of her. Xander noticed her hand tremble as she reached for the beer bottle. She raised the bottle to her ridiculously full lips and instead of the sip he thought she would take, she chugged down at least a quarter of the beer before she brought it back down to the table. *Wow, she really is nervous. Is it us, are we that intimidating, or does she act like this around all men?*

"So tell us about yourself, Simone." Xander tried to open with.

"Uh, there's really not much to say." Simone started self-consciously.

"Sure there is. How about why exactly are you so interested in learning about the Tanana Tribe?" Xander asked, not willing to give up.

"Well I guess it's because that was my mother's tribe." Simone shrugged.

"'*Was* your mother's tribe?'" Jackson finally joined in.

"I don't have any family. Both of my parents are dead, I have no siblings and both my parents were only children, so no aunts and uncles. The only family on my dad's side are distant relatives. So the only possible family I have left are those on my mother's side. The Tanana Tribe." Simone said sadly.

"I'm so sorry. I didn't mean to bring up a painful subject." Jackson apologized.

Xander looked at Jackson. The look was one of reluctant excitement, sympathy for the obviously lonely woman sitting in between them, but excitement over the fact that she had no one to make her feel ashamed of a polyandry relationship. That was an issue they had had in the past. Women were attracted to them both and wanted them, but fear of what their parents or family would think, stopped them in their tracks.

"It's okay, I've pretty much gotten used to it." Simone reassured him.

"What do you do for a living?" Jackson asked, genuinely interested in the woman sitting between them.

"I just graduated from nursing school. I'm a certified RN. But I haven't started working yet. I got a job at a small family doctor's office, but they let me take the time off between school and work, to take this trip before I start in March." Simone said proudly.

"Wow. Congratulations, Simone! That's a pretty big deal." Jackson smiled at her, and she blushed in response.

"So what about a boyfriend? Don't you have someone back home that's going to miss you for the two weeks you're here?" Xander chimed in, making Jackson give him a death stare at his lack of finesse.

"Uh...um...no, no boyfriend. Just my best friend and roommate, Amber." Simone blush deepened.

"Seriously?! You're gorgeous. You must have a ton of guys chasing after you." Xander exclaimed.

Simone looked up in surprise at the compliment, for the first time making full eye contact with Xander. Her dark brown exotic bedroom eyes stole his breath away.

"No. Guys don't chase me. And don't joke, I know I'm not gorgeous." Simone responded angrily.

"He's not joking, Simone. You're a beautiful woman. Any man would be lucky to have you in their life." Jackson said with authority, his tone clearly conveying that he was not to be argued with.

Simone's eyes swung from Xander's to Jackson's. Jackson's breath caught as well at the first full contact of their eyes.

"I didn't mean to be rude. Thank you for the compliments. It's just that I've spent the majority of my life with my nose in a book and generally being ignored by men." Simone finally broke the connection with Jackson's intense gaze.

"It might be time for that to change." Jackson said matter-of-factly.

Simone's head shot up again to look at Jackson. But Jackson wisely looked away to take another swig of his beer, letting her stew about what he could've possibly meant by his last statement.

Xander took that moment to reach out and clasp her hand. He thumb caressed her knuckles gently.

"Jackson's right. Maybe it's time you got some attention." Xander smiled and winked at her.

Simone ripped her hand away from Xander's and jumped up suddenly. The quick movement tipping over her beer bottle.

"I'm sorry! Uh...I'm not really all that hungry. I'm just gonna go unpack." Simone mumbled quickly and then fled out of the room, not caring about the mess she's made or that she had already unpacked.

"I told you she would run if you moved too quickly, Xan." Jackson shook his head as he sopped up the spilled beer with his napkin.

"Whatever man! You didn't help either with your creepy stalker stare you were giving her." Xander joked.

"Forgive me for being the serious one. Someone has to counteract your knuckle-headed jackass ways." Jackson punched his friend playfully.

"Do you really think I scared her away for good?" Xander asked, worried.

"Nah. She'll come around. We just need to be patient, which I know patience isn't your strong suit. But I do believe she's attracted to us. So it's just a matter of time," Jackson reassured his friend. "But in the meantime, let's send some lunch up to her room. I'm sure she's still hungry. And I don't want her to starve because of her fear of us."

Simone slammed the door to her suite and leaned back against it, trying to calm her breathing and pounding heart. *OMG! What was that?!* Never in her life had she felt an attraction to a man quite like what she felt for *both* men. And she may have zero experience with men, but she was pretty sure that both of them were flirting with her. Jackson was more subtle than Xander, but still no less obvious.

What she didn't know was if they were just messing with her. Was she a joke to them? A little harmless fun to pass the time? But Jackson had seemed dead serious when he'd told her she was beautiful. So then was it a game to them? Who can get the girl first? And if so, she'd have no idea which one to choose, she was equally attracted to both. *Who am I kidding, there is no way either of those two gorgeous men could be interested in me. I have to be misunderstanding their intentions. But Amber would kill me if I didn't at least try to open up to at least one of them.*

A knock at the door startled her and she jumped away and turned around to open it. When Simone saw that it was one of the girls on the staff her heart dropped in disappointment at the fact that it wasn't one of the guys. *Really Simone?!*

"Uh hi." Simone said awkwardly.

"Hi. Mr. Cole asked that you be brought your lunch." The girl said sweetly as she handed Simone the tray of food.

"Oh, thank you. If you could tell Mr. Cole, 'Thank you' for me, I'd really appreciate it."

"Sure, no problem." The girl said and then turned, heading back downstairs.

Well that was thoughtful, Simone thought as she took the lid off of the tray and the smell and sight of a burger and fries hit her, one of her favorites. *Hmm, he made a good choice. I didn't even say what I wanted.* She sat at the small dining table and tucked into the delicious food.

She decided to stay in her suite the rest of the evening, opting to order in her dinner. She didn't want to have any more awkward run-ins with the handsome men. She knew she'd have to deal with them completely alone for two full days. At least that would be on a more professional level. Learning how to work the dogsleds and checking out the land that her mother's tribe occupied was what she could focus on, instead of Jackson and Xander. Well, at least she hoped she could.

Chapter 3

Simone woke up to her alarm clock blaring at five in the morning. They were set to head out at eight, but Xander wanted her downstairs and outside at six to bond with the dogs.

Simone jumped in the shower, threw her hair in two quick French braids and put on her brand new snowboarding pants that Amber had insisted she get. They went shopping at *R.E.I.* for extreme winter gear. And Amber had forced Simone to get the more stylish clothing, better suited for ski bunnies, than bookworms. But Amber had promised she'd be warm and cute at the same time. Simone just took her word for it.

The pants were a bright turquoise, fitted in the hips and butt and flared at the calves. She had gotten the matching jacket in white with turquoise piping with a faux fur trimmed hood. And last she slipped on her faux fur lined black boots. Grabbing a knit hat and gloves, she left her room and headed outside and around back to the kennels in the back of the lodge.

It was of course dark out, but the bright overhead light posts brightened the area like it was daylight. Xander was already there feeding the dogs, and Simone's stomach flip-flopped at the sight of him. He was wearing a slightly fitted winter jumpsuit in navy blue with lime-green trim. The top half of the suit was hanging around his hips and he was just in a fitted thermal long-sleeved shirt that clung to his strong back.

The dogs yelped at the sight of Simone, alerting Xander to her presence. He turned around and his eyes ate her up from head to toe as she walked towards him. She had never been looked at like that before. On one hand it was totally flattering and on the other it was seriously intimidating.

"Wow! What you do for ski pants should be illegal!" Xander admired her lower half.

At the compliment Simone did something she had never done a day in her life. She giggled like a schoolgirl.

Her giggle turned instantly into a scowl, unhappy with her reaction to the handsome man.

"I appreciate the compliment, but if you could refrain from making comments like that in the future, I would greatly appreciate it. I don't like sounding like the very girls I can't stand. I don't do giggly." Simone said in a no-nonsense tone.

Xander's mouth hung open in shock. Simone assumed it was because he'd never been spoken to like that by a woman. They all probably fell at his feet. *Well, get used to it buddy.*

"Huh? Well I've never gotten quite that reaction from a female before." Xander said, confirming her thoughts. "You're gonna be one tough nut to crack." Xander said, clearly showing he wasn't giving up.

"You don't need to crack anything. Maybe you should just start introducing me to the dogs." Simone stood her ground.

"Yes ma'am." Xander straightened his back and saluted Simone militantly.

Simone held back a chuckle at his silly antics as he led her over to the Alaskan Huskies. *Is he ever serious?*

"Rarely. People take life way too seriously. Where's the fun in that?" Xander answered the question that Simone had thought she'd only said in her head, with a shrug.

"I…uh…I thought I only said that in my head." Simone responded sheepishly.

"It's okay. I've heard that all my life. I was the class clown in school. I think that's why Jackson and I became friends. I help him loosen up and he brings me down to earth." Xander smiled absentmindedly as he scooped more dog food into a metal cup that he handed her to pour into one of the dog's bowls.

"Why is Jackson so serious?" Simone asked shyly as she poured the food into the bowl and scratched at the dog's head.

"Well I probably shouldn't say, but basically Jackson, his parents and younger brother were in a horrible boating accident when we were in the third grade and Jackson was the only survivor." Simone gasped and covered her mouth with her hands, dropping the metal cup. "He was raised by his grandparents. He was a carefree kid until that day. We became best friends that year and have been ever since."

Simone saw an actual glimpse of seriousness in Xander as he finished the story, reaching down to grab the cup she had dropped. As he stood back up, the Husky she had just fed jumped up on her back, pushing her into Xander. Instinct made him wrap his arms around her to steady her.

Simone froze as her body started to react like it never had before. All of a sudden her heart started to beat so hard, it felt like it was going to come out her chest. Her whole body started to tremble uncontrollably. Her skin became overheated and flushed, like she had a sudden fever.

And just when she thought that her body had betrayed her beyond reason, Xander relinquished one arm from around her waist and raised his hand to her chin lifting her face up to look at him. His eyes locked with hers and he caressed her full bottom lip with his thumb and her body committed further treason. Her heart seemed to split, because now not only was her heart pounding in her chest, it also felt like it was pounding down "there" too.

"God, you're so beautiful!" Xander said as his face descended towards hers.

Simone drew in a sharp breath, in anticipation as his full lips came closer to hers. His lips made contact, brushing softly against hers. The feeling sent shocking tingles all threw her body and the jolt made Simone stagger backwards. Not realizing the dog was still there, when the backs of her calves hit the Husky, Simone lost her balance trying to avoid stepping on him and landed on her ass in the snow.

Before Simone could get mad or embarrassed the dogs converged on her. A lick fest commenced on her and before long, she couldn't stop from laughing at the playful wet laps the dogs were giving her.

"I'm so sorry Simone. I didn't mean to get so carried away." Xander apologized as he extended a hand to help her up, as he gave her a reluctant grin. "I guess that was a little unprofessional of me to make a pass at you." He said looking a little bashful, like a little boy caught with his hand in the cookie jar.

"Uh…it's okay. But please don't do it again. I need to stay focused on finding my family. I don't have time for men, romance and flowery stuff. I have my career to think about and my family. And that means more to me than love." Simone said as she brushed off the snow from her pants and wiped the dog drool from her face. *Great! Now I'm going to smell like dog. Ah well, that's probably a good thing, maybe that will keep him away.*

"Mmm…," was his only reply, like he wasn't willing to agree one way or another.

~~~

Simone had no idea how right she was. Xander wanted her, wanted both of them to have her unlike any other woman they had encountered since he and Jackson had started this unusual arrangement. The moment he had seen her come out of the lodge with the fitted snowboarder pants and jacket accentuating her ridiculous curves, and her long hair contained in schoolgirl braids resting against her pert breasts, he'd thought he'd lose his mind if they couldn't have her.

No matter what she said in regards to not wanting love and men in her life, he knew from the brief brushing of their lips that she wanted him. He just hoped that she was equally interested in

Jackson. Because if she was, they'd have her in every possible way they could.

Considering their unusual setup, they didn't think of themselves as one or the other. They were one. A package deal. If you wanted one, you better want the other as well. They didn't do relationships without the other. They weren't into each other, they weren't gay. But they preferred to share a woman's affections. They wanted to pamper, protect and pleasure their woman. And they were comfortable enough in their masculinity to share and be naked around each other during their numerous sexual acts with any particular woman they were dating. And Xander couldn't think of anything better than being naked with this particular woman.

But this woman wasn't going to be easy. Simone had an intense focus on her career and she seemed extremely innocent. *I wonder how old she is, because she seems almost virginal. But she's a graduate, so she has to at the very least be twenty-two. So there's no way that she could still be a virgin!* Though when he contemplated the slight kiss they'd just shared, it seemed as if Simone didn't even know what she was doing. *Fuck! And that was just a* kiss*!!!*

Trying to keep his passion under wraps, Xander started introducing Simone to all of the dogs.

"So this is Sampson and Delilah and they are leaders of one sled team. They're mother and father to the rest of the dogs on their team." He pointed out and named all of their pups. "This is Midnight and Snow. Midnight is the male and Snow is the female, a brother and sister duo and they lead this team of rebel rousers." Xander said pointing to the jet black male and pure white female and the rest of their group.

Simone petted and cooed to each dog he named off. "And last of the leads of the teams that we're going to use is Romeo and Juliet." In which the whole team had names from the classic play.

"They're beautiful Xander." Simone exclaimed as she scratched the scruff of Romeo's neck.

"And so are you." A deep voice said from behind them.

Xander and Simone both turned around to see Jackson watching them, but mostly his eyes were on Simone as he leaned against the kennel fence reflectively.

"Hey Jax! It's about time you made your way out here. I thought I'd have to drag your ass out of bed for a minute there." Xander taunted Jackson, as Simone just blushed.

"I didn't want to take away from Simone bonding with the dogs. But I thought I'd come out and get you for breakfast. I know you can get carried away with your babies and I didn't want our guest to starve to death during the trip." Jackson shot back.

"Aw whatever man! I didn't starve you, did I Simone?" Xander smiled down at her and not making eye contact she just shook her head no. "See, she's fine. The dogs make you forget everything, they're so cute." Simone smiled up at him at that, and he just winked at her. "Come on, let's go eat. We have a long ride ahead of us, and you'll get hungry. Trust me." Xander said to Simone, leading the way into the lodge.

Once inside, Xander sat Simone at his favorite table and then asked Jackson to help him grab their food.

"What? What happened? I know you didn't ask me in here just to help you with food, when you could've asked the staff to get it for you." Jackson prodded Xander anxiously as they walked into the kitchen.

"I kissed her…well kind of." Xander blurted out.

"And…?" Jackson waited impatiently.

"Well, it's hard to tell. She was definitely into it, but something spooked her. I swear to God Jackson I think she's still a virgin!" Xander loudly whispered.

"Get the fuck outta here!" Jackson exclaimed.

"I'm tellin' you man! I don't think she's ever even been kissed before. It was like she had no idea what to do." Xander said, still in shock.

"Well...shit! It's hard enough to find a woman who has experience to not get freaked out about having a relationship with two men. But a *virgin*?! I mean, I like the idea of us being the only men she's ever been with-"

"Fuck yeah! It's hot!" Xander cut Jackson off.

"But...I know we're going to scare her away." Jackson looked at Xander with worry.

"Yeah. And she kinda snapped at me. She told me that she doesn't have time for men or romance. Man, she's got some fire under that shy exterior. She'll probably be magnificent when she comes out of her shell." Xander smiled plotting all the ways he wanted them to do it.

Jackson smiled and wrapped his arm around Xander's neck, putting him in a brotherly headlock. "I know what you're thinking…'we're just the men to do it'. Hell, I'm willing to give it a shot." Jackson roughed up Xander's hair before releasing his neck.

"Good. You have to try to see if she's attracted to you. And if she is…game on!" Xander rubbed his hands together with glee.

"Dude, this is not a game. And she's not like the other girls we've been with. We can't go barreling in like bulls in a china shop. This may take some finesse, which I know you have little of." Jackson shook his head at his best friend as he grabbed some plates and headed back out to the dining room.

~~~

"Can I walk you to your room to help you bring down your bags for the trip?" Jackson asked Simone after they finished their breakfast.

"Sure, that would be really nice. Thank you." Simone accepted bashfully.

Jackson stood up and pulled out Simone's chair for her. He gave Xander a quick look and his friend gave him the thumbs up as they headed out of the dining room.

They walked to the elevator in silence. Once inside, they both reached to press the button for the third floor at the same time. Their skin made contact and Jackson felt a jolt at her touch that radiated through his body and straight to groin. *God, I want her. Please let her give us a chance.*

He silently watched her under his lashes as she faced forward, avoiding eye contact with him. Jackson noticed that her chest rose and fell heavily, as if she was out of breath. *So you aren't immune to me. You feel it too.* Jackson knew that if she felt this way about Xander as well, that it would only be a matter of time before they convinced her that the relationship they sought with her would suit her perfectly. *But how do you tell a possible virgin that you want to share her with another man? That some nights we would take turns pleasing her, and other nights we would take her at the same time. Double penetration isn't something you just bring up in polite conversation.*

The elevator reached the third floor and they both got off. Jackson tried to think of safe subjects to talk about, to get her to open up. He knew he only had a small window of time to make sure she was into him individually from Xander. She had to be attracted to both equally in order for this to work, but most women weren't going to show that she was into two men at the same time if they were in the same room. This moment alone with her was pivotal.

"I know this is rude to ask a female this question, but I wanna ask it anyway…how old are you, Simone? I know you just finished school, so you have to at least be twenty-two or twenty-three, right?" Jackson looked down at Simone as they walked along the hallway to her suite.

"Oh I don't mind saying my age. I'm twenty-nine." Simone said softly.

"Really?! You seem so much younger, especially with these braids." Jackson reached out to touch a braid as they came to a stop in front of her suite door.

Jackson watched as Simone's breath hitched in her throat. He faced her and gently grabbed both braids that were lying against her breasts. The backs of his fingers barely grazed the tops of her breasts. He noticed the pulse in her neck quicken and her body start to tremble slightly. Jackson pulled smoothly on the braids, forcing Simone's head back to look up at him. Her already sloped bedroom eyes looked even more heavy-lidded behind her glasses. Her full lush lips were parted and her breath rushed out in anticipation.

"I...I...I waited 'til later to get m...my undergrad in Biology. Then...then I took a br...break, working full-time to...to save up more money f...for nursing school. That's wh...why I'm so much ol...older." Simone said nervously, obviously trying to distract Jackson from his apparent intent.

"You've worked hard, and I'm sure your parents would be really proud of you." Simone's eyes widened slightly at Jackson's thoughtful words. "And I know your career is very important to you. But don't you think you should enjoy yourself sometime? Enjoying life makes all the hard work worth it, don't you think?" Jackson finished, caressing his knuckles down her cheek.

All Simone could do was nod her head yes, mesmerized by his piercing gray gaze.

"I thought so." Jackson replied as his lips descended towards her.

Jackson gave Simone a soft gentle kiss on the side of her mouth and her breath drew in sharply. He pulled back just enough to brush his lips across hers and then kissed the other side of her mouth. Simone held her breath the whole time. *She's gonna pop a lung if she doesn't breathe soon.*

"Breathe, Simone. Just enjoy it." Jackson whispered against her lips.

Simone blew out a ragged breath and then drew in much needed oxygen.

Jackson rested his forehead against hers, as he too drew in a breath to calm his pounding heart and cool down his raging need for her.

"Have you ever been kissed before Simone, besides today?" Jackson asked as his breathing calmed, not giving away the fact that he knew Xander had a small taste of her earlier.

"Well, kind of, one time in high school." Simone tried to look away, but Jackson brought her face back up to look at him with his index finger.

The answer to that one simple question, they both knew revealed so much more than she wanted to admit. *Shit! She is a virgin!*

"God, your innocence is killing me. I want to kiss you more, but I don't want to scare you." Jackson squeezed his eyes closed, trying to contain himself.

"It…it's okay. I…I…want you too." Simone shyly raised her face up.

Jackson looked down at her, wondering how he'd be able to remain in control if he kissed her the way he really wanted to. "Just breathe through your nose." Jackson said, reaching up to gently remove her glasses before placing his lips on hers. *Jesus, I'm teaching a twenty-nine year old how to kiss.*

He started with a soft peck. The peck developed into soft nibbles on her bottom lip. Jackson reached for her clenched fists at her sides and brought them up to rest on his wide chest, and they grasped his shirt in a death grip. He clasped her face in either hand, bracing himself to take the kiss to the next level.

Jackson flicked his tongue against Simone's firmly closed lips and they opened on a gasp. He took advantage of the access and plunged his tongue into her mouth. She gathered more of his shirt into her fists as if she was going to pull him closer or push him away. Her tongue stayed still, not knowing what to do. Jackson flicked and caressed hers, coaxing it to do the same.

Slowly and timidly, Simone touched her tongue to his. Jackson's tight control slipped a little and he pulled Simone in closer and deepened the kiss, growling in the back of his throat. Getting the hang of the intense kiss, Simone started to mimic his tongue, diving into his warm mouth shyly when his retreated from hers.

When her hands slowly snaked around his neck and her fingers made their way into the hair at the nape of his neck, what little control he had left, snapped. He walked her backwards towards the wall, pressed her against it and his hips thrust instinctively into hers, his painfully hard erection aching to get inside of her.

But the first touch of his hardness against her broke the passionate spell. Simone gasped and pulled away from his lips.

"Stop…stop please." Her voice shook with need and fear.

"Oh God! I'm so sorry Simone. I didn't mean to lose control like that." Jackson apologized looking into her large dark brown eyes that were filled with confusion, as they both panted trying to calm their pulses.

Jackson knew that she must have been confused with her body's reaction to his. She probably didn't understand what was going on inside of her body. She was more than likely afraid of him and her need for him.

"I…I better get my bags, so we can get going. I'm sure Xander is wondering what is taking us so long." Simone looked anywhere but at him.

"Ah…I doubt he's too worried." Jackson hedged.

Simone just gave him a perplexed look, not sure of what he meant by the comment. She turned and put the keycard in the lock, opening the door. Jackson walked in slowly behind her, not wanting to get too close and freak her out.

"Here let me take those down for you." Jackson offered.

"Thank you. Uh…can you give me a second while I call my friend Amber? I need to let her know that I won't be able to call her for a couple of days. I don't want her to worry." Simone said, shyly looking at him from under her lashes, too afraid to make full eye contact with him again.

"Sure. We'll be downstairs waiting. Take your time." Jackson said, the timid look making him want to drop her bags, throw her on the bed and ravish her curvy body for the rest of the day.

"Thanks." She said as she grabbed her phone.

Jackson looked longingly at her before he closed the door. Still grasping the door handle, he took a deep calming breath, clenching his jaw before releasing the handle and walking down the hall. *Fuck! The next couple of days are going to the best and most frustrating days of my life, being in such close proximity to that body.*

~~~

Oh holy hell! Simone fell back on the bed. *Shit, shit, shit, shit, SHIT!* Simone wasn't in the habit of cursing, but she felt that now was as good a time as any. *Plus, it doesn't technically count if it's just in my head.* Before she could overthink it, she grabbed her phone that she'd dropped on the bed and immediately pulled up Amber's number.

"Hey stranger! How's the-?" Amber started cheerfully, before Simone cut her off.

"Amber! I don't have too much time, but I needed to talk to you…to get some advice." Simone said in a rush.

"Oh my God! What? What?! You never ask for advice, so this has to be about a guy!" Amber shouted.

Simone could imagine Amber jumping up and down in excitement.

"Well…spit it out!" Amber said impatiently after Simone stayed quiet a moment.

"Uh…well. It's not just one guy…it's…it's two." Simone said cringing because she knew what was coming.

"WHAAAAAT?!?!" Amber shouted into the phone. "Holy shit! You've only been gone twenty-four hours! Two guys?! Now you've *got* to tell me. I need the deets!"

"Amber, I really don't have time to give you too many details." Simone implored, but knowing there was no use.

"Well then get to talkin', cause you're not getting off this phone until you've told me everything." Amber pressed on.

"Fine. Fine. Well the owner of the lodge is Xander and his best friend that is helping him this week is Jackson. And-"

"Damn! Just their names sound hot. And best friends too! You've hit the jackpot!" Amber interrupted.

"Are you going to listen or not?" Simone smiled into the phone, teasing her friend.

"Oh sorry…continue."

"Okay. So Xander is tall and lean like a swimmer and has blond hair, greenish hazel eyes, with crazy plump lips and dimples to die for. And Jackson has this beautiful unruly curly chestnut brown hair with crazy gray eyes and built like a Mac truck. He owns a lumber mill and it looks like he was given an ax the moment he came out the womb." Simone told her friend.

"Wow", was Amber's only response, just imagining the beautiful men.

"And…and…uh…they both kissed me today." Simone said quietly.

"WHAT!?!?! Amber shouted again into the phone. "You go from never getting any action…ever, to getting kissed by two men in the same day?! And two gorgeous men at that!"

"I know! First it started with Xander when he had me bond with the dogs. One of the dogs jumped on me and pushed me into him. It really wasn't a full kiss, just a brush of his lips against mine. But just a few moments ago, Jackson walked me to my room to get my bags to take downstairs for the trip and he kissed me. Like *really* kissed me! Like *French* kissed me!" Simone said in wonder.

"You are *such* a virgin." Amber said exasperated.

"I know. But it was amazing. I've never felt anything like that before. But then he rubbed his…his…you know what…on me?" Simone tried to come up with a good word for "it".

"No, I don't know. He rubbed what on you?" Amber refused to back down, making Simone squirm.

"He rubbed his *penis* on me." Simone whispered the offensive word.

"And…?"

"Well…it…I can't be sure, but it felt *huge*! And I got scared, broke the kiss and told him to stop." Simone finally finished.

"It sounds promising to me." Amber said happily.

"But Amber, don't you get it?! They're best friends! Am I supposed to choose? And if so, how do I?" Simone said with worry.

"Well you don't have to choose yet. Just enjoy it…the attention. Have fun with it. You're only there for a few weeks. If it doesn't work out, you'll just come back and never have to see them again." Amber reasoned.

"I guess. But I'm not really comfortable with all this. How do I go from no experience at all, to being sneaky and fooling around with *two* guys? It just feels wrong." Simone said sadly.

"Just go with it one day at a time and see what happens. And try not to overthink it, though I know that's hard for you, since studying and analyzing is your thing." Amber advised.

"Okay, I'll try." Simone said with a voice filled with doubt. "I better go, they're waiting for me."

"God, this is *so* exciting! My big sister from another Mister, finally coming out of her shell and wanting to have 'girl talk' with me. It makes me want to cry." Amber sighed dreamily. "Oh hey, make sure you get a pic of them and send it to me!" Amber said at the last minute.

"Uh...okay. If there's cell reception at the next lodge that we stay at, I'll try to call you to give you an update."

"You better. Alright girl, go to your men. Hehehe...I love it! Bye!"

"Bye." Simone said nervously, and then hung up the phone.

Simone left her room, walked to the elevator and took it down as if she were going to her execution. She had no idea how she was supposed to act normal in front of both men that she had kissed. For one, she didn't know how to act in front of *one* man that she had kissed. *Am I supposed to act like it never happened?* For another, was she supposed to tell one that she had kissed the other? *God, this is so confusing.*

~~~

Xander was loading their gear on the sleds when Jackson came out with a shit eating grin on his face. Xander hadn't seen the serious man that happy in a long time.

"What's with the goofy grin, Jax? Xander smiled at his friend.

"Oh, I'd just say things are lookin' good brother." Jackson came up and clapped Xander on the back happily.

"So she's into you?" Xander asked anxiously.

"You have no idea." Jackson replied, deliberately making his friend stew a bit.

"Well...give me details. Did you kiss her? Did you find out if she's a virgin?" Xander asked impatiently.

"Yes, to all of the above. And life never tasted sweeter." Jackson grinned.

"Shit! Really?! What else...what happened?" Xander wasn't backing down.

"Well I kissed her. And not just a pussy brush of the lips either." Jackson taunted Xander. "I could tell that she wasn't experienced, so I asked her if she'd ever been kissed before, and she said 'kind of, once in high school'. So she is definitely a virgin. Hell man, I had to teach her how to fucking breathe while kissing. She's a complete innocent. And it's sexy as hell."

"Damn! You got more action than I did!" Xander punched Jackson in the arm, happy that things were working in their favor, but wanting more of a taste of her himself.

"Oh shit! And I almost forgot. She's fucking twenty-nine!"

"No freakin' way! And she's still a virgin?! That's gotta be some kind of record or something!" Xander shook his head in wonder.

"Yeah, how anyone can go that long is beyond me, especially with a body like that. What the hell is wrong with the guys down in the lower forty-eight?!" Jackson shook his head.

"Beats the hell outta me. But it worked out in our favor." Xander replied.

"Anyway, I told her she needs to enjoy life every once in a while, and I think that helped her loosen up a bit. And we can definitely help her along with that." Jackson said thoughtfully.

"It's a dirty job but somebody's got to do it." Xander winked at Jackson, cracking his knuckles, more than willing to help "loosen" her up.

"You're such a turd." Jackson chuckled at Xander. "I just don't know how to go about explaining our particular relationship preferences to her." Jackson contemplated.

"Well buddy, it's not always about words. We might just have to show her how it works. Once we get her engines revved up, in the heat of the moment she may not care. And then after when she's on cloud nine from all the sweet lovin' we'll give her, we can explain how it all works." Xander suggested eagerly.

"You know what Xander, I think for the first time you thinking with your 'little' head might be a good idea." Jackson wrapped his arm around Xander's shoulder and gave it a firm squeeze.

"Hey sometimes the big head and the little head have to come together and make really tough decisions." Xander replied cheekily.

"Ha!" Jackson laughed, just as Simone walked out of the lodge towards them.

Both men held their breath as she walked timidly towards them. Her head was down in embarrassment, obviously not knowing how to act in front of the two men she had kissed. She was a breath of fresh air to both Xander and Jackson.

"Hey, Simone! Come on over. I want to teach you the ropes of working the dogsleds." Xander called out to her, trying to break the ice, helping her ease into being comfortable around them by talking work instead of flirting.

It worked, because she finally looked up at them and smiled brightly. "Okay", she replied softly.

"Alright, so I have you with Sampson and Delilah's team. Their pros at this and will practically lead you." Xander walked her over to the team of dogs that were waiting impatiently to be attached to the sled.

"They're really excited aren't they?" Simone said in wonder as they all sat obediently next to the spot on the gangline where they were normally positioned, wagging their tails in anticipation.

"Oh yeah, they love it." Xander smiled fondly at the dogs. "So before we hook them on to the gangline, I'm going to teach you some basic commands."

"Okay." Simone said, ready to learn.

"To get them moving you'll shout out 'HIKE'. And to stop them you'll say 'WHOA'. Okay, repeat for me." Xander instructed.

"To start: 'HIKE'. To stop: 'WHOA'." Simone repeated.

"Good, now-", Xander started before Simone chimed in again.

"Turn right, 'GEE'. Turn left, 'HAW'." Simone said with a shy smile.

"Nice! So I see you've done some research." Xander said impressed.

"Well, research and studying is a big part of what I've done for several years." Simone said with a shrug.

"Alright then tell us what else you know." Xander said looking back at Jackson, who had a front row view of the show leaning against the fence quietly observing.

"'EASY': to slow down. 'STRAIGHT AHEAD': to keep straight on an intersecting trail. 'ON BY': to pass another team or distraction. And 'LINE OUT': to keep the lines from getting tangled when we're stopped." Simone easily rattled off.

"Wow! Good girl. There's just a few other commands that might help you out in a pinch. 'GEE OVER': to move right past another team or to the right of a trail. 'HAW OVER': to move left to pass or left of a trail. As well as 'GEE or HAW COME': to have the leaders come to you and turn the team around." Xander further instructed.

"Okay. I think I got it." Simone said.

"Good, but just in case we'll practice out front before we head out. I'm sure you'll do fine. You seem to love animals and you're smart, but you have to be confident in your commands. Let them know that you're the boss." Xander coached.

"Alright, I'll try." Simone said doubtfully, apparently not trusting her ability to be commanding.

"You'll do fine, Simone." Jackson finally said, straightening up from leaning on the fence and walked towards them. Once he stood in front of Simone he touched a finger under her chin and lifted her face to look up at him. "There's some fire in there. I can see it and Xander can too. Just think of yourself as part of the team. You got this." Jackson said, infusing confidence into Simone.

"Thank you, Jackson. I think you're right." She took a deep breath and stood up a little straighter.

"I know I am." Jackson smiled down at her.

"Alright, now let's get this party going!" Xander called out, ready to harness the dogs to the gangline.

Simone and Jackson walked over to the dogs. Xander instructed Simone on how to check to make sure the harnesses were on the dogs properly and then how to secure them on the gangline. Once the six dogs were attached and ready to go and her gear was loaded onto the sled, Xander stopped Simone in front of the dogs.

"Now I have a few other commands that you may need at a moment's notice." Xander whistled and the dogs stood at attention. "When things are going rough just say: 'SMILE'." And at that moment all of the dogs on the team pulled back their lips in a doggie version of a smile that looked more like an angry snarl. At which point Simone burst into unexpected laughter.

"When that's not good enough to brighten a tough moment, then just say: 'GOOFY FACE'." All of the dogs hung their tongues out the side of their snouts in an impression of a goofy face. And Simone clapped with joy at their antics.

"And last but not least, for the finale just call out: 'CONGA LINE'!" All of the dogs adjusted their position and when they were close enough to each other one by one except the two in the front, the dogs jumped up to put their front legs on the backs of the dogs in front of them, forming a doggie conga-line.

"Oh my goodness, how talented you all are! That was amazing Xander!" Simone wiped at the tears of laughter at the corners of her eyes. As her giggles calmed, she pulled out her cellphone. "So I was wondering if you two wouldn't mind if I took a picture of you with my phone for the start of the trip?" Simone asked hesitantly.

"Sure! Wait, I'll grab one of my staff and so that way you can be in the pic too." Xander said excitedly.

"But how about a selfie first?" Jackson piped in, surprising Xander.

"Alright." Simone said bashfully.

"You? A selfie? I didn't even think you knew what that meant." Xander teased Jackson.

"Just because I don't take them or participate in social media doesn't mean I've been hiding under a rock, dick!" Jackson shot back, while Simone's head turned back and forth like at a tennis match, trying to keep up with their banter.

"Are all men that are friends, this mean to each other?" Simone asked perplexed.

"For the most part. It's how we show we love each other. We can't hug and say 'I love you, BFF', like you girls do. We're too tough for all that." Xander winked at Simone, as a boyish grin spread across his face and his dimples deepened, making her breath hitch.

"Alright 'tough' guy, enough flirting. Take the picture, so we can get on the road." Jackson said as he reached for Simone's phone and handed it to Xander.

Xander pulled Simone close into his side, wrapping one arm around her shoulders. Jackson stepped in close on her other side and wrapped his arm around them both, pulling them even tighter together, until Simone was sandwiched between them like a sardine. Xander held up her phone and they all smiled big as he snapped the picture. Xander flipped the phone around and brought up the picture to show Simone and Jackson.

"So what do you think? Good enough?" He asked Simone.

"Uh…yeah." Simone ogled the picture on the screen, as the two men smiled knowingly over her head.

"Do you want one of my staff members to take a regular picture of us still?" Xander asked Simone.

"No, this one is perfect. Thanks guys." Simone said as she sent the pic out to Amber.

Seconds later as Xander and Jackson readied the other dog teams and sleds, Simone's phone chimed with a new text message.

HOLY SHIT!!! You lucky bitch! Those two are drop dead gorgeous!!! Good luck trying to choose! I can't wait to get there to meet them in the flesh!

Simone just shook her head at Amber's text and quickly responded before it was time to head out.

Thanks a lot! You're no help, whatsoever. Anyway, I'll text you in a day or two.

Simone shook her head as she shut off her phone and put it away in her back pack on the sled.

Chapter 4

After about thirty minutes of practice out front of the lodge, they were well on their way to another lodge that was about four hours away by sled. The Tanana Tribe's village was spread out between the two lodges. Xander wanted Simone to become familiar with the area, so it would be easier for her to come and go as she pleased.

Simone was happy that she felt like she was getting the hang of commanding the dogs, though the dogs mainly just followed the sled in front of them, led by Xander. Jackson was following several yards behind her.

The temperature was a little chilly, but Simone enjoyed the landscape of the snowy white plains and the silhouette of the mostly white mountains in the semi-lightened sky. She found beauty even in the stark terrain and perpetual darkness. It was so quiet, peaceful and serene, especially with the sounds of rushing water in a nearby river. It was easy for her mind to drift off and wander. And her thoughts went straight to the men with her.

She thought of how Jackson was so rugged and handsome. So serious compared to Xander's lighthearted demeanor. She could relate to him though, having lost both of her parents as well, but not in such a tragic way. Plus, losing a sibling had to be equally tough. *I wonder how close they were before his little brother died.* Jackson seemed like the protective sort, and if he had been like that with his little brother, then his death had to weigh on him. Yet Simone did see how Xander lightened Jackson up a bit. It seemed easy for him to joke around with his best friend. *A lot like Amber and I. She brings out the silliness in me.*

But in all of his seriousness, it seemed easy for her to talk to him. *Like he understands me.*

Now Xander, his carefree easy-going ways, made her laugh. Half of the things he said were inappropriate, but it was hard to get mad at him. He just had a way of making weird situations bearable and fun. *And that face...God that face is beautiful!* Simone couldn't pinpoint what it was. Most men were considered handsome, gorgeous, hot or sexy. But beautiful wasn't an adjective she'd ever thought to use to describe a man, but use it she did.

Simone was so wrapped up in both men's equally pleasing attributes that she barely noticed Xander slowing down and waving her over to pull up next to him.

"GEE OVER!" Simone shouted out to the dogs, commanding them to come up to the right of Xander's sled and team. "WHOA!" They both called out as their dogs and sleds pulled up next to each other.

"Hey, I figured you'd need a little bit of a break. Dogsledding can be more tiring than you realize, especially at first and we've been going for about two hours now. I also wanted to show you some of your tribes land." Xander said as the dogs came to a stop.

"We stopping for a break?" Jackson asked stopping on the right side of Simone's sled, putting her in the middle.

Why does it always feel as if they are constantly putting me in the middle of them? What am I, the meat in the middle of a hot guy sandwich?! I'm already having a hard enough time choosing which one I want. Ha, me *having a choice between to incredibly hot guys?! Inconceivable!*

"Yeah, I figured Simone might be getting a little tired. And I wanted to show her part of the Tanana land." Xander pointed to a group of small homes. The lights in the windows glowed and smoke from the chimney tops floated up from the roofs. "All of that is where many of the tribe still lives. A lot have moved into the city, but the diehards will never move. I don't blame them." Xander finished.

"Thank you for showing me." Simone said shyly, looking at the outskirts of the village, wondering if her family was there.

"Oh, and I brought some energy bars to snack on. You need to keep up your energy while sledding. We don't need you distracted from hunger." Xander grinned at Simone.

I doubt it would be hunger that would distract me. More like two ridiculously sexy men. God, what is wrong with me. I have never ever been concerned with men and sex. Ever! School, yes. Nursing, yes. Work, yes. Men, never. Sex, I don't think so. I always thought I was Asexual, because I had just as much sex drive as a freaking cactus. Now, it's like the men turned on a light switch and now I can't shut it back off. Ugh!

"Well, you're the expert. I'll listen to your judgment. I am a little hungry." Simone admitted, slightly embarrassed by her appetite after the large breakfast they'd had, thinking that she probably shouldn't be eating so much. And she was afraid that they'd think the same thing.

"Good. We can't have you losing any of those curves. For one, you have to have meat on your bones around here or you'll freeze to death. And two, they just look too good to change." Jackson said, looking at her appreciatively, making her blush to her roots.

"I concur!" Xander cheered, sending the blush from her face to spread down her neck and chest.

"Um, guys…I…I uh, I'm not every comfortable with compliments. I don't mean to be impolite, but…but could you please refrain from saying those kinds of things." Simone said awkwardly, looking down at the snow.

"Um, yeah, I don't think that's gonna happen." Jackson said matter-of-factly.

"Exactly. If anything I think you better get used to being complimented, because as long as you're here around us, it's inevitable." Xander said as he handed her a protein bar. "We'll have lunch once we get to Northern Lights Lodge."

Simone took the bar, but remained quiet, contemplating how they could both be volleying for her attention and not get mad at each other for it.

"So Simone, if you don't mind me asking what other nationality are you mixed with? You're definitely not full-blooded Native American." Xander asked curiously, while Jackson looked on equally interested.

"My father was black." Simone said in between bites.

"Hmm…a lovely combination, especially where you're concerned." Jackson smiled approvingly.

"Why is it that you two find me so attractive when others have not? Were you dropped on your heads as children? Because I seriously don't get it." Simone said truly baffled by all the attention from the gorgeous men.

"We know a beautiful woman when we see her. But we see in the movies, TV and social media, what is considered beautiful down in the lower forty-eight. And women like that can't make it up here. Like we said before, you have to have meat on your bones to survive Alaskan winters." Jackson said.

"And you can't look like you just stepped out of the salon or a fashion show. Heels, makeup and fancy clothes don't work up here. So we've spent a lifetime seeing women for who and what they really are. How beautiful you look without all the camouflage." Xander added as Jackson nodded his agreement.

"We just see *you*, Simone." Jackson said her name quietly, almost seductively.

"Oh," was Simone's only response. The men had left her speechless.

"Are you satisfied now? Are we now free to compliment you and be attracted to you without you biting our heads off?" Xander teased her.

"Uh…well…I didn't mean to be rude. I'm just not used to men saying such things to me." Simone blew out a huge breath.

"You guys talk like you're twins or like you're one person or something. It's weird." Simone blurted out.

"Hahahaha!" Both men laughed.

"You have no idea sweetheart." Xander winked at her, in his usual playful way.

Simone had no idea what their reaction or that statement meant. So she just shrugged it off as some other aspect of dating and men that she didn't know about or pretend to understand.

"So, how are you feeling, Simone? Any aches and pains yet?" Jackson asked after Simone shifted trying to stretch her aching muscles without them noticing. *Apparently I'm Captain Obvious.*

"I'm a little sore, but I'm okay. I can keep going." Simone said putting up a brave front.

To be honest, my hips are aching from balancing on the sled. My shoulders and arms are throbbing from trying to hold on. But other than that, I'm peachy. Simone said to herself, but not willing to admit that she couldn't handle it. They had about two more hours to go and she didn't want to look weak or incapable in front of the strong sturdy men. *I can hang with the boys, just you wait and see.*

"I know you can do it. Plus, we've got a surprise for you at the lodge that will help you later too." Xander smiled at her.

"Okay…thanks." Simone said uncertainly.

~~~

Jackson watched Simone appreciatively as he followed behind her sled. The mostly dark sky couldn't hide that form. *Good lord, that ass and those hips can make a man parched! How in the hell did no guy notice those particular attributes before us? Or was she just too blind and focused on her studies to notice?*

He was pretty sure that it was the latter, because there was no earthly reason otherwise and he was sure of it. *But she's noticing now.* Jackson smiled to himself. He knew when a woman was attracted to them, and Simone definitely was. They just needed to make sure they approached her in the right way.

She was shy but spirited, and Jackson adored that about her. She was smart and goal-oriented, and had no thoughts of finding a man to take care of her, which made him want to take care of her all the more. For the first time in maybe ever, Jackson looked forward to the future.

He had been afraid to want or have his own family again, but now he was able to see it. As unconventional as his idea of family was, the meaning was still there and meant no less. And he was starting to want it really badly with the beautiful woman in front of him and his best friend.

Jackson could tell that this first novice run was wearing on Simone. She kept trying to adjust her position, to find a more comfortable stance. They only had about thirty minutes left before they got to Northern Lights Lodge. So Jackson pushed the dogs harder to catch up with Simone's sled, just to keep her company and distract her from her aches.

"Hey stranger, come here often?" Jackson joked as he pulled up alongside of her, trying a classic cheesy Xander approach to make her laugh.

"Huh? Oh, you sound like Xander…though that kind of stuff sounds better coming out of his mouth, and barely even then." Simone said seriously.

"Ow, burn!" Jackson said impressed.

"Ha! Psych!" Simone laughed at his shocked face. "You guys aren't the only ones with jokes and surprises. I have a sense of humor too." Simone smiled shyly at him, as he stared down at her intently. Her smile faltered a little. "You stare a lot don't you?" *Must I really say nearly everything I'm thinking?*

"You're just stunning and I can't stop staring at you." Jackson said seriously.

"Oh."

"So, we've only got about a half hour left before we get to the other lodge. Do you have enough energy in you to make it a little longer? Otherwise, I can attach your dogs to my sled and you can ride with me." Jackson offered.

"Oh no, I can make it. If I've made it this far, I can go another couple of minutes." Simone said firmly.

"I'm impressed. Most girls from the lower forty-eight would be complaining or passed out by now." Jackson said.

"Well, I'm not like most girls." Simone shot back.

"There's no doubt about that." Jackson said still shocked by her determination.

"Plus, not all girls in the 'lower forty-eight' as you call it are spoiled brats. There are quite a few of us that have had to work hard. They just don't happen to make a trip to Alaska, either from lack of interest or funds. Now if you had made the effort to go down there, maybe you would've been able to meet the tougher girls, and could've brought one of them back with you." Simone said logically.

"Well, maybe I was just waiting for the right one to make her way up here." Jackson fired back, looking at her with meaning.

"Oh. Well…uh…ah…I…um…oh nevermind!" Simone finally gave up trying to find a clever comeback.

Jackson just threw his head back and laughed at her discomfort. "You are a breath of fresh air, Ms. Staton. One minute, your sharp tongue cuts like a knife and the next minute, you're all tongue tied. It's adorable." Jackson smiled down at her.

"I'm glad you find me amusing." Simone said a little disgruntled.

"Oh, don't be mad. You just keep me on my toes, and I like it." Jackson tried to pacify her.

"Uh, huh," was Simone's only response. "Oh look! I see light up ahead!" Simone pointed in excitement.

"Good. Then we're here. I'm sure you'll definitely be ready for your surprise at this point." Jackson said, noticing Simone's shoulders slump in relief and fatigue.

"Whatever the surprise is, if it involves relaxing for a little bit, I'll be overjoyed." Simone replied. "God, how are the dogs still going like it's nothing?" Simone said with wonder.

"They're used to it. They can go all day and night." Jackson said as they neared the lodge and Xander slowed his team to let them catch up to him.

"Hey guys! Ready to call it a day?" Xander shouted over to them, all smiles.

"Yes!"

"Yeah."

Simone tried to keep the desperation out of her voice, but Jackson could hear it. And as they pulled up to the lodge, Jackson noticed her body slump slightly and knew what would happen once she let go of the sled. Jackson instinctively jumped off of his sled towards Simone, and caught her around the waist in mid-faceplant.

"Whoa." Xander exclaimed as he too jumped off his sled towards them.

"I'm okay. I'm okay. I just didn't realize that my knees were going to give out on me." Simone said trying to break free of Jackson's hold.

"Are you sure?" Jackson said, as he slowly released her.

"Yeah, I got it." Simone said, standing up straight.

"Well I was going to say that we could eat lunch before the surprise, but I think you need it first." Xander said with concern.

"Well what's the surprise and I'll tell you for sure?" Simone said looking over tiredly at Xander.

"We have a full-body massage planned for you." Xander told her.

"Massage, please. I'm hungry, but that can wait." Simone said without hesitation.

"I figured as much." Xander chuckled. "Come on, let's head in."

Both men stepped to either side of her to walk her into the lodge, sandwiching her once again.

"Hey boys!" Rachel, the lodge owner shouted out as they came through the door.

Rachel was a short round feisty older woman, who ran her lodge like a well-oiled machine. Xander and Jackson loved her like a favorite aunt. She had given Xander advice and guidance often when he was first starting his lodge. And they regularly found themselves getting dating advice from the cantankerous woman as well. She was a permanent fixture in their lives, and they wouldn't have it any other way.

"Hey, Rachel!" Xander shouted back. "How's our favorite lady doing?"

"Oh, I'm alive and kickin'." She replied as she walked up to them to receive her customary hugs and kisses on the cheek from the two large men. "So, who's this adorable creature you have with you today?" Rachel said, looking intently at Simone as she blushed profusely.

"This is Simone Staton. She's an RN from Washington. She's gonna be here for a few weeks to meet her mother's family." Xander introduced.

"Simone, this little spitfire is Rachel Thomas. She owns this lodge and runs it like a drill sergeant." Jackson teased, as the two women shook hands.

"Oh hush. You're not too old to be put over my knee, young man." Rachel warned.

"Yes ma'am." Jackson grinned down at her, not afraid of her empty threat.

"So are the pups out front?" Rachel asked Xander.

"Yeah." Xander answered.

"Well I'll get some of the staff to come out and put them in the kennel." Rachel said as the very staff she had mentioned that were hovering nearby, sprang into action.

"We can come out and help in a minute. We just wanted to make sure that we setup a full-body massage for Simone. It was her first sled run and she did a wonderful job, but it was longer than most novice runs and she's tired and needs to relax." Xander told the older woman.

"Sure, I'll get her situated. You just leave it to me. She'll be in good hands." Rachel said, putting her hand on Simone's back and guiding her out of the foyer.

The men looked on with big grins on their faces, knowing that Rachel could be a big help in their plans to get Simone to agree to a relationship with them. Rachel looked back, catching them staring, and gave them a knowing smile.

~~~

Rachel led Simone down a hall lined with different rooms with different types of spa treatments. The sounds of soothing water and low relaxing music reached Simone's ears. The atmosphere was very calming and relaxing.

"So just strip down and put on this robe and I'll take you to the room you'll get massaged in." Rachel said leading Simone into a posh changing room and handing her a white fluffy robe.

"Totally naked?" Simone whispered.

"Of course, honey. Haven't you ever gotten a massage before?" Rachel looked at Simone curiously.

"No, ma'am. Never had the money for one before." Simone said truthfully.

"Oh well then, you are in for a treat. My masseurs are the best in the region. Xander tries to steal them from me, but they're loyal. I told him that he can have them when I'm cold and dead in the ground, but until then, don't even think about it or I'll have your balls in a vice." Rachel smiled deviously, as Simone giggled.

"Wow, I bet you keep Xander in line." Simone said amused at Rachel's gruffness.

"Hell, I keep both of them in line. Two peas in a pod, those two." Rachel grinned at the thought of the men. "You have a lot of work cut out for you with those two, but it'll be worth it. If only I was younger…" Rachel said shaking her head.

"What do you mean? They're just helping me find my mother's tribe." Simone denied.

"If you believe that you're either blind or dense, honey. Those two couldn't keep their eyes off of you. I noticed the moment you walked through my front door." Rachel said, looking at Simone like she was an idiot.

"I'm neither blind nor dense. I just don't have any experience with men. I don't understand them and don't pretend to." Simone said in a huff.

"Good, you're shy buy feisty. You'll keep them on their toes and won't let them completely walk all over you." Rachel grinned happily.

"Why do you keep saying them? It's either one or the other, and I have absolutely no idea how I would ever choose between the two. So it's best if I choose neither and just stick to finding my family." Simone said matter-of-factly.

"Ha! We'll see about that. But I'm not gonna explain things to you, that's their job." Rachel wisely stated, keeping the boys' secret, knowing they must not want it shared if they hadn't told the girl yet. "So would you prefer a woman or a man masseur?" Rachel asked, changing subjects.

"A woman, please." Simone replied, still trying to figure out what Rachel meant.

"Damn, I was hoping you'd say a man. There's nothing like a little jealousy to keep a man on his toes. But I have a great female masseuse for you. I'll let her know and make sure the room is ready for you while you change. Oh, and take down your hair. Part of the full body massage is a to-die-for head and scalp massage." Rachel said walking out of the changing room so Simone could have some privacy while changing.

Once Simone had stripped down, put on the comfy robe and taken down her braids, she stepped out into the hallway where Rachel was waiting to take her to the right room. They walked down a couple doors and Rachel opened the door to the room where Simone would be getting her massage.

The large room had the same rich brown wood that made up the whole lodge. It was decorated in calming shades of blue, tan and brown. A babbling water fountain was in the corner and soothing music was playing from cleverly hidden speakers. The atmosphere alone was making Simone relaxed enough to pass out. The only thing that kept her slightly tense was the fact that there were three padded tables setup side-by-side. *Oh God, please don't let the guys get a massage at the same time as me!*

"Gretchen will be in in just a second. Go ahead and take off the robe and lay down on your stomach on the table." Rachel instructed, as Simone looked at her with trepidation. "Don't worry, I won't look, just lay down." Rachel said holding up a giant towel to Simone's body as she turned her head away.

"Okay." Simone said blushing.

She took off the robe and Rachel held up the towel to her, covering her naked form. Simone laid down on the middle table that Rachel had pointed to, as the older woman covered her lower half with the towel.

"Now just relax. You're in for a treat young lady." Rachel said before she left the room.

~~~

"That child is about as innocent as a newborn baby. You two would do good not to scare her half to death with your...*charms*." Rachel said with a raised brow, looking Jackson and Xander up and down in just towels wrapped around their waists, as they stood outside of the door to the massage room. "You two are a whole lot of man individually, but combined you'd scare a seasoned prostitute half to death! Just take care." Rachel warned before opening the door for them.

The men just quietly chuckled at the older woman, before they entered. Both inhaled sharply at the sight of Simone's oiled naked back and narrow waist that the tall blonde masseuse was in the process of working on. Simone's insanely luscious hips and ass were barely concealed by the towel. And her jet black wavy hair also slick with oils from a deep scalp massage, spilled over the side, practically touching the floor.

They both adjusted their towels, in a poor attempt to cover their arousal. Gretchen looked up at them when she realized they were in the room. Her eyes widen perceptively at their 'situations' barely hidden behind their towels, and she grinned knowingly. Both men actually blushed at being caught with their proverbial pants down around their ankles.

Xander took the table to the right of Simone and Jackson took the one on the left. Both took a moment to adjust themselves comfortably on the tables. But they were finding that it wasn't easy to lay on their stomachs with massive erections. And just when they thought they had their passions under control, Gretchen must have hit a good spot on Simone's back, because she moaned passionately in the back of her throat. And both men quickly glanced at her and grimaced in pain. They looked at each other, empathizing with the other nonverbally.

"Oh my God Gretchen, thank you so much. I was already tense when I got on the dogsled, but by the time I got off my muscles were screaming at me. You're hands are like a miracle. Am I allowed to tip you?" Simone said in between groans of ecstasy.

"We'll take care of the tip." Jackson said to Simone, startling her.

Simone quickly scrambled up on her elbows at the sound of Jackson's voice. Swiping her hair out of her face, she realized that she was naked and likely giving him a show and just as quickly flopped back down on the table and then covered her face in mortification. Jackson caught a quick glimpse of the side of her pert breast and a dark brown nipple before she dropped back down. The peek was enough to make him weep inside with need.

"What are you doing in here?" Simone said through her fingers that covered her face.

"We needed a massage too. We have more experience with the dogsleds, but still get achy too." Xander piped in.

Simone whipped her head around to her right to see Xander smiling over at her.

"Well aren't there other rooms that you two could use? Do you have to be in the same room as me?" Simone asked in frustration.

"Sure. And no, but where's the fun in that?!" Xander answered her two questions, giving little notice to her aggravations.

"Well I would appreciate it, if you guys could give me some privacy. I don't feel particularly comfortable laying here naked with you in the room." Simone said looking back and forth at the guys.

"Alright, if you say so." Xander said with a sigh, as he went to get up from the table without trying to cover himself.

"Stop! Stop. Fine, just stay. Whatever." Simone yelled and covered her eyes before he could completely show her the goods.

Outside of nursing school, Simone hadn't encountered a naked male body in a non-clinical atmosphere. No matter how hard Amber tried to change that. She was always trying to get Simone to watch porn so that she could get some tutorials on sex, so that she'd know what she was doing when it finally happened. And there were a couple of close calls when Amber had her boyfriend of the month over to stay the night and they would happen to saunter out of her room naked to use the bathroom.

Simone may not have seen what sex actually looked like when it was happening, but she sure knew what it sounded like. Amber was not quiet about it in the least.

Hell, to Simone it sounded like she was dying or being murdered. The loud banging of the bed, the smacking sounds of skin and the groans and screams. Half the time, Simone wanted to run into Amber's room with a bat to beat the shit out of whoever was attacking her friend. She couldn't fathom why anyone would want to do something that made them sound like a wounded dog. *It can't be* that *great!*

But just the quick glimpse she got at Xander's body would have made Amber swoon and had Simone considering what it would be like to have sex with him. *Even I can recognize how amazing their bodies are, and I've never even noticed men before. What the hell is wrong with me lately?*

"Tsk…tsk. You boys have ruined all my work. She is all tense again. And I have no time to work the knots back out, I have another appointment in a few minutes." Gretchen scolded, in a slight Swedish accent.

"Don't worry about it Gretchen, we'll take care of it." Jackson said, getting up from the table and rewrapping the towel tightly around his waist. "You just go to your next appointment."

Xander quickly got up as well, following Jackson's lead.

"Uh…what are you two doing?!" Simone looked up glancing nervously at both of them, trying to keep eye contact with them and not their packages that were only a few feet away from her face.

"We're going to redo all the work that Gretchen has done. Just relax, we'll behave." Jackson said, brooking no argument.

Simone dropped her head back down and shook it from side to side. *What have I just gotten myself into?* She knew that she was trapped, considering she was naked and couldn't get up without flashing the men.

Jackson looked at Xander and nodded his head towards Simone's bottom half. Xander understood instantly and walked over to Simone's legs. Jackson grabbed the oil that Gretchen had been using and poured some in his hands before passing it to Xander. Xander also poured oil onto his palms and rubbed his hands together. They looked at each other, took deep breaths and lowered their hands for the first touch of Simone's smooth butterscotch skin.

The moment they touched her, Simone tensed and breathed in sharply. Jackson started at her neck and firmly smoothed down her back to her tailbone. Xander began at her ankle and slid up her leg to her upper thigh, just below the edge of the towel.

The men's hands were rough and sandpapery from years of hard labor and the feel of them on her sensitive skin sent a fire raging through her veins that she didn't understand. Her pulse raced like she was running a marathon. And her breathing became labored. A strange flutter started in her tummy as Jackson's hands lightly caressed past the sides of her breasts and Xander's fingertips came dangerously close to her most intimate place. And Simone couldn't stop the sounds that escaped her lips.

Their seductively rough hands delicately kneaded her tense muscles. But Simone realized that the tension in her muscles was not from stress, but building from the contact of their skin against hers. The fluttering in her stomach gained intensity as the pounding in her nether region sped up and she felt moisture flood the area.

Never in her life had she felt feelings so intense and they scared the crap out of her. As she felt the tension reaching a crescendo, she couldn't take it anymore and was afraid of what would happen if their magic hands continued.

"Guys please…please stop…I can't!" Simone cried out.

Something in her voice must have warned the men that she was serious, because they instantly stopped.

"Can you give me my robe please?" Simone said with tears clogging her throat.

Xander grabbed her robe and handed it to her. Simone took it gratefully.

"Can you please turn around?" Simone asked softly.

The men stayed quiet as they turned and she put on her robe and fled the room.

"Fuck! She was so close!" Xander said slamming his fist against the padded table, once she was gone.

"Calm down, Xan. This is just going to take time and finesse. She's innocent-" Jackson said calmly before Xander cut him off.

"To be twenty-nine she's more innocent than a five-year-old! It's like she's been sheltered all her life. But Jesus, that was hot. Did you hear her? I know she was about to come, if she would've held out just a little longer. God, I'm still hard just thinking about it!" Xander exclaimed, trying to adjust himself under the towel.

"I know. Just be patient, we're working on her, wearing her down little by little." Jackson sighed, rubbing his hands down his face, not as calm as he seemed.

"You know it's killing you too. You know you want her so badly you can taste it. So don't give me that 'be patient' shit." Xander scowled.

"Of course I want her, dipshit. But that doesn't change the fact that she's not ready…for even one of us, let alone two." Jackson glowered at Xander.

"I know, I know. I'm just worried that she's going to say no and I've never wanted someone so bad in my life. Women don't usually act like this around us. They may pretend to be hesitant about entering into a relationship with two men, but they usually give in pretty quickly. But she doesn't even know yet that we want to share her and she's already running. That doesn't bode well for us." Xander stated dejectedly.

"Yeah. Fuck!" Jackson finally exploded with frustration, knowing that there was a distinct possibility that they wouldn't 'get the girl' this time around.

Simone ran into the changing room, slamming the door and falling back against it. Tears that she had been holding back started to slowly slide down her face. *What is wrong with me?! FUCK! I reacted like such a slut from a simple massage. And with* two *men! Is that even normal?!*

Simone swiped angrily at the tears on her face and pushed off of the door. She threw off the robe and quickly dressed. She braided her oiled hair back up and wound it around in a bun so that the oils didn't get all over her clothes.

Once she was ready she walked over to the door and opened it a crack and peeked out, making sure the guys were nowhere in sight. She didn't think she'd be able to face them again for a while.

When she saw that the coast was clear she high-tailed it back out to the front of the building to the front desk to get her room key. As the girl at the front desk handed Simone the key, a now familiar gruff voice spoke behind her.

"So how was the massage? Did it help you relax any?" Rachel asked.

Simone turned around as a blush spread quickly across her cheeks.

"Oh it was lovely. Gretchen was wonderful." Simone replied softly.

"I hear that the boys finished up for her. That must have been nice." Rachel said knowingly.

Simone's blush spread to her roots and down her neck.

"I…I…uh…it was interesting," was all that Simone could find to say.

"I'd say!" Rachel laughed delightedly. "You're one lucky girl."

"Well…I think I'm going to go up to my room and wash the oil off of me." Simone tried to dodge the subject of the two men.

"You should take a bath. We have wonderful jetted tubs, and it'll help you to relax further." Rachel said, letting the subject slide.

"Thanks. I think I just might take you up on that." Simone smiled at the older woman.

"Will you be taking lunch in your room or are you coming back down to eat with the boys? I think you should come back down, if only to spend time getting to know them. They can be a little overwhelming, but once you get to know them, they're some really great guys." Rachel said before she walked away.

Simone stared after her and in mid-step a few feet away, Rachel turned and looked at Simone thoughtfully.

"You should give them a chance. I think you'd be good for them. Oh and if you do come down for lunch, make sure you wear your hair down. Men love long flowing hair." Rachel smiled and then turned and walked away.

Why does everyone, including the guys refer to them as a whole?! Simone wanted to shout across the room to the retreating lodge owner. Instead she just shook her head in confusion and headed to her room.

Chapter 5

After serious deliberations, Simone decided first not to call Amber. She was so embarrassed over her reaction to Jackson and Xander, she really didn't want to talk about it. And second, she mustered up enough bravery to take Rachel up on her suggestion to spend more time with the guys. Avoiding them wasn't going to work, if they had anything to do about it. And at least if she spent more time with them she could decide which one she may want.

Another big decision she had made while taking a relaxing bath, was that maybe losing her virginity to one of the men, wasn't necessarily a bad thing. She had never really thought much about keeping it from a moral standpoint, whether to wait for love or marriage. It was more of a lack of interest. She had never been a sexual person, so she didn't care to have sex, didn't seek out learning about sex.

But now that the sexual side of herself was finally making an appearance, due to the gorgeous men, she thought that maybe it wasn't a terrible idea to take advantage of it. *Who knows if I'll ever feel this way again about a man?*

So with a deep fortifying breath and a final swipe to her thick hair, Simone walked out of her room and headed to the dining room in an outfit that Amber had picked out that reached *way* beyond her comfort zone.

~~~

"The lights are going to be pretty bright tonight. So it'll be a perfect time to show Simone. But it also looks like we're going to be hit with a major snow storm coming in a couple of days." Xander said looking at the weather on his cellphone. "That's just great. I know that'll delay several flights coming in with some of my guests. I have a big group coming in in a couple of days." Xander said with frustration.

"It'll be fine. They'll get here eventually." Jackson said knowing how the weather worked in Alaska and reminding Xander of it. "But we better make sure we get Simone back to your lodge before it hits, of course after we show her the lights tonight."

"Definitely." Xander agreed, and then looked up when he sensed movement in the doorway. "Well, speak of the devil." Xander said as Simone walked into the dining room and then whistled when he got a good look at her.

Simone was wearing black leggings that fit her thick legs, hips and ass like sin with knee-high brown boots. Over the leggings she wore a form fitting long cream cowl-neck sweater that accentuated her full perky breasts, smaller waist and ridiculous hips and ass. And her hair hung loose in inky black waves down to her tailbone. She had even foregone her glasses for the afternoon.

Both men swallowed audibly and adjusted uncomfortably in their seats.

"Jesus." Jackson whispered under his breath.

"Are you trying to kill us?" Xander asked as they both stood up as she walked up to the table. "J-Lo and Kim Kardashian have got nothing on you!"

Simone ducked her head down and blushed profusely. "You guys are so weird. I'm shaped like a pear, which isn't the normal standard of beauty."

"Please. And who is it that decides what the normal standard of beauty is? You have heard the phrase 'beauty is in the eye of the beholder', haven't you? And what Xander and I see is stunning." Jackson said seriously.

"Hell, if you're shaped like a pear, than call me the Fruit Guy, because I love it!" Xander exclaimed, making both Jackson and Simone laugh. "I'll have to keep that in mind the next time I eat one, because I'm going to savior every juicy bite." Xander teased her, as he pulled out a chair for her to sit.

"Uh, thanks…I guess." Simone said as she sat down.

Xander brushed her hair back from her face with gentle fingertips and slid the hair through his fingers to the ends. A shiver coursed down Simone's spine at the subtly intimate touch.

"You have beautiful hair, Simone. The braids are adorable and most men's fantasy, but it's sexy as hell down." Jackson said to her.

"Why would braids be a fantasy for men?" Simone asked, perplexed.

"It's the whole schoolgirl thing. Put a girl in braids with a plaid skirt and knee-high socks and black strapped shoes and most men are a goner." Xander added.

"Really?!" Simone scrunched up her face in confusion. "Why would looking like a little girl interest a grown man? That's kind of sick."

"It's just a fantasy, Simone. The forbidden. But most men that aren't pedophiles, like the idea of a *grown* woman dressing up like a little girl." Jackson explained.

"It's just like woman wanting their man to dress up like a fireman, police officer, or some other guy that wears a uniform that protects and serves. It's an authority/hero worship thing." Xander further explained.

"You guys might as well stop now. Because I'm not your average girl that has ever even thought of that kind of stuff." Simone shook her head in wonder.

"Really? You've never had a fantasy of your own?" Xander asked skeptically.

"Nope. My mom kind of sheltered me growing up. And I was okay with it, because I was more fascinated with school, studying and reading. I was a nerd. Am a nerd. I prefer books to fashion magazines. Studying to going out. Etcetera, etcetera, etcetera." Simone said uncomfortably for the first time in her life on her lack of experience.

The men just stared at her in disbelief.

"My roommate and best friend is the exact opposite of me in every way. She's girlie, loves fashion and men, and tall and skinny and beautiful like a model. You guys will get to meet her in about a week when she gets here. She might be more to your liking than me." Simone said somewhat sadly, thinking about not getting as much attention from the handsome men when her gorgeous scene-stealing friend showed up.

Simone didn't begrudge Amber her out-going ways, heck it kept the spotlight completely off of her, which she preferred. But now that she was somewhat getting used to the attention they bestowed on her and she still hadn't chosen which guy she really wanted, she didn't want one or both of them to fall for her friend. *Selfish much?!*

"Nah, I think we're good. We like what we've got right here in front of us." Xander pointed out.

Taking a deep breath, Simone brought up the subject she had been trying to avoid with both of them.

"Well, it's not like I can have both of you or anything. So it would be okay that one of you might find interest in Amber." Simone said quietly. "I can't believe I'm having this conversation right now!"

"Well Simone, here's the thing…OW!" Jackson yelled out as Xander kicked him under the table, stopping him from admitting what they really wanted from her.

"What Jackson is trying to say is, you don't have to pick between us right now. Just spend some more time with us, and we'll figure it out." Xander said, giving Jackson the death stare.

"Oh, okay. I think I can do that." Simone said softly, a pretty blush spreading across her cheeks.

"So we have another surprise for you tonight." Jackson said to Simone with excitement.

"What is it?" Simone asked curiously.

"We can't tell you or we'd have to kill you." Xander joked.

"But we can tell you that you have to stay up really late tonight for it." Jackson chimed in.

"Is it okay if I take a nap after lunch? That sled ride wore me out and I'll never make it that late if I don't." Simone said, stifling a yawn.

"Of course." They both said in unison.

Simone just looked at them in wonder as they gestured for the waiter to finally come over to take their orders. *They're not even related and they act like brothers, they're so in sync with each other. So weird!*

~~~

Strong rough hands caressed all over her naked body. Her skin was on fire and tingled everywhere. Soft lips and wet tongues whispered over her glistening skin. Warm sweet breath fanned over her face as she gasped in passion. Hard teeth grazed her stiff nipples. No inch of her soft flesh had been untouched and her clit throbbed with need. Her eyes were clenched shut in ecstasy, her heart was pounding out of her chest and sweat trickled down her neck. A fingertip caressed at her opening and her eyes flew open at the sensation and she looked down in shock at two faces that were smiling up at her.

Simone's eyes flew open for real and she sat up so quickly that she became lightheaded. She was covered in sweat. Her heart really was about to pound out of her chest. And her clit drummed out a beat so hard that she thought she'd go crazy. So she squeezed her thighs together trying to stop the torment, but it only enhanced the sensation. She flopped over on the soft mattress, moaning in exasperation. *What the hell is wrong with my body? And what* was *that?! I've never had a dream like that before.* Two *men?! Why all of a sudden am I becoming a slut now? Oh yeah…Jackson and Xander. Yep, it's official…they are ruining my life. I'm turning into an irrational sexed-up hussy.*

Besides a few R-rated movies, Simone hadn't even seen the likes of which she felt and experienced in that dream.

"What random fucked up part of my brain did that shit come from?" Simone uncharacteristically cursed and shouted to the empty room.

Simone shook her head in defeat, getting up from the bed, knowing that her body had won the battle over her head. She couldn't shake the arousal coursing through her body, so she stripped off her panties and tank-top she had fallen asleep in and got in the shower and turned the water to cold to help cool her need, like she had heard people say in numerous movies, television shows and elsewhere. But all she accomplished was jumping ten feet out of the shower, leaping and dancing around naked and wet, rubbing her hands up and down her arms.

"God! Why would anyone think that was a good idea?!" Simone chattered as she dried off, foregoing the cold shower altogether.

She quickly reapplied some lotion from her earlier bath and threw back on the clothes she had on before and made her way back down stairs to reluctantly find her two tormentors.

"Hi, Rachel. Where are the guys?" Simone asked the lodge owner who was talking with her staff at the front desk.

"Hey, Simone! They're at the bar waiting for you." Rachel winked at her. "It's connected to the dining room. Just go through the doors of the dining room and turn left, go down the short hallway and the bar is on the other side."

"Okay, thank you." Simone said, as she left the front desk to follow Rachel's directions.

The bar area had a surprising and slightly sleek modern look to it, considering the rustic feel of the entire lodge. The bar was in the middle of the room in a square. The lighting on the walls and bar were lowered to give a soft almost seductive glow. And sitting at the bar facing the entrance were Jackson and Xander. Both had their eyes on her the instant she walked in from the hallway.

They took Simone's breath away, especially after the dream she had. She could still feel their hands and mouths on her skin. Xander had on a blue and black flannel that was undone with a white thermal underneath that hugged his lean frame. His hair hung down in his face like a classic surfer boy. His strong jaw had a fresh coating of blond stubble that was a major contradiction to his boyish dimples that deepened as Simone drew closer to them, making her stomach flip flop uncontrollably.

Jackson had on a gray thermal that clung to his upper body in ridiculous ways, with every muscle on display. Simone marveled over the span of his shoulders and chest, a force to be reckoned with. As usual his curly chestnut hair flopped down on his forehead and curled around his ears and neck, making her fingers twitch at her sides wanting so badly to plunge into the curls. *How can I possibly make a choice between these two? There's just no way!*

Simone took in all of their details in just a few seconds, but couldn't compete with the weight of their stares and looked down at the floor as she walked the rest of the way to the bar.

"Hello, Simone. How was your nap?" Jackson said deeply as he stood up to greet her and place a soft kiss on her cheek.

"Hi. Good." Simone squeaked out, as a blush spread across her face thinking of the dream she had while she napped.

"Hey, beautiful." Xander also stood up and kissed her other cheek.

"Uh…hi, Xander." Simone said bashfully as he moved over one stool to the right to let her have the one in the middle of them, as usual.

"Sit with us, have a drink before dinner. It'll help you relax." Jackson said with authority, not to be argued with.

"Okay."

The bartender walked up and placed a coaster down in front of Simone.

"What can I get for you?" The handsome forty-something bartender asked.

"Umm…I don't really know. I don't drink very much." Simone said shyly at the man that Amber would have categorized as a 'Silver Fox'.

"Well then, I'll just make you up something nice. Nothing too strong…at least not yet." He winked at her. "By the way, I'm Jake." He introduced, holding out his hand for Simone to shake.

"Simone." She said looking at his chin, not able to make eye-contact as she shook his hand.

"A beautiful name to go with a beautiful woman." Jake said, making Simone's head pop up at the compliment.

A blush spread across her face as the men next to her scowled at the bartender.

"We'll take it from here, *Jake*." Xander said with a sneer at the bartender's name.

"She's already spoken for." Jackson added with complete confidence and a hint of aggression.

"I meant no offense. I'll just make her drink." Jake held up his hands in surrender at the ill-concealed threats the guys directed at him.

Simone looked back and forth between the three men in complete shock. *I can't get one single guy to look my way in the 'lower forty-eight' as they call it, and now I'm surrounded by men that blatantly flirt with me?! Maybe I should've come here a long time ago. And what's with these two. They practically piss on me to mark their territory in front of the bartender, but they're totally fine with the each other flirting with me? It makes no sense what-so-ever.* Simone shook her head at the strange turn her life had taken.

"So tell us more about you and your family." Xander asked Simone curiously.

"Like what?" Simone said, at a loss of what to say, as Jake placed a pretty pink drink in front of her.

"Like...why you haven't met your mother's family before?" Xander suggested.

"Well, from the way my mother told it, she was always restless." Simone said, taking a sip of the drink and finding it delicious. "She wanted to see more of the world. She wanted to go to the "big city" and meet new and exciting people. So when she was eighteen, she packed a bag and moved to Seattle, against the express wishes of her immediate family and tribe. They said if she left, not to come back. But she left anyway. Shortly after getting to Seattle she started nursing school at a community college, met my father who was stationed in Seattle, and they quickly fell for each other. They got married a year later and shortly after my mom became an RN and then had me.

"My dad went to the Desert Storm war and never came back. He was a fighter pilot for the Air Force and his plane got shot down. I was five." Simone said sadly.

"I'm so sorry, Simone." Jackson said rubbing a soothing hand down her back.

"I don't really remember him that well. I just remember that he smiled a lot and made me and my mom laugh all the time. Kind of like you Xander." Simone said with surprise at the sudden realization.

"Then I bet he was a pretty amazing man, if I remind you of him." Xander said with a cocky grin.

Jackson reached around Simone and smacked Xander on the back of the head playfully.

"You're an over-confident jackass." Jackson teased Xander. "Go on Simone. What happened with your mom? Did she ever remarry?"

"Oh no! She was completely heartbroken over my dad's death. She tried dating a few times, but nothing worked out. I think she kept comparing them to my dad and I guess they all came up short. I'm sure I missed out on a lot of things without a dad. And since I had no uncles, brothers or any male figures in my life, I've just never learned how to act around men." Simone just shrugged.

"We noticed." Xander grinned at her.

"So anyway, my mom raised me the best she could on her own. She still never contacted her family for help. I don't even think they know I exist or that she has passed on. She died of an aneurysm when I was eighteen. She told me a little about her tribe when I'd ask, but didn't bring them up often. I think it hurt her too much to talk about them. So here I am. I saved up money throughout the years to get up here and finally meet them. Though I have to admit, I'm a little nervous." Simone finished.

"We'll go with you the first time, if you'd like?" Jackson offered her sweetly.

"Hell yeah! I'm in!" Xander exclaimed, agreeing with Jackson.

"Thanks guys. I really appreciate that. And I just might take you up on your offer." Simone smiled timidly, sipping down the rest of her drink and placing the empty glass back on the bar.

"So, what did you think?" Jake said coming back over to get the empty glass.

"It was really good! I could barely taste the alcohol." Simone said in delight.

"Therein lies the danger. When you can't taste the alcohol, you usually drink it faster and it sneaks up on you. So be warned. Now…would you like another?" Jake advised, trying to inflect a more professional tone instead of a flirtatious one, under the watchful eye of Xander and Jackson.

"Yes, please." Simone answered, hoping to get a little tipsy to endure the next several hours in the company of the guys.

After Jake walked away to make her drink, Simone turned her attention back to the guys.

"So you're always asking me questions about my life, what about you two?" Simone sat back and looked back and forth between the two men.

"Xander? You can go first." Jackson looked to his best friend to start, avoiding talking about his depressing life.

"Well…I'm the oldest of five. I have two sisters and two brothers. Or should I say three brothers, since Jackson is considered family. He's my brother from another mother." Xander said, smiling at the popular turn of phrase.

"Wow, that's a big family. I always wanted siblings. That's why I love being around my friend Amber and her family. She calls me her sister from another mister." Simone smiled back at Xander.

"Yeah, my parents wanted to have a big family and planned to make it through the entire alphabet starting with me, Alexander. Then there's Bethany, Christopher, Delanie and Ethan. But after the complications my mom had giving birth to Ethan, they decided to stop. Which is funny considering where they stopped, because their names continue the alphabet, Frank and Gail.

"My parents have been married for forever. My dad was a fisherman and was gone several weeks at a time, which I think helped keep the fires burning at home. They didn't have enough time to get on each other's nerves. And my mom is a sweet but tough lady, raising us half the time on her own. We didn't get away with much. And that's about it." Xander finished.

"They sound like wonderful people." Simone said.

"Maybe you'll get to meet them while you're here. They come and go often from the lodge." Xander smiled fondly, thinking about his family.

"So…what about you Jackson?" Simone asked hesitantly, not wanting to give away the fact that she already knew a little about his tragic life, but also wanting to know more about the serious man straight from his own mouth.

Jackson cleared his throat, preparing to talk about something painful.

"Well, there's not much to say. Just like you, I lost my family, but all at the same time. We were in a boating accident and my parents and little brother died and I unfairly made it out, barely without a scratch." Jackson said tightly.

"Oh my God! I'm so sorry Jackson." Simone exclaimed still saddened by the story, especially hearing it straight from him. And for the first time, she touched his arm on her own.

"It's okay. It was a long time ago. I'm over it." Jackson lied.

"No it's not okay. And you're not over it. I don't believe you ever fully get over the loss of close family…I know." Simone said with tears in her eyes.

Jackson flexed his jaw several times as he looked down at Simone, both bonding over shared loss. Slightly choked up by buried emotion, Jackson turned away and started chugging down the rest of his beer.

"Jake." Jackson called out to the bartender. "I need something a little stronger." Jackson said when Jake came over.

"How about a whiskey?" Jake suggested.

"Yeah…Johnnie Walker, please. Neat. Three fingers." Jackson ordered.

"Coming right up." Jake grabbed a tumbler and filled the glass three fingers full.

"Don't stop talking on my behalf." Jackson said after Simone and Xander just sat in silence pretending not to notice his melancholy.

"Uh…so what were you two like when you were little? Causing trouble I presume?" Simone smiled looking at both of them.

"No doubt!" Xander smirked at her. "I came up with the ridiculous schemes and Jackson would only follow to make sure I was okay. Then I'd end up getting him in trouble with his grandparents and I'd smooth it over with my charm and general adorableness."

"Ha! You mean with your big mouth and golden tongue." Jackson shook his head at Xander. "He was always talking his way out of trouble, which was often." Jackson smiled down at Simone with a faraway look on his face, remembering their past exploits.

"Like what? Tell me one of your stories." Simone asked, truly interested in what the men were like as kids, having a pretty sheltered and mundane upbringing herself.

Xander and Jackson gave each other a look, both deciding and agreeing without words that they would give her a tiny taste of their "background".

"Well…there was this one time…the night we lost our virginity. We were thirteen-" Xander started before Simone cut him off.

"Thirteen!? Holy crap, that's young!" Simone exclaimed.

"Not really for a guy." Jackson reasoned and Simone just shook her head in wonder.

"So anyway, we were thirteen and we both liked this girl Brittany. She was seventeen and liked us both. We looked a lot older for our age, especially Jackson. Hell, he already looked like a grown man. So I stayed the night at Jackson's grandparents' house that night because we knew they'd be asleep early. Then we snuck out and met her at a nearby park in the middle of the night. We were in the middle of…well, you can imagine I'm sure. So anyway, we were going at it like rabbits and a flashlight shined on us."

"Oh no!" Simone gasped and giggled under her breath.

"Yeah, 'oh no' is right. It gets worse. It was the local sheriff and her *father*! They had been searching for her, worried that she had been kidnapped or something. We hightailed it out of there buck ass naked as they chased us through the woods. And unfortunately without our shoes on they were able to catch us in the rough brush. They handcuffed us and made us walk naked in front of the squad car all the way home with the spotlight shined on us. But unfortunately for them, the walk of shame caused such a commotion that most of the town got a peek and made all the girls and some of their mothers want us even more." Xander chuckled to himself. "That was a *good* summer!"

Xander high-fived Jackson over Simone's head as they both laughed over the memory.

"You guys are terrible! That was completely over the top. Are you sure you didn't make that up?" Simone questioned them skeptically.

"No we swear!" Xander said as they both held one hand over their hearts and the other raised in the air.

"Wow! Tell me more! My life was so boring growing up…still is as a matter of fact." Simone said, wanting more fun stories.

"We'll see about that." They both said in unison under their breath.

"What was that?" Simone asked, not fully hearing what they'd said.

"Nothing." They said again in unison but this time loud enough for her to hear this time.

~~~

They spent the next several hours talking, eating, laughing and drinking. Jackson and Xander regaled her of their most outrageous exploits and Simone told them about the times she had to bail out Amber in her friend's frequent sticky situations she'd gotten herself into.

Simone had developed a nice hazy little buzz, the first in quite a few years. The last time was when her and Amber had first became roommates and she'd let Amber talk her into drinking. After that horrible night she'd vowed never to drink that much again. But wanting to relax and be herself around the guys, Simone had decided tonight was as good a night as any to throw a little caution to the wind.

At about three in the morning Jackson excused himself, leaving Simone alone with Xander in the somewhat busy bar. A slow song started playing on the jukebox and Xander reached over brushing Simone's hair away from her face and caressed a finger down her cheek to her neck. She closed her eyes and a soft sigh escaped her lips.

"Dance with me?" Xander leaned over and whispered the question in her ear, his lips slightly grazing the shell of her ear.

Simone just nodded, breathless. Xander took her hand and led her onto the dance floor. Once on the floor, he spun her out and back to him, leaving little room between them. Her body felt so soft and appealing against his hard flexing muscles. His arms wrapped around her and his hands caressed up and down her back as their hips swayed together. His large hands slowly made their way down to her wide hips, pulling her closer into his erection. She looked up on a gasp at the feel of him against her. He looked into her heavy-lidded exotic eyes and brought his hands back up to clutch her face.

"Si…" Xander murmured her nickname, no smile was found on his ridiculously full lips this time.

Something in her eyes must have given him the permission he needed, because a second later his was pulling her off of the dance floor and guiding her to a dark corner of the bar. He pressed her up against the wall and without hesitation his soft lips were on hers. His warm wet tongue plunged into her mouth, finally getting the taste of her that he'd been craving. His stubble scraped at her delicate skin as he devoured her mouth. His aggression and passion was so intense that Simone was barely able to kiss him back. A throat clearing behind them broke the spell and they wrenched apart.

"Everything is ready for the surprise, you two." Jackson said with one raised dark eyebrow.

Simone broke eye contact with Jackson, totally ashamed of the display he had just witnessed. *He'll never want me now that he knows I've kissed Xander too. I guess I just made my decision really easy. Xander it is.* Simone's heart broke at the thought that she would never have a chance with Jackson. They both appealed to her, but on different levels. Xander made her laugh and brought life to wherever he went. And Jackson was like her kindred spirit, having both been left as orphans.

One moment she was in the throes of passion and the next she was hit with a wave of melancholy as she followed dejectedly behind Jackson as he led them through the lodge. He stopped at a door and turned to Simone with a winter scarf in his hands.

"I'm going to blindfold you so that you won't see the surprise until the perfect moment." Jackson said holding the scarf up to her face.

"Are we going outside? Shouldn't I take my coat?" Simone asked as he blindfolded her.

"Nope. I have it all taken care of." Jackson said to her softly.

Jackson looked at Xander and Xander brought his clenched fist up to his face and bit it in a sign of blissful agony at the passionate kiss he'd finally had with Simone. Jackson silently chuckled at Xander's usual antics as he gently guided Simone outside to the little wintery oasis he had created just for her. When Jackson had her right where he wanted her he removed the scarf from her face.

As Simone's eyes adjusted she saw three comfy looking cushioned chairs with blankets and a raging bonfire with the rustic lodge as the backdrop to the very romantic scene.

"Jackson it's lovely." Simone said quietly.

"Well if you love that, then you'll faint over this." Jackson said as he grabbed her shoulders and turned her around to face the other direction.

"OH MY GOD!" Simone gasped in awe at the most beautiful sight she'd ever seen.

In front of her were the vibrant greens, blues and fuchsias of the Northern Lights that lit up the night sky. Instant tears clouded her vision and then the hot tears started to drop down hitting her cheeks.

"Never in all my life did I think I'd see something so beautiful." Simone said in a wobbly voice filled with tears.

"Neither did I." Jackson said looking directly at her and not the lights.

Simone blushed deeply, not sure why he'd still want her after what he'd witnessed earlier.

"Come on, let's sit and enjoy the lights." Xander said pointing over to the chairs.

They sat with Simone in the middle as usual and she wrapped the blanket around her shoulders and stared at the lights in wonder.

"Thank you so much for this. You didn't have to do all of this for me, but I'm glad that you did." Simone finally took her eyes off of the lights to look at both the men.

"It's our pleasure. It's something that you'll always remember and we wanted it to be perfect." Jackson said reaching over to grab her hand firmly.

"Yeah, and I thought it was best if Jackson set it up for you, he's the romantic one." Xander smiled brightly.

"I...I don't understand you guys. You practically bite the bartenders head off for flirting with me, yet you two flirt with me in front of each other all the time and you don't get mad at one another. I don't understand how this works. You're making it really hard for me to choose. That is...if either of you actually want me that way." Simone said unsure of herself and their feelings towards her.

"You don't have to choose, Simone." Xander said softly.

"What do you mean? I don't understand." Simone looked at one then the other, in confusion.

"Here, we'll show you." Jackson said, pulling her out of her seat and onto his lap. "Straddle my hips." He instructed her.

"But..." Simone looked over at Xander as she put both knees on either side of Jackson's hips.

"It's okay." Jackson coaxed, raising his hands to her neck and pulling her in for a soft kiss.

Jackson flicked his tongue over Simone's lips and as she gasped he took advantage of the access she provided and plunged his tongue into her awaiting mouth. Xander stood up from his chair and walked up behind Simone and softly pulled her hair back from her neck and leaned down to give the soft sensitive skin just beneath her ear a gentle kiss. Simone released Jackson's lips on a gasp at the feel of Xander's lips on her.

Xander put his index finger under her chin and lifted her face up to his as she looked at him in bewilderment. Xander leaned in and took her mouth in a blistering kiss, as Jackson put his hands on her hips pulling her closer to his steel heat aching to be inside of her.

Jackson continued to guide her heat back and forth over his hardness confined in his jeans as Xander plundered her mouth. Simone started to moan seductively in the back of her throat at the sensations they were giving her.

Xander's hand that was cupping her face, slid down her neck and into the collar of her sweater and further still, until his hand reached into her bra to caress her naked breast. Simone's moans became louder at the feeling of her breast being touched for the first time.

Jackson took the moans as a good sign and started to slowly raise the sweater up her body. Xander released her plump breast and helped Jackson draw the sweater up until her white cotton bra was exposed. The virginal bra nearly sent them over the edge. Lace, satin and vibrant colors couldn't have given them a stronger reaction.

Jackson pulled down the bra, trying to be gentle, but in his excitement he accidentally ripped the bra in two with his large hands. He felt like a randy clumsy teenager with the feelings she was evoking in him. And her bare breasts and little brown nipples didn't help the situation. With shaking hands he reached up and gently cupped her breasts, positioning them for his eager mouth. He leaned forward and flicked a tongue against her turgid nipple and Simone bucked her hips and cried out.

    Xander watched as Simone's passion was unleashed and it was the sexiest thing he'd ever seen. To watch a woman that was so unsure of herself, shy and timid lose all control, was almost more than he could take. His hands dove into her hair and he pulled her face up to his once more. He bit and nibbled at her full lips like they were his last meal. Her moans and cries as Jackson continued to rub her clit against his jean-clad erection, rippled against Xander's tongue.

    "Ah God, Simone!" Jackson shouted out as her hips now moved over his without his help, seeking release just as much as he was.

    Simone was mindless to everything around her. All she knew, all she felt were the feelings and sensations coursing through her body. Something was building inside her that was ten times as intense as the massage earlier that day. It was like her dream that afternoon was a premonition, a prelude to what was happening to her now. She was on fire, yet her body was exposed to the cold night air, but she couldn't feel it. All she felt was them.

    Her body started to tingle and the feeling was mostly concentrated at her wet core. The inner walls of her vagina started to pulsate. Jackson suddenly grazed her nipple with his teeth at the same time as he thrust up against her clit and Xander flicked his tongue against hers just right. The onslaught of pleasure all at the same time combined to send her body over the edge. She bucked out of control against Jackson's imprisoned manhood and screamed into Xander's mouth as she reached her pulsating climax.

    The moment it was over, instant shame crashed down upon Simone so hard that she could barely breathe. She quickly pulled down her sweater and crossed her arms over her breasts, still feeling completely naked.

"Simone? Are you okay?" Jackson asked with concern trying to look at her face, but she kept her face turned away from him as she tried to hold back tears.

Jackson looked up at Xander completely dumbfounded by the change in Simone.

"Si. What's wrong?" Xander tried next.

"Please don't call me that." Simone said with a shaky voice, trying to keep it together. "Xander can you please give me some room so I can get up."

Xander immediately stepped back a few paces. Jackson reached out to grip Simone's hips to help her up, but she flinched away from him.

"Don't touch me." Simone said with underlying anger in her tone, as she scrambled off of his lap.

"Simone please, let us explain?" Jackson implored, holding his hands up so she could see he wasn't going to touch her.

"I don't want to hear it. You don't have to explain anything to me. You used me. Turned me into *that* girl! You just made me feel like a slut." Simone choked out the last sentence.

"God, no Simone! That wasn't our intention. You're not a slut. And we don't think of you that way. We never intended to make you feel bad about what just happened. We were trying to make you feel good." Xander tried to explain, coming towards her.

Simone stepped back quickly, too afraid to let one of them touch her again. She lost her footing in the snow and fell into the white slush. The men leapt to help her.

"Oh God! Please don't touch me!" Simone sobbed, finally breaking completely.

She clumsily got up out of the snow and raced to the lodge, nearly falling again in her hurry to get away from the two men.

"What did we just do?" Jackson said putting his face in his hands.

"I thought that she enjoyed herself. What woman gets upset over an orgasm?" Xander said with exasperation.

"Well, she's obviously not like other women, Xan. When was the last time you had sexual relations with a twenty-nine year old shy and sheltered virgin?" Jackson looked at Xander like he was an idiot.

"Never." Xander said in defeat.

"That's what I thought. She's the type of person that is used to analyzing, studying and observing things. We should have explained it to her first and then let her make the choice." Jackson reasoned.

"I don't buy that. Yes, you're right she is someone that thinks about how she's supposed to feel. But if we would've sat her down and told her about how we like our relationships, she would've run for the hills. She needed to know what it would feel like to be with us. She can't analyze what she's never experienced. She might be upset now, but when she starts to think about what it was like, she'll want more. And we have the trip back alone with her tomorrow. She can't get away from us then and we can talk to her about everything." Xander suggested.

"I hope you're right." Jackson said, sadly looking up at the fading Aurora Borealis and thinking about how well the night had started. "We better put out this fire and head in."

Chapter 6

Simone woke to the sound of gentle knocking on the door. She had barely gotten any sleep, and looking over at the clock that read nine in the morning she knew she had to get up and moving.

When she had ran back to her room the previous night sobbing uncontrollably, the instant she came in she jumped in the shower trying to wash away the memories and the feel of their touch from her skin. She felt so humiliated over the spectacle she had made of herself. So she had cried herself into a fitful sleep.

The knock sounded at the door again and Simone got out of bed walking slowly to the door, afraid that it might be Jackson or Xander.

"Who is it?" She asked hesitantly.

"It's Rachel. Can you let me in for a moment?" Rachel's gruff voice reached Simone's ears through the door.

Simone unlocked the door and let the older woman in.

"I'm guessing you had a rough night if those puffy eyes and dark circles are any indication." Rachel observed.

Simone just looked at Rachel sadly, too afraid to speak or else the waterworks would start again.

"I'm guessing those fools botched everything." Rachel shook her head, as Simone just looked at her with a perplexed look on her face.

"I know what the boys like. I've known them for years. And I know their tastes. They like to share their women." Rachel finally said and Simone's eyes bugged out of her head and a blush spread over her entire face and neck. "Don't be embarrassed, Simone. It's the way they've always been." Rachel stopped talking when Simone held up her hands.

"I don't want to talk about it. Was there a reason you came up here, besides defending those two?" Simone asked tightly.

"They just wanted me to tell you that they want to head out by ten. They wanted to let you sleep in as much as possible, but there's a snow storm coming and they want to get you back to the Drake Lodge before it hits." Rachel relayed the message.

"Thank you." Simone said, as she purposefully walked Rachel back to the door.

"Just hear them out is all I'm saying. Let them explain, and then make a decision based off of that." Rachel said lastly before shutting the door.

Simone walked back over the bed and flopped back onto the mattress. *How am I going to face them today? I've never been so humiliated in all my life.* But no matter how hard she tried to focus on her anger at being used like a common whore, her mind kept creeping back to the sensations she had felt last night. *God, it felt so* good*!*

"Oh shut up Simone!" She yelled to herself, trying not to remember their touch.

Simone got up from the bed to start packing up her things, knowing that she had to face the inevitable sooner or later. She braided her hair in a side braid that rested against her neck and breast. She threw on her black pair of snowboarder pants with white piping down the sides of the legs and grabbed her white jacket. Picking up her duffel bag, Simone reluctantly left the sanctuary of her hotel room.

~~~

Simone thankfully ate her breakfast by herself when Rachel told her that the guys had already eaten and were outside readying the dogs for the journey back. Once she was done she gloomily headed outside to face Xander and Jackson.

The dogs and sleds were ready to go and the men stood talking quietly together. The moment Simone laid eyes on the tall handsome men, her breath caught in the back of her throat, her stomach flip-flopped and her heart started pounding. Apparently her humiliation was no match for her attraction to them. So she just shook her head in disappointment at her weakness, took a deep breath and walked over to the men.

Jackson and Xander stopped talking mid-conversation and watched silently as Simone made her way towards them. They seemed sad and more reserved than normal, causing Simone further confusion because they actually made her feel bad, like she was the bad guy in this scenario.

"Good Morning, Simone." Jackson said gently, as if she'd break.

"Mornin'." Xander said at the same time.

"Jackson. Xander." Simone acknowledged.

"Ready?" Xander asked.

"As I'll ever be." Simone said shortly.

"Just let us know if you get tired. We can stop when you need to. You'll probably still be a little sore from the trip yesterday." Xander suggested.

"Thanks." Simone responded, not giving an inch.

"Alright then, let's get going." Xander said, backing down for the moment.

~~~

Xander stopped his team after two hours for a break, since it seemed Simone was going to refuse to show any sign of weakness and ask to stop.

"WHOA!" Simone shouted the command to the dogs as they came up beside Xander's team. And a few seconds later, Jackson's team stopped beside hers.

"I thought now was a good time to take a break to stretch and eat a snack." Xander said handing Simone another protein bar that he pulled from his pack on the sled.

"Thank you." Simone said grudgingly.

Jackson walked over to Xander to get his bar. They gave each other a meaningful look before they both turned to Simone.

"Simone, can we please talk about last night?" Jackson started.

Simone gave no sign that she even heard him, other than the tightening of her jaw.

"Simone, please? Give us a chance to explain." Xander implored.

Simone slowly laid her half eaten protein bar down on her bag in front of her and turned to look at the men. She stared quietly at them for a moment.

"You had all the time in the world yesterday, to explain. Hell, even the day before that! Because if I'm not mistaken you started in on me even then, trying to wear me down from the moment we met. But no, you both just flirted with me and stole kisses here and there driving me to distraction and making me believe that I had to choose between the two of you. When all along you wanted to use me like some chick you picked up at the local bar, and do God knows what to. And if you haven't noticed, I don't operate that way. I don't just jump into bed with a man, let alone *two*! You had your chance and now it's passed." Simone ended her tirade as the men looked down in shame.

Not wanting to spend any more time in their presence, Simone turned back to the sled, grabbed the reigns and shouted out to the dogs.

"HIKE!" And like a gunshot the dogs took off.

"Simone! Stop!" Xander shouted.

"Shit!" Jackson exclaimed at the same time.

Both men ran to their sleds and jumped on, shouting out commands at their teams. And they took off after her. By the time their dog teams were up to full speed Simone was already several yards away.

The cold air whipped at Simone's face as her dogs speed through the snow. Something unseen or heard to Simone caused the Huskies to growl, bark and whine collectively. And without her command the dogs turned left and careened through the woods that ran along the path they were taking.

"GEE GEE!" Simone shouted at the dogs trying to get them to turn back to the right, but they kept going at a break neck pace through the woods.

Simone held on for dear life as she tried to look around at what had spooked them. To her right she caught a glimpse of something running. Gripping the sled tighter, she looked again and saw about four loose dogs running a few paces away from them. And then realization hit. They weren't dogs, they were wolves. *Oh my God, oh my God!* Simone's heart started to pound with fear.

Her team broke free of the woods and started running straight for a rushing river that ran along the middle of the forest.

"GEE GEE! Simone screamed trying to get the dogs to turn away from the river.

At the last minute the team turned sharply to the right and the sled started to tip. The momentum of the dogs, the off balance sled and the sharp turn flung Simone through the air.

Simone felt weightless for a split second and then bone chilling cold enveloped her as she plunged into the ice cold rushing river. Her body instantly seized up from the freezing temperature of the water. Her muscles locked, making it nearly impossible to swim against the current of the rushing water. And within seconds her clothes were soaked through and she started to lose feeling in her fingers and toes.

Her body started to shake uncontrollably and she quickly started to sink down into the water like a stone. The ice cold water enveloped her, enclosing her in an icy tomb. Simone's lungs started to burn with the need for air. Instinctively, she took a breath trying to get precious oxygen, taking the frigid water into her lungs and her world went black.

  Jackson and Xander saw the wolf pack chasing down Simone's sled, and their hearts raced with panic. They knew there had been some wolves uncharacteristically hanging out in the Fairbanks area killing local pets, but they never imagined that they'd be so bold as to chase down a dogsled team.
  The men watched helplessly as Simone's team careened through the woods. Jackson shouted out at his dogs to go faster, trying fervently to catch up with Simone. But her team was going at a breakneck pace.
  Xander watched as her team cleared the forest and he and Jackson followed closely in pursuit, gaining a little speed on the erratic sled. The wolves still gave chase alongside her sled team. Simone tried to command the dogs to turn right before they plunged into the river and at the last minute they made a hairpin turn that set-off a chain of events that sent Simone sailing through the air and into the raging river.
  Her team kept going trying to get away from the wolves, but they surround them forcing them to stop. Sampson tried to defend his team and attacked what looked to be the alpha male. Xander and Jackson's sleds came to a halt near the scene and they jumped off their sleds and sprang into action. Jackson ran straight for the river, ripped off his coat and shoes and jumped into the frigid water without a second thought, watching helplessly as Simone struggled against the current. Her limbs flailing uselessly until her movements became sluggish and she started to sink. *No, no, no! God, I can't lose another person I care about like this.*

Please just let me save her. I couldn't save them, I couldn't save my family. I wasn't strong enough. Please, let me be strong enough now.

Jackson reached her a few seconds later, the adrenaline pumping through his veins kept him from feeling the glacial temperature of the river and he swam like an Olympian in his desperation to save her. Jackson reached out to grab her arm and pulled her to the surface. He wrapped an arm across her shoulders and began to pull her to the river's edge.

As Jackson rushed for Simone, Xander jumped off of his sled grabbed the gun that he always brought with him on sled tours, in case of this very scenario, and shot it off a couple of times into the air. The wolves immediately ran off back into the forest.

As soon as the threat of the wolves was gone, Xander ran to the edge of the water to meet Jackson as he pulled Simone in. Xander grabbed Jackson's collar on his coat and started to pull him out of the water as Jackson held on to Simone.

Jackson fell back in the snow catching his breath for a moment while Xander pulled Simone to lay her flat and ripped off his gloves to feel her pulse and leaned his ear to her mouth to check if she was breathing. When he quickly assessed that no air was passing through her mouth or nose he lifted his head, pinched her nose and opened her mouth that was an unsettling shade of blue and started to perform CPR.

He released her mouth after forcing two breaths into her lungs, clasped both hands together and started to pump her chest for about sixty seconds. He pressed his ear to her mouth again, but still there was nothing. Xander started to panic, fear of losing someone who had become important to him and Jackson made him refuse to give up.

Jackson knelt beside them helplessly waiting for any signs of life from the beautiful woman, as Xander continued to work on her. And finally, Simone choked and sputtered out the water that was trapped in her lungs, gasping for breath.

"Oh, thank God!" Xander exclaimed, dropping his forehead to her heaving chest.

"Simone!" Jackson cried out as she came to.

"Are the dogs okay?" Simone's voice rasped out in a whisper.

"Oh baby, they're fine." Xander said, rising up to look at her. "Sampson is a little torn up trying to defend the team, but otherwise fine."

"Good." Simone wheezed before passing out again.

"We need to get her to the hospital." Jackson urged. The worry of losing her to drowning now transferred to losing her from hypothermia.

"There's no time. The hospital is too far and we're not that far from my lodge." Xander reasoned. "But first we need to try to get her out of these clothes. Check her bag, to find another coat and pair pants. And grab some of the blankets, while I get her out of these wet clothes." Xander instructed Jackson.

Xander worked at removing her wet outer clothing from her limp body, while Jackson riffled through her duffel bag to find something warm and dry. He grabbed her extra ski pants, the sweater she wore last night and a couple of blankets from all the sleds and ran back to Xander and Simone.

"I couldn't find another coat and we didn't bring any extras either, but I've got some blankets." Jackson said as he knelt down on the other side of Simone.

They worked quickly to keep her bare skin from being exposed to the cold air for too long. They got her in her dry pants and wrapped her tightly in the blankets in place of a coat. Once she was completely covered from head to toe like a burrito, Jackson carried her to his sled and made a makeshift bed to lay her on in the front.

Xander attached her team of dogs and sled to the back of his sled as Jackson also quickly stripped out of his wet clothes, swapping them for dry ones.

Xander placed Sampson on Simone's sled and securing him to it, since he was unable to walk because of the injuries he sustained from the fight with the wolf.

When they were ready, they took off at full speed knowing that they had very little time to get Simone to warm shelter before it was too late and to get the injured dog to the vet right away to tend to his wounds before he lost too much blood.

They made it to the lodge in record time. The instant the sleds came to a stop both men hopped off, Jackson grabbing Simone and Xander picking up Sampson. They both hurried into the lodge. The lodge staff was hanging out at the front desk when the men burst through the front door.

"Mike, I need to you to get Sampson to Dr. Bennett's, he was attacked by a wolf. After that you can go home." Xander ordered, as Jackson grabbed the master key and strode quickly to Simone's suite.

"Are all the guests checked out?" Xander continued.

"Yes, sir." They responded.

"Good. The rest of you should head home now, the storm that's about it hit is gonna be brutal. Our new wave of guests are going to be delayed, so there is no reason for you to get stuck here for however long this blizzard is going to last." Xander further instructed his staff.

He passed the injured dog to Mike and as the rest of the staff headed out Xander locked up the lodge and quickly made his way up to Simone's suite to see how she was doing.

When he entered the room, Jackson had Simone laid on the bed still wrapped tightly while he stroked a blazing fire in the fireplace. They knew the key to warming her up was to slowly elevate her temperature. So Xander walked over to the bed, unwrapped her feet from the blankets and started to rub vigorously from her feet to up her calves to jump start the circulation. When Jackson was finished with the fire, he also came over to start at her hands and arms.

"Let's get her in front of the fire." Jackson suggested.

"Yeah, good idea." Xander agreed.

Jackson grabbed the blankets off the bed and made a pallet on the floor in front of the fire. Once done, Xander lifted her off the bed and laid her down on the pile of blankets. As her temperature started to slowly increase her body went from completely still to violent tremors.

"Okay, I think if we undress her and we strip down too and lay on either side of her it'll help bring her temp back up to ours." Jackson proposed.

Xander just nodded his agreement and they started to remove her clothing, not thinking of how beautiful they thought her thick body was. All they could think about was if she made it out of this okay. Once she was bare they continued to massage and rub warmth back into her body.

"Do you think we should've stripped her completely naked? Because when she wakes up she's going to go ape shit on us." Xander asked as they stripped down to only their boxer briefs.

"Hell, if she's feeling good enough to rip us a new one, I'll be the happiest man alive." Jackson smiled grimly as they both laid next to her, pulling her in close to receive their much need body heat.

Slowly her body's racking shivers subsided, the alarming blue of her lips started to fade and her lowered heart rate started to pick back up to normal. Both men realized that she was going to make it, and with the drop in adrenaline through their veins they snuggled in tighter to her, pulled one of the blankets over the three of them and passed out from exhaustion.

~~~

Simone felt like she was dying in the fires of hell from all of the heat surrounding her. Her eyes fluttered open and they took a moment to clear and focus. At first she saw a blazing fire and looking down she saw two heads lying on her chest. One with chestnut curls, the other shaggy blond. In the instant she realized it was Jackson and Xander, she also realized that she was completely and utterly naked. *Holy shit! What happened and why am I naked in the middle of these two. What the…did they roofie me this time?!*

Simone started to panic. But then the events of the day all rushed back to her; her anger with the men, the wolves chasing her sled team, and the rushing artic river. *They must have saved me. Well…crap! How can I be mad at them after all that?* Simone grudgingly looked down at the two sleeping men and a warm fondness enveloped her that one could only feel for someone that risked their own life to save yours. *It's just hero worship.* Simone tried to convince herself of the feelings coursing through her.

She must have stirred a little because both men's heads popped up and looked up at her at the same time. Two sets of eyes stared at her for a moment, steel gray and mossy green.

"Simone! You're awake!" Xander exclaimed.

Jackson said nothing, but with lightning speed he went from staring at her one moment and his lips were on hers the next, in a desperate kiss.

"You're okay." Jackson breathed against her lips, when he finally released them.

Simone's heart pounded, not sure of how she was supposed to react to the kiss.

"Yes." She whispered back.

"How are you feeling?" Xander asked in concern.

"Hot." Simone said shyly.

At the same time they all became exceedingly aware that she was completely naked in between their mostly naked bodies. Apparently they were all hot in more ways than one.

"Simone." Xander said softly, placing an index finger under her chin and turning her face to his. "May I?" He asked.

Simone could do nothing but nod her head, since it seemed she had suddenly lost her ability to speak.

Xander gently placed his lips to hers. He gave her soft pecks, easing her into the kiss.

"Is this okay?" Xander asked, afraid to scare her off again.

"Y...yes." Simone stuttered out nervously, as Xander placed his lips to hers again, but this time deepening the kiss.

Oh God, this is it. This is about to happen. I'm going to lose my virginity to two men. Oh God...oh God! I never thought I'd lose it to one!

Simone's mind went wild, but she knew that it was inevitable. After the orgasm she'd had last night, finally feeling what all the fuss was about, she couldn't turn back. Her body craved more of that amazing sensation. And she realized now that she had been trying to hold on to her anger at the men to keep from admitting what she was really feeling. What she really wanted.

"Stop, Simone. You're over-analyzing everything. Just enjoy it." Xander said pulling back to look her in the eyes.

"Sorry." Simone said, taking a deep breath trying to calm her nerves. "I...I've never had...s...sex before." Simone confessed, closing her eyes not wanting to see the look on the men's faces at her admission.

"We know. We'll take it slow." Jackson said nuzzling her neck.

"How-" Simone turned to look at him in surprise and he claimed her lips in a searing kiss.

Xander took that opportunity to pull back the blanket, exposing her upturned plump breasts tipped with brown quarter-sized areolas. He stroked a finger down her neck, past her collar bone to the slope of her right breast. He caressed the tip making her nipple pucker as she moaned, and his mouth watered to taste her skin.

Leaning down, Xander flicked his tongue against the stiffened peak and she gasped into Jackson's mouth. Jackson stroked her tongue practically in time to gentle laps that Xander gave her sensitive nipple. Of their own volition, Simone's hips moved restlessly, seeking something that she didn't understand.

Xander saw her hips pumping, in search of relief. So obliging her needs, he slowly and softly slid his hand down her curving tummy under the covers to the thatch of hair at the apex of her thick thighs. Easing the way, letting her know what his intentions were. Her hips stopped and tensed in anticipation of what was too come.

Stroking over her damp curls, wet with her arousal, he sought out the sensitive nub nestled underneath. Xander caressed her clit with the barest of touches and Simone cried out, releasing Jackson's lips and throwing her head back in ecstasy.

With Simone distracted by the sensations Xander was inflicting on her clit, Jackson joined him at her breasts, making a meal of her left nipple.

Simone was overwhelmed with the passion the two men were stirring in her. She looked down at their two heads as they licked, sucked and nibbled at her stiff nipples. She felt Xander's fingers dance across her clit, only to retreat and dip into her tight vagina. Her hips shook in response.

"Ahh…please, please, please!" Simone begged.

"What, Simone? What do you want?" Jackson asked her, as they both looked up at her.

"I…I don't know!" Simone cried, confused by all the feelings that were coursing through her.

"Let us show you." Xander said, kissing the side of her breast.

"O…okay." Simone said shyly.

Jackson pulled back the blanket, completely exposing her naked body. Simone's instincts made her immediately try to cover herself with her hands and arms.

"Don't hide from us. Your body is beautiful." Jackson said, gently brushing her arms away.

"No it's not." Simone argued, turning beet red with embarrassment.

"How can you tell us what we find beautiful? I think we know our own minds." Xander scolded her.

"Because I know what my body looks like. I've looked at it in the mirror for twenty-nine years." Simone argued.

"Simone, your body is made for what we're about to do to it. Maybe it's because you're still a virgin that you can't see the appeal you have to us." Jackson explained.

"We can show you just how much you appeal to us." Xander said sitting up to kneel next to her.

Jackson followed suit on her left side. Both men were only in boxer briefs and their manhoods strained against the material. In all her years of study for nursing Simone had never seen an erect penis up close and now she was about to see and *feel* two. Simone held her breath as both men clasped the waistband of their underwear and slowly pulled them down, revealing their erections, as they sprang free of their confinements.

Simone nearly passed out at the sight of both monstrous appendages. Jackson's was nearly as thick as his wrist, and if she had to guess, about seven to eight inches long. And Xander's was thick but not quite as thick as Jackson's, but a bit longer by an inch or so and had a slight upward curve. *Sweet Mary Mother, I'm never going to survive all that!*

"Now, does it look like we find you unattractive?" Xander asked looking down at her.

Since words had completely escaped Simone, she just quickly shook her head.

"That's what I thought." Xander responded.

Jackson laid back down beside her, seeking her lips for another searing kiss. Pulling back a little, he rested his forehead against hers, his breath harsh and fanning her lips.

"Touch me, Simone." He breathed out.

Simone knew exactly what he was talking about, but too nervous to touch him 'there' right away, she placed her hand on his burly chest. The springy dark hair that covered his massive chest and ran down his rock hard abdomen to his equally hard member, Simone could only describe as blatantly manly.

Simone brushed her fingers over his defined pecs and the flat disks of his nipples and he hissed in response. Her hand eased down his stomach, going over each rise and valley of his abs. Once she got to the bottom of his abs, only inches away from his intimidating hardness, she hesitated.

"It won't bite you." Jackson chuckled

His chuckle quickly died in his throat when she finally reached down to grasp him tightly.

"Ahh…gently. Gently. I don't want to finish before we've even gotten started." Jackson gasped at Simone's touch. "Here, like this."

Jackson placed his hand over hers, showing her how to lightly stroke over his flesh, as his body shuddered from restrained pleasure. Her hand didn't even come close to wrapping around his girth. And her heart rate picked up at the thought of trying to fit him inside her tight body.

Xander moved to Simone's legs, bringing her knees up and placing his hands top on them. Simone looked up at Xander from watching her hand glide over Jackson's length.

"Now Simone, we've made it our mission to understand what women want and how the female body works. All we want is to give you pleasure, but we know that it can be difficult for a woman to orgasm. And since this is your first time we know it'll take more effort, so I want to get you ready and make sure you get yours before we even think about getting ours. Is that okay? Can I show you?" Xander asked, still nervous that she would change her mind and stop them.

"Y…yes." Simone said softly in anticipation of what he had planned for her.

Xander grabbed her knees firmly and started to pull them apart as she tried to clench them together.

"Don't fight me, Si. Just relax." Xander scolded.

Simone took a deep breath and let him separate her legs. She flushed with embarrassment as he lay between her thighs and gazed at her most intimate place. Xander took a deep breath and then blew gently against her heated flesh and all thoughts of mortification evaporated at the sensation.

Simone watched as Xander spread her labia and his tongue flicked out against her clit. She cried out and tried to crawl back away from him, shocked at the feeling of his tongue against her. She didn't get far because of Xander's hold on her wide hips. He pulled her back and growled in the back of this throat as he aggressively latched onto her clit, holding her down tightly as she went wild.

Simone screamed at the sweet torment Xander caused her. Her hips had a mind of their own. They pushed down into the blankets, trying to retreat from Xander's persistent tongue, only to pump back up, wanting so much more.

"God, you're magnificent!" Jackson said, as he watched her buck against Xander's mouth.

Adding to her torture, Jackson flicked his tongue against her left nipple as he caressed and lightly pinched her right. Simone was in the middle of sensory overload. The culmination of the sensations coursing through her veins centered at her core.

Xander and Jackson were like a well-oiled machine. When one retreated the other advanced, never leaving her skin. Jackson drew her breast into his warm mouth and his tongue lightly swiped at her nipple. Xander sucked on her clit and slid one finger into her tight opening, caressing her inner walls. The tense knot at her core began to expand, her heart pounded out a beat in her ears blocking out all sound.

As the intensity built Simone's thighs started to tremble so hard that her entire body started to shake. And her world shattered. A piercing scream ripped through her throat as her back bowed in release.

Simone collapsed out of breath, as her hips continued to reflexively pump against Xander's mouth until she could take no more.

"Stop…please." She begged, and Xander released her clit on a gasp.

Jackson kissed her lips gently as Xander came up from between her legs. When Jackson relinquished her lips, Xander came in to give her a deep kiss, dipping his tongue into her mouth so that she could taste her own nectar.

Jackson reached out to unwind the hair-tie at the end of her long braid. He threw it to the side, unraveled her hair and combed his fingers through it.

"You have amazing hair. You should show it off more." Jackson complimented.

"Thank you." Simone said shyly, after Xander released her lips, overwhelmed by the two men.

Xander and Jackson looked at each other, silently communicating their next move. Xander slid from between her legs, stood up and walked over to the bed and laid in the middle, reclining his back against the headboard. His lean and sculpted muscles moved gracefully under his skin. What little body hair he had was blond and blended in with his golden skin tone, making him look like a blond Adonis.

Simone marveled over how confident both men were completely naked, as if it was a normal occurrence to strut around nude. *But then again, if I was a guy and looked like them, I'd strut too.*

Jackson slid his hands under her back and knees and lifted her gently off the makeshift pallet on the floor. He walked her over to the bed and placed her on her knees in the middle of the bed.

"Come here." Xander instructed, holding out his hand for Simone to take.

Xander pulled her over to him, placed her between his legs, adjusting until her head and back laid against his chest and stomach. He brushed her hair to the side and down her shoulder, covering her left breast.

Jackson gazed down tenderly at them, seeing his future laid out before him. Simone looked up at him bashfully and he knew in that moment he'd do anything to make this work. He just hoped that Xander was on board and that Simone would be willing. He knew she had a life in Washington, but prayed that she'd be willing to stay with them.

The bed dipped down as he crawled onto it, towards Simone.

"Are you okay?" Jackson asked. Simone nodded her head slightly. "Do you want to stop?" Again she just shook her head no. "Okay. This may hurt you a little and I'm sorry for that. I'll try to be gentle, but make it quick." Jackson cautioned.

"O…okay," was Simone's only reply.

Jackson looked at Xander. Xander nodded his head in understanding. It would be his job to soothe and relax her as Jackson took her virginity, which Xander was okay with not being first. He knew that it would be his turn to take her virginity in other ways. But that would take more time and finesse. He knew it was hard to convince an experienced woman to engage in anal sex, but in order for them to have her at the same time it was something that they had to coax her into.

Xander slid further down, reclining more on the pillows behind him, positioning Simone at a better angle for Jackson.

"Bring your knees up, Si." Jackson commanded, using her nickname for the first time.

Simone did as she was told, and Jackson pulled her knees apart as Xander did earlier. Jackson knelt between her legs and gently caressed her opening with the tip of his finger. She was still wet from her recent orgasm, making access easier as Jackson slid a finger into her tight canal. Simone took in a sharp breath as her muscles clenched around his finger.

"God you're so tight! I think I'll lose my mind if I can't be inside you right now." Jackson moaned at the feel of her around his finger.

Jackson slid his finger back out of her wet entrance, positioned his thumb against her clit and eased two fingers into her wet pussy. For the first time since their passionate lovemaking began, Jackson actually worried about truly hurting her when he finally did take her. He could barely get two fingers inside of her and his cock was *way* bigger around than his fingers.

"Jackson!" Simone gasped as his thumb danced across her clit.

Removing his hand from the slick heat, Jackson grasped his rock hard erection firmly and stroked the large head up and down her cleft. He knew that there was no amount of prepping he could do to lessen the pain and shock of the first initial breach of her hymen. So he eased his engorged tip into her snug opening, not wanting to waste any more time.

Xander slid his hands over Simone's as she panted with fear and entwined his fingers with hers as Jackson shallowly stroked his mushroom capped tip in and out. Her back tensed and she whimpered softly as Jackson stroked deeper finding her barrier.

"Shh…easy. It's okay, Si. It's okay." Xander soothed, kissing her temple.

Jackson looked to Xander for some help. Xander understood and released her right hand, brought his fingertips up to her chin, tilting her head back and raising her face up, he bent his down and took her lips in a passionate kiss. As she lost herself to the kiss, Jackson took the opportunity to pull out practically to the tip and then plunged in swiftly past her cherry.

Simone groaned in pain in the back of her throat as she bit down on Xander's lip and squeezed his left hand in a vice like grip. Tears escaped her tightly shut eyelids and slid down her cheeks.

Jackson held perfectly still, buried inside Simone's warmth to the hilt, letting her get accustomed to his length and girth. He gritted his teeth in restraint, wanting nothing more than to pound into her and lose himself in her tight heat.

After a few moments had passed and Simone's body had relaxed enough to release Xander's lip and ease up on the grip she had on his hand. Her inner walls expanded to accommodate Jackson's immense size. The sharp pain of him breaking her hymen eased enough for her to feel the fullness of him inside of her.

Jackson noticing her body relax, he pulled back again to the very tip and thrust back in deeply. Simone cried out in pleasure this time, as Jackson hit the perfect spot. Taking his cue from her reaction, Jackson continued to pump into her slowly. His forehead dropped to her chest and groaned as her muscles flexed round him.

"Oh my God! Jackson! Jackson…please!" Simone pleaded.

"What, baby? What do you need?" Jackson panted, as he tried to hold back.

"I…don't…I don't know." Simone whimpered.

"How about faster?" Jackson asked, as he increased his speed.

Simone's back bowed off of Xander as continuous cries escaped her throat. Jackson leaned down to suck a taunt nipple into his mouth as he continued to stroke in and out at a steady pace.

"Xander, hold her legs back." Jackson instructed.

Xander grabbed hold of Simone's legs, wrapped his hands around the back of her thighs, right above the crease of her knees, pulled them back to her chest and spread her wide open for Jackson's assault. Jackson sat up on his hunches, gripped her hips and pounded into her mercilessly. The sounds of lovemaking; flesh smacking, masculine moans and feminine cries filled the room.

"Shit!" Jackson shouted out as Simone's walls started to ripple over his cock.

Xander ground his teeth together as Simone's back moved back and forth over his painful erection. The sounds of her cries nearly making him mad with want.

"Ahhh….yes…yes…yes…YES!!!" Simone screamed, as she exploded, her entire body tensing.

Wave after wave of ecstasy washed over her as Jackson continued to thrust into her, extending her climax. The lust that they brought out of her turned her into a completely different person in the heat of the moment. She didn't even recognize herself. She was wanton, passionate and lustful.

Jackson tensed and shuddered above her.

"Fuck…Simone!" He shouted out, as his raging steel spilled his seed into her.

Jackson collapsed on top of her, his body covered in sweat and his breath came out harshly as his chest heaved.

As his head cleared from the haze of lust, Jackson realized what he had just done.

"Shit! I'm so sorry, Simone. I didn't use any protection. Fuck!" He said with shame, looking up at her in apology.

"It's okay. Well, that is if you're disease free. I've been on the pill since I was sixteen, for atrocious acne and excruciating menstrual cycles." Simone said with a blush.

"No. No diseases here. We've rarely went without using condoms. And the last relationship we had, ended on a bad note. So we went to get tested just in case and we both got a clean bill of health." Xander responded.

"Okay. I trust you." Simone said quietly, her shy nature creeping back in once her passion had subsided.

Simone adjusted awkwardly as Jackson laid on her legs and abdomen and Xander hissed in pain. She realized at that moment that Xander still hadn't found his release.

"Oh God, Xander! I'm so sorry!" Simone exclaimed.

"It's okay. I'll live." Xander grimaced.

"But what about you? I don't know men very well, but I'm assuming you need some kind of…relief." Simone looked back at him sweetly.

"You need a break. I'm sure you're very tender right now." Xander said considerately, kissing her forehead.

"I'm okay. That is if you want me?" Simone said, looking at his chin, not able to make eye contact for fear of rejection.

"Are you crazy?! I'm dying to get inside you…to feel you." Xander blurted out.

"Then I'd like to please you too." Simone smiled timidly at him.

"Dear God, I think I've died and gone to heaven." Xander declared, happily.

"No you haven't. You won't know what heavens like until you've been inside her." Jackson said flopping down on the bed next to Simone as she blushed profusely.

"I don't know if you're ready for this so soon, but I'm an ass man myself. And ever since we met you, I've imagined you in this position a hundred times." Xander said as he slid from behind Simone.

He grabbed her around her waist, flipped her over and pulled her up onto her knees in front of him.

"Xander?" Simone asked warily.

"It's okay. This position is a little rougher and deeper. If you don't like it or if I hurt you, just let me know okay?" Xander prepared her.

Simone nodded her head and looked up at Jackson as he watched them. Simone felt the head of Xander's erection rub along her labia and the passion that had subsided earlier came back to the forefront.

Xander slowly glided the tip of his cock into her tight warm sheath and she gasped in response. He slid into the base and back out again. The suction of her body around him, nearly made him weep. His hips shook as he eased in one last time, before his restraint snapped.

Bringing the tip back out to her slick opening, Xander gripped her hips tightly and slammed back into her. Simone threw her head back on a scream, and still Xander continued his assault on her. With each slam of his hips to her, her ridiculously round ass rippled with the force.

Unable to resist, Xander raised his hand back and brought it down with light force against her right cheek. She cried out as her body tensed around his manhood, making him groan loudly. Her inner walls began to flutter and convulse around him. And Xander was glad for the empty lodge because he was sure they were bringing down the roof with their cries and screams of ecstasy.

Xander thrust into her a few more times as his scrotum drew up and then exploded with his climax.

"Fucking shit, Simone!" Xander shouted out as they both collapsed.

Xander rolled to the side, not wanting to crush her. They both panted with exhaustion, trying to catch their breaths.

"Jesus! You were right Jackson. Absolute heaven." Xander panted, trying to catch his breath.

"Yeah, and she's all ours." Jackson said, grinning from ear to ear.

A soft snore sounded from the subject of their conversation. Jackson looked down at Simone, who appeared to of passed out on her stomach in the same position she had collapsed in.

Jackson had to rein in his passion. Having watched Simone and Xander together had gotten him rock hard again. But he knew she needed some serious rest. So he took a deep breath, resigned to wait.

"I think maybe we wore her out." Xander chuckled, as he too looked over at the sleeping beauty.

"Wouldn't you be? She went through a traumatic ordeal today and then when she woke up, we forced three orgasms out of her, which was probably a really shitty thing to do. But I couldn't help myself. I had to have her." Jackson confessed.

"Well…I don't think she was exactly complaining. Man is she responsive! And for someone so shy, quiet and reserved any other time, she was mighty vocal and a wild cat during." Xander sighed, already reminiscing about their lovemaking.

"Indeed. And she's only getting warmed up."

Both men looked at each other happily, and they snuggled closer to Simone as they too feel into a contented sleep.

Chapter 7

Simone woke up the next morning with a nearly exploding bladder, and the body wrapped around her lower half wasn't helping. Simone tried to look back but the other body crushing her lungs that was wrapped around her top half, made movement impossible.

She shifted trying to wiggle from under the heavy men. Both reflexively tightened their holds on her, simultaneously cutting off her air supply and nearly making her piss her pants, that is if she had pants on.

"Guys! Please!" Simone yelped.

Both men popped up loosening their hold on her.

"What?! What's wrong?" Xander asked half delirious, completely releasing his hold on her abdomen and raising his head off of her ass cheek.

"I have to go to the bathroom and you were squeezing my bladder. And Jackson was crushing my lungs." Simone said as she started to move down the bed awkwardly, trying not to expose her naked body to the men.

"Sorry, you were just really comfy." Jackson mumbled sleepily.

Once she cleared the bed, she tried to cover herself with her arms and hands as she crouched down to grab a blanket. She wrapped it around her body and scampered off to the bathroom to relieve herself.

After using the bathroom and washing her hands, Simone just stared at herself in the mirror several seconds, trying to see if she looked different. Her already full lips looked puffy from numerous rough kisses. Her hair was a wild mane around her face and shoulders. Unwrapping the blanket, she looked at her naked body in the mirror, noticing loves bites all over her skin. Not understanding her appeal to the gorgeous men, she looked at her body as she imagined it looked last night in their eyes.

Her B-cup breasts fit in their hands and mouths perfectly. Her somewhat slender waist, that appeared smaller compared to her hips, cinched in right above her absurdly wide hips that were the perfect anchor for the men to hold on to as they stroked into her. Her thick thighs cushioned their hips and waist as they laid between them. Turning, she looked at her huge behind and saw it as Xander did as he plunged into her over and over again. Soft and round, absorbing every blow he delivered to her core.

Just the memory of what they did to her made Simone's heart pound and her inner walls clench in response. She realized just how sore she was from all the lovemaking. But it was the best soreness she had ever felt. Every aching muscle was attached to a memory of touch and delicious sensation, especially her tender vajayjay.

Simone took a deep breath, rewrapped the blanket around her body, preparing to walk back out to the guys. She had no idea where to go from here. She had no experience in dating and men, she'd be nervous and awkward around just one of the men. *But how do you date two? And do they want to date, or am I just a fling to them? God, this is so* weird!

Simone opened the bathroom door and slowly made her way back into the bedroom. She found the men laid out on their backs with their hands behind their heads. They were still completely naked and sporting massive erections.

Simone's eyes nearly bugged out of her head at the vision they made. She hesitated at the foot of the bed. She tried to gather her jumbled thoughts, but found she could only focus on the matter at hand by closing her eyes to the view in front of her.

"Um guys…we need to talk. Is it possible that you could show some modesty and cover yourselves? I can't concentrate when looking at *all* that." Simone said, waving her hand in their general direction since she couldn't technically see them.

"Sure." She heard them say in unison.

"Okay, you can look now." Xander said with a chuckle.

Simone slowly opened one eye at a time, to see both had covered up their happys with just pillows. She started to giggle at their antics.

"That wasn't exactly what I was thinking, but I guess it'll do." Simone took a breath and started. "So…I'm trying to understand how all this works. Do you guys just have sex with women casually? Or do you actually date…like go out to dinner and movies together as three? Do you call yourselves boyfriends and girlfriend? Are there rules? Like she can only have…um sex…with both of you at the same time?" Simone whispered the word 'sex' timidly. "Or is she free to be with you separately as well?" Simone finished.

"That's an awful lot of questions." Xander teased.

"I…I know. But I don't even know how to date one man. I've never had a boyfriend before or a casual fling. So I'm trying to figure this all out." Simone responded honestly.

"Well, it's just like any other relationship. We'll play it by ear. Get to know each other." Jackson stated. "It depends on the woman, on whether it's a casual relationship or something more serious. But I can assure you, there is nothing casual about you." Jackson explained.

"Yes, we'll take you out on dates together. Well as much as you can do around here on the outskirts of Fairbanks. But we'll take you into the city for a night out if you'd like?" Xander chimed in.

"And as long as you remain monogamous to us, you can have us any way you want. Together, separate or whatever the situation calls for." Jackson added.

"So…are you also monogamous to me, because that would only be fair?" Simone asked.

"Of course. When we enter into a relationship with a woman, she is the focus of our attention and affections." Jackson said with eyes filled with honesty.

"So um… I've never been on a date before, so I can't be too sure, but wouldn't everyone stare at us? I mean, me being with two men?" Simone asked.

"Who cares? It's none of their business what we do. Let 'em look and wish that they can do what we do." Xander smirked, just one dimple deepening in his cheek. "Now get back in this bed so we can do more of it." Xander said, patting the bed between them.

"Uh…I think I should probably take a shower first." Simone said, looking down shyly at her toes.

"That's a perfect idea!" Xander exclaimed, jumping out of the bed and throwing the pillow that was covering him to the side.

His erection bounced as he hopped up. Simone swallowed loudly as Jackson too, got up from the bed with an equally hard penis. They both strode towards her from either side of the bed as she walked backwards, away from them.

"Uh, guys…I really don't think that's a good idea." Simone said, nervously.

"No…I'm pretty sure it's a great idea." Jackson said as they closed in on her.

Simone turned and took off in the direction of the bathroom, but Xander caught her around her waist and lifted her off of her feet and over his shoulder making her squeal. He carried her the rest of the way into the bathroom as Jackson followed smiling at her as she swiped her long wild hair out her face, to look at him over Xander's shoulder.

Xander opened the glass door and leaned into the shower with Simone still on his shoulder and turned the water on to hot. He placed her on her feet outside of the shower, brushed her hair back off of her face and clasped her face in both hands. He leaned down and flicked his tongue over her lips making her gasp and her hips involuntarily pump into him.

Jackson came up behind her and slowly pulled the blanket away from her flushed skin. He pushed her hair to the side and kissed and licked a path down her neck and shoulder. Bending down, Xander wrapped his arms around her waist, lifted her and walked into the shower, never releasing her lips.

The hot spray ran over her hair and body. Jackson came in behind them, closing the glass door. Xander's back pressed against the wall as Jackson pressed into her back sandwiching her between them, his hot steel sliding between her cheeks.

"Eventually we'll have this part of you too, so that we can take you at the same time." Jackson whispered in her ear as he caressed his hardened tip against her puckered flesh.

"Ah…is…is that even safe?" Simone asked on a gasp.

"As long as we're gentle, yes." Jackson answered, licking the shell of her ear.

"Just checking. I study nursing you know. Ah God...," Simone gasped against Xander's lips as he rubbed his length over her clit. "…I've seen some weird stuff come through the emergency room. Aaaahhh…the last thing I want, is to be rushed to the hospital stuck between the two of you."

Both men laughed out loud at Simone's statement.

"We've never been sent to the ER before." Xander chuckled.

"I know you've been with other women, but I'm not sure I like hearing about it, much less thinking about it." Simone frowned at Xander.

"Then we'll do our best to keep talk about exes down to a minimum." Xander kissed her gently before releasing her legs, letting her feet slide down to the floor.

Jackson grabbed the soap, lathered it in his hands and then passed it to Xander who did the same. They stood on either side of her and placed their hands on her shoulders, smoothing the soap on her skin as they kneaded her shoulders. Simone moaned deeply, enjoying the massage.

Their hands slowly they made their way down to her breasts, soaping them and sliding her nipples between their fingers. Simone threw her head back on a gasp. Their hands followed the trail of water that ran down her stomach to her sex. Xander grabbed the bar of soap again and ran it over the thatch of hair between her legs.

Once Simone was fully lathered, Jackson ran his fingers through her labia and circled her clit and she bucked against his hand. Jackson removed his fingers and Xander's replaced them, taking turns driving her insane. Then Xander ran the soap down her back, over the large round globes of her ass and up the crease in between. Their hands alternated between dipping into her hot core, circling her clit and sliding their fingers up her ass, teasing her tight anus.

"It's too much!" Simone cried out.

"It's not even close to enough." Jackson said, before claiming her lips in an aggressive kiss.

When Jackson released her lips, Xander turned her face to his reclaiming them. Simone couldn't think, could barely process what was happening. All she could do was feel; every touch, every kiss, every sensation as they completely surrounded her. The men consumed her, overwhelmed her and left her raw.

She tried to back away from them to get her bearings, to clear her head of the haze of passion surrounding her before she lost her mind. The men stepped towards her, not giving her an inch.

"Please!" Simone cried out as she held up her hands to stop them. "I just need a moment. You both overwhelm me so much it feels like I can't breathe."

They stood completely still except for their jaws that flexed, their hands were balled up in fists at their sides, trying to rein in their eagerness.

"I'm sorry. I'm just not used to being touch this way. May…maybe if you let me get a chance to touch you, it wouldn't seem so bad." Simone whispered.

Xander quietly passed the bar of soap to Simone, silently giving her permission to touch them. Simone took the bar of soap and alternated between lathering both their chests and stomachs. The men's chests rose and fell rapidly as she stroked her hands over them. As she caressed over their nipples, they both gasped and clenched their fists tighter till they were white knuckled, resisting the urge to touch her.

Her hands smoothed down their rippling abs, she thought of them as speed bumps slowing her progress to where they really wanted her hands to go. Her fingers trembled as she lightly stroked them over their erections.

Simone marveled over how soft the skin was yet how hard they were. It was like satin covered steel. They hissed in response to her touch and she felt delighted and powerful at the ability to affect them so much. Their reactions spurred her on, to go further, and she tried her best to wrap her fingers around them. Her soapy hands glided over their hot skin and a deep groan rumbled in their chests.

Xander was the first to break. He grabbed her face and attacked her lips with a low growl. The kiss surprised her and she released their cocks. Xander squatted down, clutched her ass, lifted her off her feet and without preamble plunged into her heat stretching her to capacity.

An ear piercing scream ripped from Simone's throat and vibrated off of the shower walls, not prepared for his assault. Her nails raked across his back, leaving red welts in their wake. The buildup of tension from the bathing foreplay made them reach their peak within moments. Xander was only able to pump into her three times before they both exploded with their climaxes.

Xander released her cheeks, letting her down before collapsing against the wall panting. And Jackson immediately stepped in also squatting down, but this time he wrapped his hands behind her legs and lifted up draping her legs over his forearms, spreading her wider as he thrust into her, also lacking patience after watching his best friend take her so roughly.

"FUCKING SHIT!" Simone screamed out uncharacteristically, as her still quivering muscles from the last orgasm spasmed around his hard length. "I can't Jackson…I…" Before she could finish another shattering scream and climax ripped through her as he too erupted inside of her, after only a few pumps of his hips.

Tears streamed down her face, mixing with the spray of the water from the shower. Jackson dropped to the floor with Simone in his lap, still connected intimately. Simone's inner walls trembled around him as she crumpled prostrate on his expansive chest in exhaustion.

"Stick a fork in me…I'm done!" Simone sighed out in fatigue.

~~~

Simone woke up awhile later, alone in her bed. *Dear God, I must have passed out in the shower*, she thought to herself. She couldn't remember getting from the shower to the bed. Since her body had never been used and abused so thoroughly before, she assumed that it must have just shut down.

Having a moment alone she reached over to the nightstand and grabbed her phone, quickly calling up Amber's number.

"Finally! You kept me waiting long enough! What's happening with those two ridiculously hot men? Dear God, Simone…they are gorgeous! You hit the fucking hot guy jackpot!" Amber chattered brightly.

"It happened, Amber!" Simone said in an excited whisper.

"What?! You finally gave away your V-card?!" Amber shouted into the phone.

"Yes!"

"Holy shit! I have to break out some champagne! We are totally celebrating when I get there." Amber said excitedly. "So which one did you choose? The blond with the crazy lips and dimples? Or the one with the adorable curls and piercing gray eyes? Can I have the one you didn't pick? It doesn't matter which one, they're both smokin'!"

"Well…that's the thing. I…I slept with both of them." Simone whispered waiting for the scream that was surely to come.

"WHAT?!?!" Amber screamed as Simone knew she would, so she held the phone from her ear. "How did you pull that off without both of them knowing? It's not like you're experienced in the art of juggling two men. Hell, it's hard for me to do."

"Uh…well…we were all together…at the same time." Again Simone held the phone away from her ear waiting for the scream, but she heard nothing but silence. "Hello…Amber? Are you still there?" Simone asked bringing the phone back to her ear.

"I think I just passed out for a second there. Or maybe I just went deaf, because I swear I just heard you say that you lost your virginity during a THREESOME!" Amber said, ending on a shout of disbelief, making Simone cringe and her eardrum vibrate.

"Um…well, yeah…you heard correctly. But somehow you make it sound dirty. It was…lovely, and…and a little overwhelming." Simone whispered into the phone.

"Well hell yeah, it was overwhelming! A virgin with absolutely zero experience, hopping into the bed with two huge gorgeous men, would be a little dazed. Oh and speaking of huge…?" Amber left the obvious question open.

"Dear God Amber, I've never seen anything like it!" Simone exclaimed under her breath, trying not to be loud.

"Sweetie, I need specifics. Hell if you could draw up a diagram and send it to me, that'd be great! Or better yet…how about you send me a double penis pic?!" Amber prodded.

"I don't know if I should be telling you about their private parts." Simone hesitated.

"Spit it out woman, I need the deets! I've been waiting years to have this conversation with you!" Amber shouted out.

"Well…uh…one has to be at least eight inches long and so big around I can't even get my hands around him! And the other is even longer, by an inch or so and I still can't get my hand completely around him either! It's insane and intimidating. But Amber, it felt so…so…*amazing.*" Simone ended in awe.

"Wow! It's like you're Luke Skywalker and I'm Obi-Wan and you just surpassed me in your Jedi training. My big sister from another mister has finally become a woman." Amber said on a sigh, making Simone giggle.

"Oh God, you're making *Star Wars* references? Did you find your inner geek in the few days I've been gone?" Simone smiled into the phone.

"Shit! I've become you and you've turned into me, though I'd like to point out that even *I* haven't had a threesome before. So was it a one-time thing? A one night stand?" Amber asked curiously.

"Actually, no. It happened last night and again in the shower this morning." Simone said matter-of-factly.

"Holy shit! Can I be you for a day?! I'm so fucking jealous!" Amber shouted in Simone's ear. "So where do you go from here? I don't like the thought of them using you or taking advantage of your innocence." Amber asked with concern.

"Well, this is actually the way they prefer to do relationships. They seem to like to share one woman at a time. It's even how they lost their virginity." Simone explained.

"Damn! Where can I find a relationship like that?!" Amber sighed with envy. "So I have a very important question to ask you." Amber paused for effect. "Have you landscaped?"

"Landscaped? What do you mean?" Simone asked perplexed.

"You know? Groomed?" Amber responded vaguely.

"I don't get it, Amber. Just say what you mean!" Simone burst out, frustrated.

"Oh God, it's worse than I thought, if you don't even know what I'm talking about. Simone you can't get intimate with them with a 70's bush! You need to get your lady parts waxed or at the very least shaved." Amber exclaimed.

"Oh…well they didn't seem to mind. This is Alaska, you know. I don't know if they go by the same rules as the rest of the States." Simone defended.

"Well just try it and see how they react." Amber suggested.

"I don't even know what it's supposed to look like." Simone admitted.

"Okay, this might get a little graphic, but you shave or wax your lady lips and then leave only a cute little triangle or landing strip up top. The landing strip is hot. Guys love it!" Amber explained.

"Ew! Really, Amber?!" Simone scrunched up her nose.

"Yes, really! And don't 'ew' me! What's 'ew' is the fact that you've got a jungle down there and they've got to whack at it with a machete to get to your clit!" Amber shouted at her innocent friend.

"Whatever you say, Amber. Maybe I'll give it a try. I don't want to offend them with my obnoxious gorilla bush." Simone stated with sarcasm.

"Good." Amber said, finally pacified. "Man, I can't wait to get there and witness this with my own eyes! It's just so hard to believe that my innocent bestie has two boyfriends!" Amber cheered with excitement.

"They're not my boyfriends, Amber." Simone denied, not wanting to fill her heart with hope.

"Ha! We'll see about that." Amber stated, confident in her friend's appeal.

~~~

After taking a proper shower alone, taking Amber's advice and landscaping her nether regions and checking out the results in the mirror, Simone got dressed for the day. She pulled on a pair charcoal gray leggings and a pretty blue sweater dress that complimented her caramel skin, at least that's what Amber had told her when she'd picked it out for Simone.

Simone was sitting in front of the fire Indian style, brushing out her wet hair when the door to her room opened. Looking up, she saw both men walk into the room, Xander holding a tray of food.

The moment they saw her sitting there so sweetly with the fire light dancing across her face, they're breath caught. Xander placed the tray on the dining table and they both strode over to her. They knelt on either side of her and Xander grabbed her face and took her lips in a punishing kiss. When he was done thoroughly tasting her, Jackson turned her face to his and did the same.

"Guys stop." Simone urged, pulling her lips away from Jackson's. "You can't attack me every time you see me. There is something called the 'art of conversation'." Simone scolded them.

"Sorry. You just looked so beautiful sitting here. I don't think we could help ourselves." Xander apologized.

"Thank you." Simone smiled shyly. "So what's with the tray?" Simone said, the delicious smell of the food wafting over to her.

"We made you breakfast in bed, but you're not in bed like we expected." Jackson said, smiling at her.

"Well I thought I'd get up and get dressed. I need to stop putting off meeting my mother's tribe." Simone explained.

"Uh…you're going to have to put it off a little longer. I don't know if you noticed but there is a blizzard raging outside." Xander grinned at her.

"What?! Really?" Simone looked over to the closed curtains on the window.

"Yeah, it started last night." Jackson informed her.

"Huh. I guess I was a little distracted." Simone blushed to her roots. "In my defense I was a little incapacitated when it started. And speaking of, what happened with the wolves and how did I get out of the river?"

"Jackson jumped into the river to save you and pulled you to safety. I shot my gun off that I always carry with me on sled tours and the wolves ran off, but not before the alpha started fighting with Sampson. He sustained a few injuries and is now at the vet. And when Jackson pulled you out, you weren't breathing so I performed CPR on you to get you breathing again. You asked if the dogs were okay when you came to and then passed out again." Xander grinned at her and then expelled a harsh breath, remembering how afraid he was for her at the time. "Then we rushed to get you back here, before you died from hypothermia. And that's about it." Xander finished, quickly breaking down the day for her.

"Holy crap! You both saved my life. Thank you so much." Simone said sincerely, grabbing both their hands and squeezing tightly.

"Anyone would've done the same." Jackson said modestly.

"No they wouldn't." Simone denied.

Xander stood up and held his hand out for Simone to take and pulled her up off the floor.

"Come on. Come eat before your breakfast gets cold." Xander said before kissing her lightly on the lips.

Simone sat at the dining table and Jackson came over to whip the tops of the tray with a flourish and ended in a bow. Simone just giggled at his lighthearted mood. Looking down she saw three fluffy pancakes, scrambled eggs, crispy bacon and toast.

Simone looked up in shock at the two men as Jackson took a seat next to her and Xander across from her. "You did all this?" She said in awe.

"Yeah. Well, Jackson is the better cook, so he made the pancakes and eggs. I did the toast and bacon, you can't go wrong with toast, unless you have a faulty toaster and I don't believe there is any man in the history of the world that has burnt bacon." Xander smirked at her, deepening one adorable dimple.

"Go ahead eat up before it gets cold." Jackson said.

"Well what about you two, aren't you going to eat something?" Simone asked.

"We already ate. We wanted to let you rest for a while." Xander explained, as Simone tucked into her food.

"Wow! This is really good guys. Thank you." Simone said as she moaned around a mouthful of food.

Both men swallowed at her moans and groans, Simone unaware of the affect she had on them. Simone looked up at them when she noticed their silence. She slowly stopped chewing as she recognized the barely restrained passion in their eyes that she had seen last night and this morning.

"So…ah…where do you both live? I feel as if I'm keeping you from your daily lives." Simone said, trying to distract them with conversation.

"We live together in a log cabin that we built a few years back." Jackson said, banking the powerful need he had to lay her across the table and feast on her. "And you're not keeping us from anything. The storm has pretty much shut down the area. And besides we want to be here with you."

"Do you share the same room?" Simone asked, trying to figure out their strange relationship.

"Only when we're dating someone. We're not gay Simone, we just happen to be best friends that are attracted to the same women and instead of fighting over them, we share them. There is a huge gap in the ratio of men to women up here, so we just find our way easier." Xander explained.

"Do your families know about this?" Simone asked curiously.

"Well Jackson's grandparents have passed on, so it's just my family that's left, and yes they know. It took them a little while to get used to it. I think for a while there, they thought we were gay too and were just trying to cover it up with a female buffer." Xander ended on a chuckle.

"So you said that your last relationship ended on a bad note, what happened?" Simone asked curiously, but not sure she actually wanted to hear about them with another woman.

"I thought you didn't want to hear about our exes?" Jackson said, giving voice to her thoughts.

"I know…but I was just curious. I…I…I don't want to make the same mistake." Simone said shyly, looking down at her plate.

"God you're so sweet!" Jackson said, reaching over to grab her hand tightly. "It'll never happen." He said fiercely.

"Basically we found out that she was sleeping with someone else at the same time she was dating us. I guess she figured that since we shared her, that it was okay to be with a third guy too. Two wasn't enough, I suppose." Xander said with a shake of his head.

"Seriously?! The two of you individually are a hand full, so putting you together is the most mind-boggling experience of my life! I can't imagine trying to throw in a third." Simone exclaimed astounded.

"So tell us something…why is it that you're so innocent and went so long without a boyfriend or losing your virginity 'til now?" Jackson asked curiously.

"Uh…well…I…I don't know." Simone started bashfully. "I just wasn't interested in boys…uh…men." She said looking at both men, rephrasing her sentence because they were nowhere near boys. "My mom sheltered me from a lot of stuff because I was all she had and I guess she wanted to keep me safe. And I wasn't a pretty girl growing up. I was…am awkward. My body grew into a weird shape, so I wore baggy clothes to hide it. I've worn glasses practically my whole life and when I reached puberty, my face broke out in God-awful acne and I wore braces all throughout high school. So my looks definitely didn't inspire any sonnets, let alone invitations to go out on dates." Simone said sadly, as she pushed around the remaining food on her plate, having lost her appetite.

"And I definitely didn't have very many friends, and those that I did have certainly didn't have or talk about sex. So I just focused on school and kept my nose in a book. My interests were in biology, studying the human body and what makes us the way we are, but when my mom passed away, I decided to follow in her footsteps and went into nursing. So in college, while everyone was partying, drinking and having sex all over the place, I just concentrated on my studies. Guys never paid me any attention and vice versa." Simone finished on a shrug.

"God the guys must be blind down there! You're not Clark Kent, your glasses don't disguise your beauty. You don't have braces or acne now. Your smile is beautiful, not to mention your ridiculously luscious lips and your skin is flawless. And no matter how hard you try to hide your hair, it's obvious to anyone with eyes that it's gorgeous. And you don't hide that delectable body behind baggy clothes now, so what were the guys at your university thinking?" Xander burst out.

"Well actually, I do still wear baggy clothes. It's just that my roommate made me go shopping for clothes for this trip and wouldn't let me buy anything loose fitting." Simone scowled.

"Well thank God for your roommate. But I still don't think I, myself or Jackson would've let you pass us by on campus without stopping to ask you out." Xander stated emphatically.

"Agreed." Jackson chimed in.

"H…have you ever been in love?" Simone blurted out quickly.

"Close." Jackson said without pause, looking at her with meaning.

"Nah. We've just been having fun." Xander stated unthinking, ruining the moment. "OW!" Xander yelped as Jackson kicked him under the table and gave him a murderous stare. "Oh…sorry Si, I didn't mean that the way it sounded." Xander apologized, as he rubbed his shin.

"It's okay." Simone replied, reluctantly smiling at Xander, a little sad that he didn't appear to care for her as much as Jackson seemed to.

Well duh, you slut! You mother always told you not to give it up to a man without marriage, and now you've gone and given it up to two *without so much as a date! What am I doing?! God, I'm such a slut!*

"Why would you say that?! You are not a slut!" Jackson shouted out.

Simone covered her mouth in shock and cringed.

"I wasn't supposed to say that out loud." Simone said as she put her face down on the table, hiding from the guys.

Jackson looked at Xander with a death stare, knowing that Xander's thoughtless comment made Simone feel bad about herself. He reached under her face on the table and lifted her chin forcing her face up to look at him.

"No one in their right mind would mistake you for a slut. You are a strong, smart independent woman that deserves some pleasure in your life that you've been lacking. And there is no doubt that we care about you. Almost losing you yesterday scared the shit out of me. I knew that I couldn't lose one more person that means so much to me. I want you in my life, our life. I want to know what makes you tick. I want to know what brings you joy and what upsets you so that I know what to do to make sure you're happy."

Holy crap! He's a man of few words, but once he opens his mouth he sure has a way with them.

"And I'm sure that Xander feels the same way I do." Jackson said looking to the man who had remained quiet during his speech, silently urging him to correct his previous tactless remark.

"Of course I care about you, Si. The more I get to know you, the more I like you. I didn't mean to imply that you were just a bit of fun for us." Xander said sincerely, grabbing her hand and rubbing her knuckles soothingly with his thumb.

"Thank you. I don't mean to be so sensitive. I'm just new to all of this." Simone said, feeling bad about making such a big deal out of a harmless comment.

"It's okay. You have a right to be sensitive. We should feel guilty for sweet-talking you into losing your virginity to two men." Xander said guiltily.

"We know that's not normal, but we couldn't help ourselves. We wanted you the moment we laid eyes on you." Jackson added as he reached out to grab Simone's hand. "Come here." He said, pulling her onto his lap.

Jackson brushed back her still damp hair, caressing her cheek with his thumb. He stared into her dark brown bedroom eyes, trying to convey how much he was feeling for her.

"I know that we should give you a break and let you recover from last night and this morning, but I…" Jackson started.

"It's okay. I want to." Simone encouraged softly, before lowering her face to his, giving him a soft sweet kiss on the side of his mouth.

"Are you sure? Don't do it because you feel obligated to." Jackson said, restraining himself.

"Yes, I'm sure. I don't feel obligated. I never really thought about sex before and now I can't seem to stop." Simone looked down shyly at her hands folded on her lap, as she felt the evidence of his arousal for her on the side of her hip.

Reaching up, Jackson gently turned her face to his with his index finger, letting it slide down her cheek and neck to the V-neck of her sweater. Simone's mouth opened on a silent gasp.

Grasping Simone around her waist in one fluid move, Jackson lifted her onto the edge of the table. Standing up he wrapped his fingers around the back of her neck, tilted her face up to his with both thumbs and seized her lips in a deep kiss. His tongue dipped into her warm mouth, stroking against hers.

The intimate kiss unleashed the passion that Simone never knew she had in her until she met them. Her shy nature disappeared and she kissed him back with fervor. Her hands crept up to his face, caressing the coarse scruff on his jaw and slid back into his soft curls.

The affectionate move struck a chord in Jackson and he wrapped his arms around her, crushing her to his chest and devoured her mouth. Reaching down Jackson grasped the bottom of her sweater and pulled up, and Simone catching the hint raised her arms up and Jackson whipped it over her head and tossed it to the floor. Jackson bent his head down and nibbled at her nipples through the cotton of another virginal bra.

This time he was cautious not to rip the bra with his large hands like the caveman he sometimes became, especially where Simone was concerned. Reaching behind her, Jackson unclasped her bra and gently pulled the straps down her arms. The bra joined the sweater on the floor, and again Jackson bent his head down to flick his tongue across her hardened nipples and drew one into his mouth.

Xander sat across from them watching intently, as Simone threw back her head when Jackson's mouth covered her nipple. He patiently let them have their moment of intimacy. He knew that there was something they shared, the loss of family and being orphaned that he couldn't compete with. He brought lightness and laughter to the triad that wasn't suitable in this moment. *Hell, it was my big ass easy-going mouth that made her feel like shit a minute ago.*

He knew that Jackson was falling hard for Simone. And Xander knew that he cared a lot for her as well, but he wasn't sure if he was on the same page as Jackson yet. *Love? Am I really ready for that? To settle down with one woman?* Jackson lowering Simone's back to the table brought Xander out of his reverie.

"I had breakfast, but I'm still hungry for more." Jackson said to Simone as he slowly pulled down her leggings and panties.

"Jesus...what is this?! Hey Xan, it looks like Simone wanted to give us a little surprise." Jackson said to Xander, as he caressed a finger over her freshly groomed mound.

Xander stood up to get a better look at what Jackson was talking about. "Holy shit! Fuck that's hot!" Xander exclaimed as he took in the landing strip.

"Amber told me to landscape," a blush spread across Simone's skin as Jackson sat back down in the chair and gently lifted her legs, resting her thighs on his shoulders.

"I'm liking this Amber girl more and more. Not that we didn't like it before, this is just sexy as hell and we can see all of you now." Xander said, as he leaned over to kiss Simone on the forehead.

Xander then kissed each eyelid, cheek and her nose, saying 'I'm sorry' in every gentle kiss. Upside down, his lips made their way to hers. He nibbled on her top lip until she opened up for him. His tongue dove into the deep recesses of her warm mouth, tasting her and playfully stroking her tongue.

Jackson caressed and kissed at her newly shaved skin. His finger stroked down the side of her soft naked labia, then stroked up the middle before dipping into her slick wet heat. The feeling of his touch was made extra sensitive against her now bare skin and she rolled her hips towards him reflexively.

Drawing out the moment when his mouth touched her most intimate place, Jackson kissed up one thick thigh and then moved to the other kissing back down. Simone held her breath in anticipation of his firm mouth making contact where she wanted it the most.

Jackson finally flicked his tongue against her swollen clit and Simone gasped into Xander's mouth. Jackson's tongue stroked her gently then retreated to blow cool air softly on her heated flesh. He alternated between soft laps and hard flicks.

Simone felt the difference in both men's techniques. Where Xander was aggressive, attacking her clit with vigor, Jackson was gentle, like he was making love to her tender nub. The differences shocked her considering their size and demeanor. She would've expected it to have been the reverse. Both were wonderful in their own ways. Xander's skill brought out her orgasm like a freight train, but Jackson's delicate butterfly strokes slowly built up her climax like a slow wave washing over her.

Her hips pumped up to Jackson's talented mouth as her orgasm crested and crashed over her again and again. Xander swallowed her cries as he kissed her deeply.

In his need to bury himself inside of her, Jackson stood up quickly, undoing his belt and jeans, hurriedly pushing his jeans and boxers out of the way releasing his massive erection and plunged into Simone's tight recesses in one fluid move. Her slick tight canal squeezed his cock like a glove two sizes too small, and he grit his teeth at the delicious feeling.

"Ahh…FUCK!" Simone cried out at the feeling of being so quickly stretched to capacity.

Jackson grunted his agreement. He lifted her legs to rest against his chest and stomach, her feet bracketing his head. He kissed each of her ankles as he started to move, setting a slow easy pace. Xander released her full lips, kissing a path down to her supple breasts. Holding onto her hips, Jackson thrust into her with a swivel of his hips and her back bowed off the table with a gasp, giving Xander easier access to wrap his lips around her hardened nipples.

"Oh my God! Again! Do it again." Simone panted out.

Obeying her command, Jackson rotated his hips as he pumped into her over and over. Simone's cries became louder and more frequent as she lost all of her inhibitions. She gave herself over to the passion and sensuality coursing through her veins, not caring about anything else. It felt freeing to stop thinking for once, to be consumed by nothing but her emotions and desire.

Simone sat up, forcing Xander to release her tender breast. She reached behind Jackson's neck and pulled him down towards her, crushing her lips to his. She let go of his lips on a gasp as he rolled his hips into her again, she looked up at him with heavy-lidded eyes filled with need.

"Harder. Fuck me harder." Simone moaned.

He didn't know how it was possible, but Simone's sudden burst of confidence and aggression turned Jackson on even more than he already was, and his cock swelled further. A deep growl rumbled in the back of his throat as Jackson clasped her ass cheeks lifting her off of the table. And with the strength and agility of years of physical labor, Jackson used his whole upper body to slam her over and over again on his raging cock.

Xander stood shocked and amazed over the sudden passionate transformation unfolding before him, by the woman that couldn't even look them in the eyes half the time. But now the shy sweet virgin was nowhere to be seen. She was magnificent, a wild cat, as Jackson held her up thrusting into her, her head thrown back and her long hair hanging past her ass as her choked cries escaped through her overripe lips.

"Ah…ah…ah…Jackson, please!" Simone keened.

Miraculously Jackson increased his speed, pounding into her so hard that she couldn't even catch her breath. Simone's ass rippled through his hands with every smack of his hips to hers. Every inch of her body tensed. Her fingers dug into the muscles of Jackson's back and her toes curled. They both threw back their heads back simultaneously, as a scream ripped from her throat and a roar from his.

His legs trembling and weak from his powerful climax, Jackson was no longer able to hold both their weight and collapsed to his knees.

"Fucking shit, Simone! You've turned into a complete temptress!" Jackson burst out breathless.

Simone's head hung limp on his shoulder, their skin clung together from the perspiration of their lovemaking. A flush spread across her face at the comment, not knowing what had come over her now that the passionate coupling was over.

"I don't know what came over me." Simone said softly, burying her face further into his shoulder in embarrassment.

"Si, that was the most breathtaking thing I've ever seen." Xander said as he approached them. "Don't be ashamed. You're a naturally passionate woman, but you're just now realizing it. And there's nothing wrong with it." Xander soothed, as Simone peeked up at him.

Xander brushed a strand of hair from her face and slowly ran the back of his fingers down her cheek. Simone saw the evidence of his arousal straining against his jeans.

"I'm so sorry. I didn't mean to leave you out Xander." Simone looked up at him with concern.

"Don't worry about it. I'm fine." Xander shrugged.

"But-" Simone started before Xander cut her off.

"No, Simone. I don't want to hurt you. You need a break. And the way I'm feeling right now, I wouldn't be able to control myself. I wouldn't be gentle." Xander said firmly.

Simone's inner walls fluttered and her breath caught at the thought of another rough bout of lovemaking. But as insatiable as she felt, she had to admit that she was extremely sore from the last twelve hours.

"I know that you're innocent to the different ways of making love, but there is one way that you could…take care of him." Jackson said hesitantly, not sure of how she'd take to the idea of a blowjob.

"Like what?" Simone asked, interested.

"Uh…you could kiss him…*there*." Jackson said, trying to find a less crude or clinical way of saying oral sex.

"Do you mean a…a blowjob?" Simone asked with a blush.

"Oh, so you do know?" Jackson said smiling.

"I know that I don't know a lot, but my roommate and best friend *is* Amber and she's tried to talk to me about it a million times, though I blocked out ninety percent of it." Simone said, wishing that she would've listened more closely to her perverted friend.

Simone looked up at Xander who had remained quiet during her and Jackson's exchange about the ways to pleasure him. His jaw was clenched and his hands flexed at his sides, restraining himself, not wanting to persuade one way or the other.

"Would you like that, Xan?" Simone asked shyly, using his nickname for the first time.

"Yes." Xander responded in a low voice, not trusting himself to move or say more.

Simone slowly lifted herself off of Jackson's lap, and hissed in pain as his semi-hard erection slipped from her tender flesh. Turning, she positioned herself in front of Xander on her knees. Xander didn't make a move to touch her or undo his jeans.

"You'll have to help him Si. He's trying to contain his need for you and he doesn't trust himself to touch you without losing control." Jackson said, reading his best friend's mind, knowing him well after years of being friends and sharing women. "I'll guide you through it, if you need help."

O…okay." Simone said, unsure of herself, as she reached up hesitantly to Xander's belt buckle.

With trembling fingers, Simone unbuckled his belt and unbuttoned his jeans. She slowly pulled the zipper down and she looked up at him. Xander looked down at her with tender eyes that contradicted his earlier statement that they were just having a little fun. She recognized the look based off of the looks that Jackson gave her when he said something sweet. It encouraged her to continue.

Grasping the waist of his jeans, Simone shimmied them down his hips and legs. Once they were at his ankles, Xander stepped out of them and kicked them to the side. His erection pushed against the soft material of his boxer briefs. Gently, Simone pulled the elastic waistband away and down from his skin, releasing his hardness with a bounce.

Xander bent over to pull the briefs all the way down and kissed Simone softly on the lips, not able to resist with them in such close proximity. Standing up straight again, Xander waited with bated breath for the moment that she touched him.

"Now wrap your hand around the base to control the position you want him in." Jackson instructed.

Simone followed Jackson's command and wrapped her left hand around Xander's manhood. She noticed a pearl of liquid at the tip that begged for her to taste. She licked her lips and looked up at Xander to see his chest rapidly rising and falling. Holding eye contact, she licked the fluid from the tip and Xander hissed and pumped his hips forward in response.

His reaction spurred Simone on. Xander looked down as she opened her full decadent lips and slid them over the head of his cock boldly. She sucked gently on the mushroom cap. Xander's eyes nearly crossed at the feeling of her warm wet mouth on him.

"Ah God, Simone." Xander gasped.

"You're doing good, Simone." Jackson praised. "Now if you need help you can use your hands to give him rotating strokes down his length."

Simone gained confidence and took him further into her mouth and as instructed, rotated her hand down the rest of his length to the base and he shuttered in response. She released him on a gasp, taking in much needed air.

"If you breathe through your nose it'll help." Jackson encouraged.

Clearing her mind of everything but pleasuring Xander, Simone plunged her mouth down his length again and breathed through her nose. Xander shouted out at the unexpected move.

"FUCK, Si!" Xander yelled as he thrust towards her mouth instinctively.

The movement of his hips and his pants and groans, unexpectedly turned on Simone more than she would've imagined. Her hips reflexively started to undulate and she moaned around his hot steel. Her moan vibrating off of him made him grit his teeth and hiss in response.

Jackson noticed how aroused she was by the act of pleasuring Xander and moved towards her. Lying down behind her, Jackson slid his face underneath her, between her legs. He saw that her labia and clit were swollen and glistening with her arousal. Lifting his head up, he licked up her cleft to her distended clit.

Simone cried against Xander's manhood at the unexpected assault on her clit. Jackson grasped her hips and pulled her down to sit on his face as he made love to her weeping pussy. Simone lost her hold on all control and decorum. Her hips thrashed violently as her head bobbed up and down Xander with vigor.

Xander thought he'd lost his mind. Simone losing all control was the sexiest thing he'd ever seen, not to mention what she was doing to him. His hands dove into her hair, trying to slow down her movements before he came too quickly. But it was too late, her wild abandon made his scrotum draw up and with a force that was beyond his control, Xander exploded in her mouth before he could warn her.

"SHIT!" Xander roared.

At the same time that Xander came violently in her mouth, Simone's body tensed over Jackson's head and she released Xander on a scream. Her body was wracked with spasms as she fell over. And Xander unable to stand on his shaking legs any longer, crumpled to the floor next to her. Jackson laid where he was trying to catch his breath and licked his lips that still glistened with Simone's honeyed nectar.

"Oh…my…God! I think you both are trying to kill me." Simone said with exhaustion, as she looked over at Jackson who once again was hard as a rock. "Not again! No more!"

"Sorry." Jackson said as he pulled her towards him.

Chapter 8

    Simone woke with a start at the sound of a throat clearing. She was on her side, sandwiched between Jackson and Xander. Jackson spooned her from behind and his tree trunk like arm was wrapped around her waist and her head rested on his other arm like an extremely firm pillow. Xander faced her, his arm thrown over both her and Jackson, and her thick hair covered his face like a curtain.
    She heard a tapping sound and she looked over at where the sound was coming from and saw two pairs of feet above her, one of the four was tapping impatiently. Shocked, Simone looked up quickly to see two tall pretty blonde women standing over their naked and entwined bodies.
    "Hi." The slightly younger looking one said brightly to Simone.
    "Uh…hello." Simone said hesitantly, as Xander stirred slightly.
    Simone grasped his shoulder and shook him a little trying to wake him up.
    "Um…Xander? Wake up, there's someone here." Simone prodded him.
    "Huh?" Xander said in a groggy voice, blowing at her hair tickling his face.
    "We have company." Simone urged.
    Xander finally swiped away at the hair covering his face and looked up. Glancing at the two women, realization dawned on his face.

"Shit! Beth! Lanie! What are you doing here?" Xander exclaimed, looking around for something to cover the three of them, finding nothing.

Jackson slowly started to stir, his arm tightened around Simone, pulling her snuggly against his body. Not realizing they had an audience, Jackson ground his hips into Simone, his hardening manhood in the crease of her cheeks. He moaned into her ear and kissed her neck gently.

"Jackson! Stop it!" Simone loudly whispered. "We have guests!"

Jackson looked up and seeing who it was, grabbed Simone tighter in the need to cover his naked form and more than a little aroused body.

"Shit! Beth! Lanie!" Jackson parroted Xander's earlier words. "What the fuck, girls!? What are you doing here? And why the hell didn't you knock first?!" Jackson yelled at them.

The older one crossed her arms over her chest with a huff.

"Well, if either of you would've called or responded to our texts, during a *blizzard* I might add, we wouldn't be here to make sure you're okay. And it's not like this is a private room to knock on. You are in the great room of the lodge or were you too *occupied* to notice?" She said with a raised eyebrow, glancing at Simone.

"Um…is it possible to get introductions, it might make being naked in front of strangers a little easier." Simone said to the room in general.

"Hey! I'm Delanie." The friendlier of the two waved, as Simone tried to remember where she had heard the name before.

"Simone, these are my sisters, Bethany and Delanie. Beth, Lanie, this is Simone." Xander said, somewhat exasperated.

"Oh my God!" Simone cried out, covering her face with her hands. "On second thought, knowing just made being naked even worse! This is so embarrassing! Can one of you get a blanket or something?" Simone said between her fingers.

"Uh…well I don't want to traumatize my sisters or myself by showing my ass or anything else. And I doubt Jackson does either. So girls, could you please wait for us in the dining room? We'll meet you there in a little bit." Xander said, solving the dilemma they all found themselves in the middle of.

"Alrighty. Come on Beth." Delanie said as she pulled Bethany out of the room.

Simone collapsed back on what she kept hoping was a fake bearskin rug that was in front of the large stone fireplace in the great room of the lodge. The night before after the three of them had had fun making dinner together in the massive lodge kitchen, they'd sat with their food and some cocktails in front of the roaring fire talking. One thing led to another and they'd made love in front of the huge fireplace and then quickly passed out snuggled together.

At the time it had seemed like a good idea to Simone, now, not so much. She hastily got up and grabbed one of the throws that laid across the back of one of the couches and made a beeline for her room, without so much as a backward glance at the two men.

Once she made it to her room, she fell face forward on the bed, burying her face in the blankets in humiliation. *I wonder if they'd notice if I locked myself in here and didn't come out 'til it's time for me to go back to Washington?* Simone knew she was being irrational. For one, the guys had a master key to get into the room to drag her out. And two, she knew that she had to at least attempt to make a better second impression on Xander's sisters, since the first one was a complete bust. *Who gets caught buttnaked sandwiched between two men?! This girl! Oh my God, they probably think I'm a total skank!*

Simone reluctantly got up and walked into the bathroom for a quick shower. When she finished she piled her hair on top of her head in a messy bun and deliberated over what to wear. Finally she decided on a blue and black fitted flannel, a pair of black skinny jeans that she hated, but Amber had picked them out, and her black faux fur lined boots. She figured anything she picked to wear would be better than the birthday suit she was in when she'd first met them. Last, she grabbed her horn-rimmed glasses, that she had forgone in favor of contacts for the past few days, feeling that they would make her look like the nerd she was instead of the whore they probably perceived her to be.

She took a deep breath and made her way down to the dining room to officially meet part of Xander's family. As she walked up to the entrance to the dining room Simone heard lowered voices.

"Really, Xander? Isn't it about time that you and Jackson stop sleeping around with every easy girl you meet and find your own individual girlfriends?" Simone heard one of his sisters' say, which she assumed was Bethany, considering the fact that in the few minutes Simone had seen her, she had a face like she'd just smelled a particularly nasty fart the entire time.

"First off, Simone is far from easy." Simone heard Jackson growl.

"Yeah, right," was Bethany's smart-aleck reply.

"She isn't. She's a twenty-nine year virgin and a complete innocent. Well as of a couple days ago, before Xan and I wore her down. How many twenty-nine year old 'easy' virgins have you met?" Jackson responded in a tone that brooked no argument.

"Okay, fine. She's a nice girl. But isn't it time that you two settled down with two different women? Isn't sharing getting a little old?" Bethany persisted.

"I can't tell you why we're hardwired this way. We tried once to date separately, and we all know that didn't work out very well. It's what we do, so stop trying to change us." Xander finally spoke up.

At a pause in the conversation, Simone felt it was the perfect time to walk into the room. She walked around the corner and the four of them were sitting at a large table in the middle of the room, the men facing the doorway. When Jackson and Xander noticed her, they both stood up and Xander's sisters turned to look at her.

Head down looking at the floor, Simone awkwardly pulled at her shirt, trying to unsuccessfully hide her hips and butt, as she walked up to the table. Jackson held out his hand for her to take and she took it with shaking fingers.

"You look beautiful. Don't worry." Jackson said, sensing her insecurity.

He pulled her towards him and kissed her softly on her temple. And as she was getting accustomed to, he moved over one chair so that she could sit in between him and Xander.

"Hey gorgeous. Sorry about all of this. I told you they show up randomly." Xander winked at her, kissing her softly on the lips, before sitting down.

Delanie watched her brother and 'adopted' brother interact with the shy girl, noticing a difference in the men that her stubborn sister probably didn't. She couldn't put her finger on it, but they seemed to treat her with a type of reverence. Especially Jackson, Xander seemed a little more reserved about it, but Jackson had his heart on his sleeve, which was probably why Bethany was so sour-faced about the whole thing, since she'd always had a secret crush on the huge man. Delanie assumed that was why Beth always hated the fact that the guys liked to share their women, more than the rest of the family. Her wish would never happen as long as he shared women with her brother.

"So Simone, what brings you to Fairbanks? Since I've never met you before and I know everyone here. I can only assume you're not from around here. And are you here by yourself? Because that's unusual for a woman from the lower forty-eight - I'm assuming you're from the lower forty-eight- to come up here all by herself?" Delanie babbled brightly, finally stopping long enough for Simone to respond.

"Yes, I'm from Washington. And I'm here to meet my mother's tribe for the first time. My friend Amber is coming up in about a week to meet me." Simone answered, liking Delanie instantly.

"Oh, how exciting! Why haven't you met them before?" Delanie asked excited.

"Well, when my mom left the tribe to experience a different life, they kind of disowned her. I don't think they even know I exist or that she's past on. But since I have no family I was curious to meet them, to see where half of me came from." Simone explained.

"I'm sorry to hear about your mother. What makes up the other half? If I had to guess, I'd say you're half black. You have such great lips. And your body! Oh my God, what I wouldn't give to have an ass like that!" Delanie exclaimed, as Simone turned ten shades of red.

"Lanie!" Xander and Jackson shouted her name in shock. "You don't say that to someone!" Xander further scolded.

"Oops, sorry." Delanie said shamefully. "My family is always telling me to think before I speak. I hope I didn't offend you, it was totally meant as a compliment." Delanie tried to smooth over.

"Uh…it's okay. Um…thanks?" Simone said it as a question.

"So…am I right? You're half black, right?" Delanie clarified at Simone's perplexed look.

"Oh…yes. My dad was black." Simone answered.

"Was?" Delanie asked.

"Lanie, seriously?! This isn't a job interview. Why are you asking her so many questions?" Xander said exasperated.

"What?! I'm curious. I'm a people person. I like to know people's stories." Delanie shrugged.

Simone tried not to smile at the tenacious woman, but failed, unable to doing anything but warm to her infectious bubbly nature.

"Well did you ever stop to realize that she may not want to answer all of your questions, that maybe they might make her uncomfortable or upset her?" Xander added.

"It's okay, Xander. I don't mind." Simone said to Xander before turning back to his sister. "My dad died when I was little, in the Gulf War." Simone answered looking at Delanie.

"Oh, I'm so sorry. Do you have any siblings or anyone?" Delanie asked with sympathy.

"No, just my roommate Amber and her family." Simone replied.

"So, you're like Jax! No wonder he seems so fond of you. All shy, but hot exotic mama who doesn't realize it, that has been orphaned just like him. Mmmhmm…makes sense." Delanie grinned.

A blush spread from Simone's cheeks, to her hairline and down her neck in embarrassment. Peeking up at Jackson, Simone saw that he too had a telltale blush on his cheeks.

"Ha! I got Jackson to blush! So I'm right! Look at that, you've turned him into a gentle giant!" Delanie giggled with delight at Jackson's discomfiture.

"Oh shut it, Lanie." Jackson said in warning.

"Now the only question is, whether or not you can tame the playboy that is my brother?" Delanie continued, unaffected by the stink-eye the men were giving her.

"Lanie, I'm warning you. Keep it up and-" Xander started.

"And you'll what? I'm a grown woman, Xan. You can't go and tell mom or dad and get me in trouble." Delanie said, sticking out her tongue at him in contradiction to her previous statement.

"But I can throw your ass out of *my* lodge. So stop being so fucking irritating!" Xander finally exploded.

Simone looked at Xander in surprise, not thinking that it was possible for Xander to actually get mad at anyone. Delanie just brushed it off with a shrug of her shoulders, as only a baby sister can do.

"So…since you're an orphan trying to take care of herself, are you after them for their money? To take care of you?" Bethany finally spoke to Simone, though Simone wished she'd stayed quiet.

"Fuck, Beth!" Xander bellowed as Jackson just growled and Delanie's mouth fell to the table.

"No…I've got this." Simone said softly, deceptively.

Never in all her life had she been so insulted. Her pulse pounded out her anger and her vision blurred at the edges with red. With clenched fists, Simone stood up and for the first time looked the other woman square in the eye.

"I know you're Xander's sister, so I'll try to show some respect, though I've gotten none. I realize that you found us in a compromising position when you first walked in, so you feel that I don't deserve respect. But I'd advise you in the future to watch your mouth when speaking to someone you don't know from Adam. Though I know both Xander and Jackson own their own businesses, I assure you that I am unaware of their financial situations or how far those finances extend. What I do know is that both men have hearts of gold. Xander is sweet and funny and only wants to bring joy to any person his life touches. And Jackson has a heart as big as he is and has more love to give than any person I know. And they were probably too modest to mention that they saved my life the other day when I nearly drowned in the freezing river, in which I can never repay.

"But on top of that, I've worked my ass off since I was eighteen so that I can take care of myself, without the help of a man or the luxury of family. Up until a few days ago, I had every intention of growing into an old virginal spinster. I don't know what will happen with…this." Simone said gesturing between herself, Xander and Jackson. "But even if after this trip is over and I never see them again, I'll be thankful that for once in my life I let go and found passion…found something beautiful even if it was just for a fleeting moment in time. Now if you'll excuse me, I don't feel like being social anymore." Simone said, choking back tears and quickly fleeing the room, not wanting to show Xander's bitter sister any weakness.

"Excuse me for saying this Beth, but you were just the biggest fucking bitch! You don't even know her. She's sweet and innocent and knew absolutely nothing about men, and definitely not enough to manipulate one out of his money. From now on, stay the fuck out of my relationships!" Xander exploded.

"I'm sorry, Xan. I was just looking out for you guys. I don't want anyone to use you." Bethany said with her head hanging down in shame.

"We don't need your help. We're grown ass men. I know you have some dream of Jackson falling in love with you, but it's never going to fucking happen. He thinks of you as an annoying little sister. So give it up!" Xander said not caring if he hurt her feelings.

His words struck their target. Tears instantly filled Bethany's eyes and when Jackson looked up at her in surprise, she looked away unable to make eye contact.

"Go to hell, Xander!" She shouted and ran from the room.

Delanie sat in shock over the heated battle of words that just took place, starting with Simone. She knew that Xander more than likely didn't want to admit just how much he cared for Simone, but she had never heard him talk to any of his siblings like he just had…ever.

"Wow! That was a low blow, Xan." Delanie said to the big brother she idolized. "I know she was being a huge bitch. But I don't know if it was enough to humiliate her in front Jackson like that." Delanie said sadly, as she got up to leave, knowing that Bethany was waiting for her and needed consoling.

"Fuck! I know, I know. She just pissed me off so bad. I think I wanted to hurt her the way she hurt Simone." Xander admitted.

"I think you care for Simone more than you let on." Delanie said, leaning over the table and kissing him on the cheek.

"I like her, but it's not like I'm ready for marriage or anything." Xander said in denial.

"Just keep telling yourself that. See ya later, Jax." Delanie smirked at Xander and waved goodbye to Jackson.

Xander and Jackson sat stunned over the events of the past ten minutes.

"What the fuck was that?!" Jackson exclaimed.

"My sisters are fucking quacks, that's what! One can't shut the hell up and one is a down right hateful bitch!" Xander scowled.

"Beth has a crush on *me*, which made her lash out at Simone, really?!" Jackson said, still in shock over the revelation.

"Yep. Haven't you noticed that she's more anti-threesome than the rest of my family? She's loved you since we first started hanging out together. I found her books and notebooks for school that had 'I heart Jackson' or 'Mrs. Bethany Cole' written all over them. I never said anything because I thought she'd grow out of it, but I couldn't hold my tongue when she lashed out at Simone like that." Xander shook his head.

"Speaking of, we need to go check on her. Make sure she's alright." Jackson said with concern thickening his voice.

"Yeah, I know. I do need to feed the dogs soon, before they starve to death." Xander remembered through all of the drama.

"Yeah. Since the storm has passed, I have to head to the mill to make sure everything is fine. It'll take just a few minutes to see if she's alright and then we can go and get some work done." Jackson said, deep in thought before switching gears completely. "Hey, what do you think about having her stay at the cabin with us? Once the next wave of guests arrive we won't able to have privacy with her, especially not as loud as we get." Jackson suggested as they headed out of the dining room.

"I don't know, man. That's moving a little fast isn't it?" Xander said hesitantly.

"What are you so afraid of Xan? Why can't you see that you have more feelings for her than just a passing fling?" Jackson said, looking at his friend in frustration, as they took the main staircase up to the third floor, too impatient to wait for the elevator.

"I don't know. Why do you care so much? I like her okay. Isn't that enough for now?" Xander argued back, as they came to the landing of the third floor.

"Just don't fuck it up, Xan." Jackson warned as they walked down the hall.

Once at her door, Jackson and Xander stopped and pressed their ears to it. At first they heard nothing and then the sound of a sniffle reached their ears. They both looked at each other before Jackson grabbed the key out of his pocket and opened the door.

Stepping into the room, they saw Simone lying on the bed facedown, her body wracked with sobs. As soon as they heard her heartbreaking sobs and saw her trembling back, they strode quickly over to the bed. Both gently climbed onto the bed lying on either side of her trying not to startle her, Jackson on her left and Xander on the right. Jackson rubbed at her back soothingly with his large hand that almost spanned the entire width of her back.

"Shh…it's okay beautiful. Don't cry." Jackson cooed at her, which of course only made her cry harder.

Jackson brushed back a tendril of hair that had escaped her bun and gently kissed her temple. He looked over at Xander, silently imploring him to use his humor to stop her tears. Xander nodded his head in understanding.

"Hey, hey…stop all these tears, gorgeous." Xander said turning Simone to face him.

Silent tears continued to slip down her face as she looked at him. Leaning in, Xander kissed her lips softly, then her cheeks, nose, and forehead. Each kiss gained speed until he was giving her soft quick pecks all over her face like a madman, until her sobs turned to giggles.

"You don't have to worry anymore. The wicked witch of the east is gone. I threw a house on top of her." Xander grinned at Simone as she burst out laughing. "Now we just have to worry about her sister the wicked witch of the west, with all her incessant questions. She'd make a great CIA agent. Her specialty would be in interrogations. I'm surprised she didn't try water-boarding you. God my sisters are bat-shit crazy!" Xander finished on a frustrated sigh.

"I like Delanie. She's sweet. I just don't get why it felt like Bethany had it in for me." Simone ended sadly.

"That's because she's been in love with Jackson since we were little. And she's always held out hope that he would stop sharing with me and realize that he loves her too, which is a pipe dream." Xander explained.

"Oh." Simone said, understanding dawning. With the feelings she had for both men, she didn't think she'd act any better if someone threatened her territory. *I'd have to cut a bitch.*

"I had no idea until today, of her feelings for me. I've thought of her as nothing but my little bratty sister all these years. I don't wanna hurt her, but I've already gotten a little attached to this beautiful shy girl that turns into a complete wanton lioness in bed…or on a bearskin rug…or in the shower…or-" Jackson teased, before Simone cut him off.

"Okay, okay…I get it. Apparently I have a personality disorder." Simone said giggling, before quickly sobering up. "I'm really sorry that I was the cause of so much drama with your family Xander. And I swear to you both, that I would never use you for your money."

"Aw Si, we know that. It never even crossed our minds. And you didn't cause the drama they did, especially Beth. Lanie was just being her normal annoying little kid sister self." Xander soothed. "And I'm so sorry that your feelings were hurt. It won't happen again. I promise you that." Xander said with certainty.

"Si, what do you think about checking out of the lodge and coming to stay with us at our cabin for the rest of your stay?" Jackson broached the subject.

"What? Really?! You'd want me to stay with you? What about when Amber gets here?" Simone asked in shock.

"Yes, really. When the new guests arrive, it'll be hard for us to have alone time. And it would be unprofessional for Xander to have loud crazy sex that would cause the other guests to complain, don't you think? Also, we have plenty of room for Amber when she gets here. So what do ya say?" Jackson asked getting more excited, seeing that she was on the verge of accepting.

"O…okay, sure." Simone said shyly.

"Good." Jackson leaned in and kissed her gently against the lips. "Now, that the storm has cleared, literally and figuratively, I need to go to the mill to make sure everything's fine. So I'll see you later tonight, alright?"

"Alright." Simone smiled at him.

Jackson kissed her on the lips once more, then got up from the bed and headed to the door. He looked back before leaving the room to see her staring after him. He winked at her and then closed the door.

~~~

Xander watched his friend leave, still unsure if it was a good idea to have Simone stay with them. But since Jackson had already said it and Simone seemed happy about it, Xander wasn't going to ruin it.

Plus, throughout the years he and Jackson had only gotten into a couple of fights that had come to blows. And though Xander felt he could hold his own, being fast and nibble, he was still no match for Jackson's size and strength. And he wasn't in the mood for a beat down in the near future. He knew Jackson would kill him if he ruined things with Simone.

"So do you want to help me feed the pups? They're probably pissed at me right now." Xander said, brushing a tendril of jet black hair behind Simone's ear.

"Yeah, I'd love too!" Simone said sitting up quickly.

"Okay, let's roll." Xander stood up and reached out to help Simone off of the bed.

He grabbed her coat and helped her put it on. He snatched up her wool hat and tried placing it on her head, but her thick bun made it stick up high on her head. Simone looked up at him with downturned bedroom eyes, and a little smile playing at her full wide mouth and Xander's heart clenched. The sudden feeling scared the crap out of him.

"You look like one of the seven dwarfs with your hat sticking up like that." Xander chuckled, trying to make a joke to shake off the feelings creeping up on him.

"And which dwarf would that be?" Simone asked, as Xander took the hat off and unwound her hair.

Xander watched as her hair cascaded down her shoulders and back, framing her face in a seductive veil, making him nearly swallow his tongue.

"Hmm…I think maybe Sleepy. With those sexy as hell bedroom eyes you have, it looks like you just woke up from having a naughty dream about me." Xander smirked down at her, one dimple deepening, as Simone blushed deeply. "Huh…or maybe Bashful? You're always blushing." Xander changed his mind as he ran a finger over the flush on her cheek.

Xander pulled the hat back down on her head, playfully bringing it down over her eyes. She flirtatiously swatted at his hands and pushed the hat back on her head, smiling up at him brightly.

Swallowing hard past his tightened dry throat, Xander reached down to slowly zip up Simone's coat with shaking fingers.

"Okay gorgeous, let's getting moving." Xander said trying to distract himself, as fear and other unwanted emotions sped through his veins.

Xander opened the door for Simone and they headed downstairs. Xander stopped to put on his full snowsuit and grabbed a fifty pound bag of dog food and threw it on his shoulder as if it weighed nothing.

Simone noticed more than ever, without Jackson around that Xander was pretty formidable in his own right. He was tall, broad shouldered and muscular too, and would make most of the guys back in Washington look puny. It was just that he was always around Jackson who made absolutely everyone look like a midget.

Simone stared at his tight ass as she followed Xander outside. *What the hell is wrong with me? Since when did I start caring more about how nice a man's ass looks than trying to find my mom's family? And since when did this trip become a time for sexual self-discovery and not about discovering were half of me comes from?*

While beating herself up, Simone almost didn't notice how the landscape was more of a winter wonderland after the storm than it was when she had first arrived.

"Oh wow, it's beautiful!" Simone gasped.

"It is, isn't it? It's easy to take things for granted when you see them every day. That's why I enjoy having new guests come in, because you get to see it through their eyes, like it's the first time all over again." Xander said looking out at the snowy terrain.

"Hmm…that was pretty poetic, Xander." Simone smiled up at him.

"I have my moments." He grinned down at her.

Xander brought out a set of keys from his pocket and unlocked the gate surrounding the Huskies. Simone noticed several lumps in the snow and as soon as the keys jingled about thirty heads popped up out of the snow. Seeing Xander with food, they jumped up and shook off the remaining snow from their coats and barked and wagged their tails happily.

"They're so cute!" Simone laughed.

"Yep, they're my babies. I'm the reverse of a cat lady." Xander joked and Simone laughed. "So here's the crappy part of the job, well besides shoveling dog shit. We have to find all their dog bowls buried under the snow."

"Oh, okay. I can do that." Simone said confidently.

"To make it a little easier, each dog bowl is chained to each of their doghouses." Xander said, demonstrating with the closest dog house to them.

"Oh, that does make a difference. How about while you fill each one I'll pull out the next bowl, to make it go faster?" Simone suggested.

"Sounds like a plan." Xander said, as he sat down the large bag of food and started scooping out some into the bowl he'd pulled out.

Simone and Xander worked silently for a little while, enjoying working together. Xander was bending down filling a bowl when something whizzed by his head. Looking over quickly at Simone, he saw her petting one of the dogs, not paying him any attention.

A few moments later he heard it again, but this time past his shoulder. And once again when he looked at Simone, she was in the middle of pulling another bowl out of the snow.

This time he kept an eye on her, to see what she was up to. And sure enough, when she thought he wasn't looking, he saw her gather some snow, pat it into a perfect ball and lifted her arm in his direction.

"Caught y-" Xander started before the snowball smashed him in the face.

Xander heard choked laughter as he wiped the snow from his face. Simone had her hands over her mouth trying to cover her laughter.

"I'm so sorry, Xan! I didn't mean to hit you in the face. I've never had a snowball fight before and I just wanted to try it." Simone said between giggles.

"Well then, I don't wanna get in the way of your first snowball fight experience." Xander said deceptively sweet, as he made a show of reaching down, grabbing a handful of snow and patting it into a perfect ball.

"Xander…be nice. I didn't try to hit you in the face, you just so happened to turn at the same time I threw it." Simone said backing up with hands raised in surrender.

"Oh no, you started it woman and I'm gonna finish it." Xander said stalking towards her.

Simone turned to run and Xander wound up his arm like a pro baseball player and aimed and released the snowball safely at her back. When the snowball hit her back fairly softly she fell face down in the snow unmoving.

Her prone body made Xander panic. He ran over to her, squatted over her and turned her gently.

"Simone, are you okay?!" Xander said with worry.

A split second later, Simone's eyes popped open and she smashed a handful of snow in his face. Simone's delighted laughter rang out as Xander sputtered and the dogs looked on curiously as they ate.

"I couldn't resist!" Simone said between laughter.

"You better be glad I like you." Xander growled before he lowered his face to hers and started to rub the cold wetness all over her face, making her laugh and squirm even more.

Pulling back slightly, Xander looked down at her. They grinned at each other like besotted fools. Simone reached up to stroke a finger over one adorable dimple. Xander's smile disappeared and he lowered his face to hers again, capturing her lips in a sweet cold kiss that quickly heated up when his tongue dipped into her warm mouth.

Simone shivered from a combination of the cold snow and the passionate kiss. A cold nose and a warm tongue on Xander's cheek stalled the moment. He looked over to see Delilah waiting impatiently to get her bowl of food.

"Let me finish up here, before the dogs decide to make a meal out of me. You go on in and get dry and warm and I'll meet you in a minute." Xander said before giving her another soft kiss, promising more to come.

"Okay." Simone said quietly, in anticipation.

Xander stood up and reached down to help Simone up from the snow. She headed into the lodge, stopping here and there to pet the dogs along the way.

Once back in her room, Simone quickly stripped out of her coat, shirt and cold wet jeans. As she finished pulling the jeans off of her ankles she heard the door close. Turning in just her bra and panties, she saw Xander standing there watching her with barely concealed desire. She realized that he must have rushed through feeding the rest of the dogs in record time. There had to have been at least ten more dogs to feed and bowls to pull up out of the snow.

Simone crossed her arms in front of her, feeling awkward under his close scrutiny. He never took his eyes off of her as he slowly stripped out of his snowsuit. Once he was out of the suit, he started on his red flannel and low slung jeans, until he was in just his boxer briefs.

His striptease over, Xander quietly strode over to her, plunging his hands into her hair and he attacked her mouth with the force of his need for her. His tongue dipped and dived into her mouth, tangling with hers. He released her lips on a gasp, dropped down to his knees in front of her and grasped her panties and pulled, rending them in half. Before she could even be shocked by the barbarian move, his mouth was on her quivering heat.

"Aahh...Xan!" She shouted out at the sudden assault on her clit.

Xander swirled his tongue around her hardened clit and Simone reached down grasping handfuls of his hair in a death grip as her hips pumped out of control against his gifted mouth. He dipped a long finger into her snug slick heat and once it was fully wet with her juices he guided it back to her tight anus. Simone flinched in surprise at the forbidden touch.

"Don't fight me. Let me show you. Let me get you ready for both of us." Xander said looking up at Simone, as she nodded her ascent.

Xander continued wreaking havoc on her clit and again dipped his finger inside her, lubricating it once more. Hitting her g-spot a couple of times making her cry out, before pulling out and caressing her puckered flesh again. Slowly he pressed in and stopped at his first knuckle, letting her body adjust around him.

When her body relaxed further, he stroked his finger out and then back in a little further. Xander repeated the slow method until his finger was buried deep inside her to the last knuckle, all while continuing to pleasure her clit with teasing swirls and flicks.

Simone's body had remained still the entire time, trying to adjust to the foreign feel of her forbidden entrance being breached for the first time. And Xander having fully reached his goal began an onslaught of sensual pleasure that made Simone's body come alive.

His full lips covered and sucked at her sensitive nub, while his tongue flicked it relentlessly. His finger in her tight rear entrance started to stroke in and out. The buildup of this climax was nothing that Simone had experienced before in their other encounters. It came on stronger, faster and harder than ever before. One moment she was enjoying the pleasure and adjusting to the new sensations, and the next an almost painful orgasm ripped through her like a tornado. The unexpected climax tore a ragged scream from her throat and her legs collapsed from under her.

Xander's quick reflexes caught her and he placed her on the edge of the bed.

"See I told you." Xander smiled down at Simone, as he leaned over her.

"Oh my God! What was *that*?!" Simone exclaimed breathless.

"I think there's another g-spot in there that brings out a more powerful orgasm." Xander explained.

"No kidding. Sheesh! I think I almost blacked out." Simone said with eyes closed.

"If that almost made you black out, then you probably will when we take you at the same time." Xander smirked.

"That sounds a little terrifying. But I have to admit after that, I am the teeniest bit curious." Simone confessed with a blush.

"My work here is done! I've brought you over to the dark side." Xander grinned before lowering his head to one tightened nipple.

He lapped at the turgid brown peak, pulled back and blew cool air over the damp skin, making it draw up even tighter. Simone's hips rose from the bed trying to make contact with what she wanted most. Obliging her, Xander quickly pulled his boxer briefs down and plunged into her wet recesses.

Simone whimpered with pleasure at the sensations Xander was drawing out of her with each powerful stroke of his hips. She thought that making love with just one of them would be less intense, less overwhelming, less…everything. But she couldn't have been more wrong.

With all of her focus on Xander alone the intimate connection between them as they flexed and strained towards each other, radiated an intense warmth that spread through every inch of her of her already heated flesh. The warmth seemed to extend to her pounding heart and filled it to near bursting.

As Xander varied the speed and depth of each pump of his hips, bringing Simone closer to the crest of her climax, she looked into his golden green gaze and her heart stopped at the unguarded look of adoration in his eyes. And the look disappeared an instant later, replaced by subtle look of trepidation. He closed his eyes and buried his face in the crook of her neck. The warmth in her heart faded away, traded by a near debilitating disappointment. So much so that her orgasm that was close to its crescendo, died a sad unsatisfactory death.

Xander's body shuddered over her as he reached his release. He rolled off of her and laid next to her, trying to catch his breath. Simone felt more vulnerable and naked than any other intimate moment with the two men. Feeling awkward and just a little hurt, Simone reached for the blanket and wrapped herself in it protectively. Xander's cellphone rang from his pants pocket that had been thrown carelessly on the floor.

"Um…I…I'll be right back." Simone stammered as he answered his phone and she quickly escaped to the bathroom.

Closing the bathroom door, Simone collapsed on it and gulped several times, trying to tamp down the emotions that threatened to rise up and choke her. She knew that even with her limited experience that she was falling for the two men. She could still vaguely remember the looks of love and passion between her parents before her father was killed. And she knew that she was already starting to look at Jackson and Xander with the same look of love her mother gave to her father. And she was willing to bet her life that the brief look that Xander had given her in that unguarded moment, was at least a shadow of how her father looked at her mother.

But what does it matter? Why am I so upset? What am I gonna do…drop everything back home and move here? And it's only been a few days, how can I expect them to fall in love with me already? Stop being so stupid Simone! You're smarter than this. Take it for what it is…an amazing moment in time that I can carry with me for the rest of my life.

She knew that this experience was probably going to be the only time that she would ever encounter this kind of passion. She knew what life was like back home. She knew that men didn't look at her the way Jackson and Xander did. Once she was back home, it would be all work and no play, like before. She would cherish this moment and think on it often and fondly when she was old in her bed years from now.

A tentative knock on the bathroom door brought Simone out of her reverie. She quickly swiped at the moisture that had gathered in her eyes and swallowed hard to unblock the knot in her throat.

"Y…yes?" Simone said to the closed door.

"Hey Si, you alright?" Xander asked from the other side.

"Yeah I'm fine. What's up?" Simone answered.

"That was the vet calling. I need to go pick up Sampson. I was thinking that you might want to pack up your things and then we can go get him and bring him home with us. He needs to be comfortable and looked after closely while he heals." Xander explained.

"Oh okay. I'll be out in just a little bit. I want to get cleaned up first." Simone said with a tiny bit of hope spreading through her body at the word 'home'.

"Alright. My staff should be here by now. I'm going down to have a meeting with them, I'll be downstairs waiting for you. If you need help with your bags, just call down to the front desk and myself or one of the staff will be up to help you." Xander finished before pushing away from the door.

Simone expelled a harsh breath through her full lips, easing the tension in her limbs, now that the awkward conversation through the door was over. She released the blanket that she realized she had in a death grip around her body, as if he could see her vulnerability through the door. Shaking her head at the absurdity of the emotional ups and downs of a relationship with a man, Simone stepped into the shower, hoping to wash away some of the doubt and disappointment of their passionate turned cold encounter.

Chapter 9

Xander carried Sampson to the truck from the animal hospital, Simone had been waiting for him in the truck and now slid out to open the door for him. He gently placed the tan and white husky in the middle of the bench seat, to lay between the two of them on the way home. As Simone got back in on the passenger side, Sampson whined and slapped his tail affectionately against the seat and then put his head in her lap, looking up at her with sad eyes.

"Oh he's going to milk this for everything its worth." Xander joked, trying to lighten the mood.

Xander knew that he had messed up at some point during making love to Simone. He hadn't missed the fact that she didn't orgasm and that the moment it was over, she turned inside herself. Reverting back to her shy and extra quiet demeanor. And after an hour of the silent treatment, Xander couldn't take it anymore. So he tried to do what he did best, making her laugh.

"Yeah." She chuckled a little at the sad blue puppy dog eyes looking up at her.

She scratched and rubbed behind Sampson's ears tenderly. The dog answered with a heartfelt whine and more vigorous tail smacking. They both laughed in response.

"Oh, cut it out ya big baby." Xander scolded with a smile that deepened his dimples as he patted the dog's back gently.

Xander looked up at Simone, turning the full force of his smile on her. She swallowed hard at his angelic face, finding it hard to stay upset with him. She smiled back timidly and Xander breathed a slight sigh of relief at being forgiven for whatever had troubled her.

"So when are you going to finally go and meet your tribe?" Xander asked as he shifted the truck into drive.

"Hmm...I don't know. Tomorrow, maybe." Simone answered quietly as she absentmindedly stroked Sampson's soft thick fur.

"What are you so afraid of?" Xander asked, taking his eyes off the road for a moment to glance at her.

"God! I don't know." Simone said in frustration at herself. "I think I'm afraid that they won't accept me. They were so mad at my mom for leaving the reservation. So I don't know if her half-breed offspring would be well received. And they're the only family that I've got left." Simone finished sadly.

"All the more reason to go and meet them. They at least deserve to know that you exist." Xander encouraged.

"Yeah. But don't you see? In some ways it would be so much better if I went on believing that they would claim me as one of them...to love me, than to actually meet them and they shun me or look at me with disgust. Because then the illusion would be shattered and I could never go back." Simone admitted, though it ripped her heart in half to do so.

"Si, you can't let that get to you. Just meet them and let the chips fall where they may. If they don't want anything to do with you, then it's their loss. You're amazing and they'd be lucky to know you." Xander said, reaching over to clasp her hand that was fanatically stroking Sampson's fur in a nervous fidget.

"Alright. I'll try to get up the courage to go tomorrow." Simone conceded.

"Good." Xander said, looking at her with a tender smile.

She smiled back at him, completely confounded by his rollercoaster treatment towards her. One minute he was distant and the next the looks he gave her could melt the coldest of hearts. She shook her head in wonder as they rode the rest of the way in silence.

After a while Xander turned down a private driveway that hadn't been plowed yet. He turned on the trucks four-by-four power and they bumped through the deep snow, winding past a dense part of the forest.

They came around a curve, in what Simone assumed was a road, though she couldn't tell with all the snow covering the ground. Suddenly the trees fell away into a clearing and in the middle sat a gorgeous sprawling two-story log home. Simone audibly gasped at the sight.

"This is your *home*?" Simone said in wonder.

"Yeah. You like it?" Xander said proudly.

"Well, yes. B…but I thought you guys said that it was a cabin? That looks more like a log mansion! It's incredible." Simone said, her mouth still agape.

"Well I suppose it helps that Jackson owns a lumber mill." Xander smiled at her dumfounded reaction.

"No joke. Wow." Simone breathed in awe.

"Come on, Si. Let me show you around." Xander said as he pulled into the three car garage.

They both got out of the truck, Xander turning back to pull Sampson into his arms. "Could you get the door for me? I'm gonna get Sampson settled, then I'll show you around. And don't worry about your luggage, I'll bring them in for you after the tour." Xander said as Simone opened the door into the house.

They stepped into what Simone assumed was a mudroom that had built-in shelves for shoes, a coatrack and giant fluffy towels, if needed for coming in out of the rain or snow. She slipped off her coat and hung it on one of the rungs on the coatrack. And at Xander's suggestion, she sat on the bench and took off her boots and slid her feet into Jackson's giant slippers.

"He barely wears his anyway. Most times he walks around barefoot or in socks. The man never gets cold. I think he was a bear in his past life." Xander joked about his best friend as he led Simone into the enormous kitchen.

Again Simone was struck dumb as she took in the kitchen. It was done in tones of rich reds, burnished gold and soothing browns. The wood of the cabinets and island were a type of red wood that complimented the slightly lighter hardwood floor. The countertops were a dark tan and golden flecked stone. The ceiling was done in a dark brown wood with crossing beams. The lovely hanging light fixtures gave off a warm golden glow. And to break up the warm tones were the stainless steel appliances and the accents of dark gray stones that created a rustic alcove for the stove and the built in fireplace on the opposite side of the room, where the kitchen table sat.

Xander looked back at Simone and smiled at the look of complete awe on her face. He walked into what Simone believed to be the biggest living room she had ever seen in a house. It had twenty foot ceilings. The windows went from floor to ceiling with wood framing each one that looked out over the winter wonderland outside. And in the center was cozy seating in buttery soft brown leather, for anyone that wanted to pass the time relaxing while reading or drinking a cup of coffee. To the left of the room was a giant wood burning fireplace with additional seating in front of it.

Near the fireplace was a staircase. Simone's eyes traveled up the stairs and saw that the living room opened up to reveal a loft that spread from nearly one side of the house to the other. Xander told her to wait as he laid Sampson down on the rug in front of the fireplace and then went back into the kitchen. A few moments later, he came back in carrying her bags and motioned for her to follow him.

Xander led the way up the stairs to the loft above, where more seating was arranged to get an even better look at the landscape outside. There were doors on either side of the loft and one in the middle. Leaving her luggage on the loft, Xander showed her each room. The two on each side were decent sized bedrooms and the one in the middle was a nice bathroom with a huge stand in shower. And both bedrooms had joining doors to the bathroom.

"These are the guest bedrooms, but we're using them as our bedrooms for the time being." Xander explained as he walked her down a hall to the left of the loft. "This is the master bedroom." Xander said, as he opened the door with a flourish.

Simone walked in, her eyes bugging out of her head as she tried to take in the enormous room. A huge bed, done in a rustic masculine handmade wood frame, which was the focal point of the room. It was wide like a California king bed, but longer than the popular bed type. Simone knew that it had to be custom. *Oh…my…God! This bed was strictly made for sexual delights.*

To the left of the bed the room boasted its own floor to ceiling windows with a view of the backyard and what could only be called a babbling brook. A lovely stone hearth and fireplace faced the front of the bed. The rest of the furniture in the room was also rugged and masculine, but not so much as to make a female feel uncomfortable when entering. More like a sense of protection…like walking into a man's warm embrace.

Xander pulled Simone from her warm and fuzzy thoughts by grabbing her hand and towing her towards a door in the room. This door led to a massive walk-in closet that then led to the master bath on the other side.

The flooring was a slate gray stone that led up a raised three step dais to a sunken tub. The huge three person shower was designed in natural stone of gray and accents of tan and brown that gave the appearance of showering outdoors against a rock face. And the vanity cabinets were tan wood, the counter a dark gray granite to match the floor and shower. But what stood out most were the three copper bowl sinks. *Huh…now I've heard of double sinks…but never triple!*

It dawned on Simone that the whole master suite was designed specifically for three people. The sheer magnitude of the situation hit her and she realized that the two men that had consumed her every move, her every breath, took this relationship they had developed very seriously. They had every intention of eventually finding a woman to share their home with on a permanent basis. *Am I that woman? Can I handle this kind of relationship for the long haul? Am I really equipped to give that much of myself? Am I enough? That's a whole lot of man...a whole lot of love and attention. Sheesh...I thought I was going to be a fucking spinster a week ago!*

"Simone! What's wrong? Are you okay?" Xander exclaimed as Simone's chest rose and fell rapidly with short breaths as she clutched the counter with trembling hands.

"I…I think…I'm…having…a panic attack!" Simone gasped.

"Here…here. Come sit." Xander guided her to the steps leading up to the tub and sat her down on the second step. "Put your head between your legs and try to take deep breaths."

Simone just nodded her head in response as she did what she was told. Eventually her breathing started to calm, but her hands continued to shake violently.

"I think maybe a nice hot relaxing bath might help. Just keep breathing and I'll take care of it." Xander said, bending over to kiss the top of her head before turning on the faucet.

Once the tub was full Xander held his hand out to Simone to help her up. She was grateful that he didn't ask her what had brought on the panic attack, because she didn't know exactly how to explain to herself let alone him, why she had freaked out. She didn't understand how she could want something so badly, yet not at all. Now she understood Xander's up and down attitude towards her.

"Are you feeling okay enough to get in? Because if I stay and help you undress, I'm not so sure I'll be able to resist getting in with you. And I don't think that is what you need right now." Xander said, lifting up a hand to caress down the side of her face.

"Yeah. I think I can manage now." Simone reassured.

"Good. Then I'll leave you to it." Xander said before turning to leave the room.

"Thank you…" *For not asking. For not pushing.*

"You're welcome." He responded, giving her a look that spoke volumes. He knew she wasn't just thanking him for the bath or the alone time.

The door leading from the walk-in closet shut with a click. Simone grabbed a towel hanging from the rack and buried her face into it, muffling her mouth as she screamed into it. The scream was mixed with equal parts excitement and fear for what was to become of her new and astounding life.

~~~

Jackson's blood was filled with so much excitement for a future with Simone and Xander that he could barely contain his anticipation as he drove home from the mill. During lunch he had stopped at the only sex toy shop in town, to get something for later tonight. He knew he wouldn't have the patience to stop after work.

His fingers tapped out an impatient rhythm on the steering wheel as he drove. He fiddled with the radio as well. One minute he wanted to drown out the incessant chatter going on in his head and the next he couldn't think because of the distracting music. He was a wreck and couldn't be happier about it.

A huge smile spread across his face when the turn onto their private driveway came into view. Once he pulled into the garage he practically shot out of his truck like a rocket, when he saw Xander's truck, knowing that they were there. His long stride ate up the concrete as he strode to the door of the mudroom. He hurriedly kicked off his boots and walked to the kitchen, where he normally stopped to grab something to eat before dinner. But he was too anxious to eat anything at the moment.

"Si? Xan? I'm home." Jackson bellowed as he walked into the living room.

"Hey, Jax! Up here." He heard Xander shout down from the loft.

Jackson quickly walked over to Sampson, who was resting in front of the fireplace, gave him a quick rub and then bounded up the stairs three at a time. His dark brows drew together when he saw only Xander sitting on the loft.

"Where's Simone? Don't tell me she changed her mind?" Jackson started to panic.

"No, no. She's here. She just needed a moment to herself. She's taking a bath and I wanted to give her space." Xander explained.

"Oh…thank God." Jackson breathed a sigh of relief and started towards the master suite.

"Jackson…wait." Xander stopped him. "I think she had a minor panic attack earlier. It happened after I gave her the tour of the house. Especially when she saw the master bed and bath. I can't be too sure, but I think the scope of how we do relationships kind of overwhelmed her. So maybe we should try not to smother her." Xander finished.

"Oh…uh. Do you think it would be alright to just say hello. I want to see her first, and then I can start on dinner." Jackson said, unsure of himself now that he realized Simone may not be as on board as he thought.

"Yeah, Jax. I don't think that would be a problem. She'd probably be happy to see you." Xander reassured his friend, feeling bad for deflating his good mood.

Jackson walked down the hall to the bedroom at a much slower pace this time. He walked through the closet to the bathroom. He looked over at the tub and his heartbeat stuttered and then started to pound at this chest when he saw only her nose peeking out from the water.

"Si!" Jackson shouted in fear.

Her eyes popped open and she sat up quickly. Jackson's heart relaxed but only a little as he took in the vision of his very own sea-nymph. As the water sluiced down her body; Simone's ebony hair cascaded down her back, her warm dark eyes stared at him through sooty eyelashes that were wet and spikey. Her caramel skin glistened and her little brown nipples stood erect on her small plump breasts.

"Jackson." Simone breathed his name, like a caress.

Without thinking; Jackson strode over to her, dropped down to the top step and grabbed her face between his massive hands and kissed her soundly. They broke away on a gasp and Jackson searched her sleepy eyes, trying to gauge what she was feeling.

"Are you okay? Xan said that you freaked out a little." Jackson said, still holding her face gently like he was protecting fragile glass.

"Yes. I'm okay." Simone looked down, breaking eye contact, unable to hold his piercing silver gaze.

"Simone, look at me." Jackson commanded softly. "I don't want you to feel pressure to try to be someone you're not to fit this obviously unorthodox relationship. Just be yourself and trust me it'll work. You're perfect as is." Jackson spoke gently.

"Okay." Simone nodded her face in his hands, closing her eyes and breathing deeply.

"In any new relationship between a man and woman, gay, lesbian or otherwise; they have to get to know each other and figure out what works for them. And it's the same here. Just like you have to adjust to us, we'll adjust to you. But I want you to know that I want this. More than anything I've wanted in a long time." Jackson said passionately as he gently stroked his thumbs over her cheeks. "I don't want you to decide right this moment if you want to stay…for good. Well, that's a lie. Of course I'd love it if you said you wanted to stay right now, but I know this is a lot for you to take in. I just want you to give us a shot and to really consider staying and making this work." Jackson finally finished his heartfelt plea.

"Alright. I'll think about it and take everything you said into consideration. Thank you…for being so thoughtful and patient with me." Simone said shyly.

"It's nothing." Jackson said before placing his firm lips on her forehead.

His lips moved from her forehead to her damp eyelids, cheeks, nose and then her soft wide mouth. Hesitantly testing the water, Jackson's tongue tentatively flicked out against Simone's full lips. And she gasped at the sensation, opening to him instantly. Jackson took her assent and ran with it. His tongue stroked boldly into her mouth. His hand traveled down her cheek, past her neck and cupped her breast in his hand. He stroked his thumb over her sensitive nipple and she gasped against his mouth.

"Jax." She said breathlessly, almost like a question.

Jackson's hand continued a path down her body, into the water, cupping her hot sex. Her hips reflexively pumped into his hand. He slipped his middle finger inside her tight heat and his thumb made circular motions over her hardened clit. Simone's bottom lip trembled with need and she looked up at him with such naked passion and love that Jackson's heart clenched and jumped into his throat. His only reaction was to bury his other hand in the hair at the nape of her neck, holding her still so that he could devoured her mouth in desperation. His hand continued its assault on her quivering flesh. And Simone exploded with her climax. Her inner walls flexing against his fingers and her cry of ecstasy absorbed into his mouth.

As she came down from her high, Jackson released her lips and they rested their foreheads against each other, catching their breath.

"Better." Jackson asked with a grin.

"Yes." Simone sighed happily, the much needed climax that she was denied earlier in her distress, finally released the pent up tension in her body that the hot bath had failed to do. "I feel like a noodle now."

"Come on. Let me get you out of there, before you turn into a prune." Jackson said as he got up to grab a giant fluffy towel.

He helped her to stand and wrapped her up like a burrito before lifting her out of the tub like a small child. He held her tightly against his wide barreled chest as he walked into the bedroom. He sat her on the gigantic bed, walked out of the room and came back a minute later with her bags and opened one of the suitcases. Simone sat quietly watching him rummage through her bag, a small smile playing at her lips.

"May I ask what exactly are you looking for?" Simone asked with a chuckle.

"Your p.js. So you can relax for the evening." Jackson said looking up, the side of his mouth lifting up in a heart melting crooked smile.

"Ah, I see. Those would be in the other bag." Simone pointed to her other piece of luggage.

Jackson opened the other suitcase and grabbed her fleece pajama pants and a long-sleeved undershirt. He brought the clothing over and unwrapped the towel.

"Arms up." Jackson instructed.

"You know I'm a big girl. I can dress myself." Simone said as she raised her arms.

"I know. I just like taking care of you. Is there something wrong with that?" Jackson said, and then bent down to place a soft kiss on the end of her nose.

Simone just shook her head no. Too overwhelmed to speak. It had been a long time since someone had wanted to take care of her. It made her think of her mother and she had to squeeze her lips together to keep from crying. She stood up and he helped her step into the comfy pants. When he was finished he looked down at her and saw her eyes were glassy from unshed tears.

"What's wrong, Si? Did I do something wrong?" Jackson asked anxiously.

"No…no. You've done everything just right. So right, it's a little scary. Like you can read my mind or something. I was just thinking about my mother. She was the last one to pamper me like child. And you dressing me, brought back memories. Good ones, though." Simone gave him a watery smile and she brushed away the wetness from her eyes.

"Yeah, it hits you at random times, doesn't it? The loss?" Jackson looked down at his feet, understanding exactly what she meant. "It doesn't completely go away. I still miss them." Jackson turned and stuffed his hands into his pockets.

"Now I've upset you." Simone said, coming up to him and placing a gentle hand on his broad back. "I'm sorry."

"It's okay. It's nice to talk to someone that understands how I feel." Jackson turned to her and grabbed her hand, pulling her to him in a warm embrace. She felt safe from the world in his strong arms. "Alright, I have to get dinner started. Wanna come down with me? Have a glass of wine?"

"Yeah sure. That sounds nice."

~~~

Five minutes later, they had all migrated to the kitchen. Xander sat on one of the three stools at the island and he pulled Simone in between his wide spread legs to sit on the edge. He wrapped his arms around her and rocked her gently for a moment and kissed her temple lightly. And they watched as Jackson rummaged through the refrigerator and cabinets, gathering things to make dinner.

"So you mean to tell me that you cook *every* night?" Simone asked Jackson, incredulous before she took a sip of delicious red wine they had poured for her.

"Well not *every* night. Sometimes we go out to eat or get takeout. But that's a bit tough considering how far we live from the city. So I cook most of the time." Jackson answered, glancing up from his work to wink at her.

"So what do *you* do then?" Simone asked looking back at Xander.

Xander took a sip of his beer and then leaned back on the stool, placed his hands behind his head, in a pose of complete relaxation. "Nothing. He's my bitch." Xander sighed with bliss.

Simone and Jackson burst out laughing. "You're full of shit, Xan!" Jackson chuckled. "Don't let him fool you, Si. He cleans the house and washes the dishes after I cook."

"Hmm…actually I think Jackson has the better end of the bargain." Simone said after thinking it over a bit.

"Oh just wait. He blasts music and dances while he cleans. So I think it's more like *Saturday Night Fever* than actual cleaning." Jackson laughed at the scowl Xander gave him.

"So…*if* I were to stay…what would I contribute?" Simone broached.

"Nothing. We'll take care of you." Jackson said seriously.

"What?! I have to do something!" Simone exclaimed.

"You would. It's a lot of work to deal with two grown babies. We need lots of affection and attention." Xander squeezed her tightly.

"Wait. What about work? I can work, right?" Simone asked, standing up and stepping away from Xander so that she could look at both their faces and wouldn't be distracted by Xander's warm embrace.

"Well, I mean you don't have to if you don't want to. We'll take care of you financially too." Jackson pointed out.

"I'm not some freaking concubine! Or sex slave! To just laze around all day reading magazines, eating grapes or any crap like that, while I wait for you to get home!" Simone railed, her relaxed mood completely obliterated.

"It doesn't have to be grapes and magazines. You could always watch soaps and eat bon-bons." Xander joked, not picking up on the queue that she was about to lose it.

"It's not fucking funny, Xander!" Simone finally exploded, making the smile quickly dissolve on Xander's lips. "If I'm really going to consider this relationship, I have to have something to do. I have to have my own identity outside of you two. I did not go to school for nothing. I did not work my ass off to sit around all day to find ways to please you two!" Simone finished in a shout.

"We didn't mean to downplay your needs." Jackson tried to soothe, at the same time, giving Xander a look for making a joke out of the situation. "You can do whatever makes you happy. We're just saying that you don't *have* to do anything if you don't want to. Or you have the choice to do whatever you want to do. It's up to you." Jackson explained as he poured more wine into her glass, hoping to bring back her peaceful mood.

Simone accepted the refilled glass and sat on her own stool, keeping her distance from both of them. She took deep breaths, trying to calm her frazzled nerves.

"I'm sorry, Si. I wasn't serious. That was just my tasteless way of always trying to get a laugh. I was being an ass." Xander apologized and reached over to squeeze her hand.

"I know. I'm just a little on edge, trying to figure out where I fit in this…this…" Simone didn't know exactly what to call what they were doing.

"Triad. Threesome. Triangle. Tripod. Three peas in a pod. Whichever. You pick." Xander listed off, finally drawing a reluctant laugh from Simone.

"Okay. Triad, then. So I'd like to help around the house and with the cooking. And *if* I decide to stay, I have to find a job." At the hopeful look Jackson gave her, she continued. "But I'm not at that stage…yet." His shoulders slumped a little in disappointment at her words.

"You're only here for another week and a few days. Are you really going to be able to decide by then?" Jackson said quietly, somewhat shyly like a little boy. The big chestnut curls hanging on his forehead, didn't help.

"I honestly don't know, Jackson." Simone admitted.

He just nodded his head and continued to work on dinner, staying silent. Simone downed the rest of her wine and hopped off her stool. She walked around the island and laid a hand on top of Jackson's as he chopped mushrooms. His hand stilled and he looked down at her with melancholy gray eyes.

"How can I help? Point me in the right direction, Master Chef." Simone tried to lighten the tense atmosphere.

"You could start a pot of water to boiling. And then if you want, you could start dicing up those tomatoes." Jackson said pointing to where the pots were.

"So what are you fixing exactly?" Simone asked curiously.

"Seafood pasta. Angel hair pasta, with a lemon zest sauce, shrimp, mussels and fresh clams still in the shells." Jackson listed off nonchalantly, as Simone gaped at him in wonder.

"Where did you learn to cook like this?" She asked him.

"Cooking shows. Plus, by the time we got into high school my grandparents were pretty elderly, so I helped out with cooking for them. Then they passed away, and I had to take care of myself. And when I moved in with this knucklehead, I definitely had to learn. Otherwise I'd be dead by now. Of either starvation or poisoning." Jackson looked up at Xander with a smirk.

"Please dude! You act like your shit don't stink because you can cook a meal. Yeah…yeah, cooking is *soooo* sexy. But if it wasn't for me you'd be turning your underwear inside out, once you ran out of clean clothes." Xander said giving Jackson the stink eye and then turned to Simone to continue. "He did that you know…before we moved in together, in our first place." Xander said smugly.

Simone turned to Jackson with her mouth hanging open in disbelief. A telltale blush spread across Jackson's cheeks. "Did you really turn your underwear inside out when you ran out of clean ones?" Simone asked.

"I hate doing laundry." Jackson said quietly, the blush spreading from cheeks to hairline and down his neck.

"And washing dishes." Xander continued on Jackson's behalf, which the big man didn't seem to appreciate, if the scowl on his face was any indication.

"Okay, okay. No more puffing out your chests and banging on them trying to prove who the better man is. It's a tie. You both obviously help each other immensely. I'm impressed with both of you, okay?" Simone said, calling a draw before the knife Jackson was gripping in his massive paw ended up buried in Xander's skull.

"Okay?" She repeated when they didn't answer.

"Okay."

"Yep."

Xander's cellphone rang, fortunately helping to end the debate.

"Hey, mom... Just helping get dinner ready." Xander said as Jackson nudged Simone and they laughed at his definition of 'help'. "What's up?" Xander said into the phone and scowling at them across the island.

"What did she tell you?" Xander said, his smile turning into a frown. "She is such a brat."

Simone had a feeling that the 'brat' in question was his sister Delanie.

"*Mom...seriously*?!" Xander groaned. "I really don't think that's a good idea." Xander paused as she said something. "But.... Alright fine." Xander grumbled before holding out the phone to Simone.

Simone wasn't exactly sure what the one-sided conversation was about, but she definitely hadn't been expecting to be involved. She looked at the phone with trepidation, like it was a living snake about to bite her.

"She wants to talk to you a moment." Xander said, still holding the phone out to her.

Simone hesitantly reached out to take the phone from him and slowly raised it to her ear. She tried her best to hide the tremble in her hand. Never having dated anyone before, the mastery of 'winning over the parents' was something she definitely wasn't familiar with. But having little choice, Simone lightly cleared her throat, trying to unblock the lump of fear in her throat before speaking.

"Hello?" She said softly.

"Hello, Simone. This is Alexander's mom, Gail. I was wondering if you would like to come to dinner tomorrow evening. The whole family takes a break in their daily lives to get together once a month to have dinner. And I would love it if you could make it." Xander's mom said kindly.

"Oh…um…sure. I would really like that." Simone said, though she wasn't so sure she was being completely honest.

I'd like to meet his family eventually. *And one at a time, but meeting* all *six of them at once. Being surrounded by a family of seven and Jackson. Even when my mom was alive, it was still just the two of us. Oh God, what have I gotten myself into?*

"Uh…what was that?" Simone quickly asked. Wrapped up in her thoughts, she had missed part of what Gail had said.

"I said, that Frank and I are looking forward to meeting you. And is there anything that you don't like to eat or allergic to?" She said thoughtfully.

"Oh, no. No, I'm not a picky eater. I'm sure anything you fix would be perfect. Is there anything that you'd like me to bring?" Simone asked, the manners that her mother had drilled into her, kicking in.

"No dear. Just bring yourself."

"Okay."

"Well, alright then. We'll see you tomorrow at seven." Gail said brightly.

"See you then." Simone ended the call, handing the phone back to Xander. "I think I need to sit down." Simone said walking back over to the stool in a daze.

"Don't worry, Simone. My family doesn't bite. I'm sure they'll love you." Xander reassured her.

Not if they're anything like Bethany, Simone grumbled to herself.

"Don't let Beth get to you." Jackson said firmly, making Simone look up in shock, realizing that once again she had voiced her thoughts out loud without realizing it. "The Drake family is the best family I know. As much as they adopted me, I adopted them. I got a ready-made family, right when I needed them." Jackson smiled fondly, with a faraway look in his eyes.

Simone smiled back at him.

~~~

They sat in front of the fireplace in the three large comfy chairs that made a semi-circle in front of the warm glow. Simone taking up the middle as usual. Sampson huffed in his sleep, worn out after eating some food and being rewrapped in fresh bandages. Stuffed from the delicious meal, they relaxed for a bit before bed. An underlying sense of anticipation coursed through them, at the thought of bedtime.

"So…is there like some unwritten rule that you two don't share the master suite on a normal basis?" Simone asked before taking a sip of wine, feeling a little light-headed from all of the wine she had consumed throughout the night.

"Kind of." Xander responded.

"The room is sort of reserved for three, if you couldn't tell." Jackson grinned at her. "I know it's weird, but for some reason it just doesn't feel right using it when we don't have someone to share it with." Jackson explained further.

"Huh… I guess I get it." Simone looked down into her glass before asking the next question, not entirely sure she wanted to know. "H…have you shared it with someone before?"

"Surprisingly, no." Jackson started.

"We only finished the house this past summer. And when we designed the house, we designed it with our future in mind. You know, building a family eventually." Xander explained further.

"The room is reserved for someone that we can see building that family with. And there was something about the last woman that we dated that we knew wasn't quite right. So the room has remained unused." Jackson finished, easily picking up Xander's train of thought again, like they were long lost twins separated at birth.

"Oh." Simone said softly. It was on the tip of her tongue to ask which room she was going to be in, but she wasn't sure what she wanted them to say. If they said one of their individual rooms, it might hurt that they didn't think more of her. But if they said the master suite, that was a lot of pressure. So she remained silent, not wanting to put them on the spot or put herself in a position to feel awkward.

Jackson and Xander looked at each other, communicating silently. They drained the rest of the scotch they had in their tumblers and stood. Jackson grabbed Xander's glass, strode over to Simone and took the glass from her hand as well. He took his free hand and stroked it down her face from temple to chin.

"I have something for you. I'll be back in a moment." He said quietly in a deep voice that sounded like honey over gravel.

When Jackson walked away, Xander stepped up and gently clasped Simone's hand and pulled her up from her chair. He reached up and unwound her hair that she had knotted into a loose bun on top of her head. Xander's eyes followed her hair as it cascaded down her shoulders and back.

"Beautiful." He said softly, and Simone felt the word in her gut, like a living thing growing and spreading warmth throughout her body.

Tipping her chin up with the tip of his finger, Xander leaned in to take her lips in a scorching kiss. His full lips molded themselves to hers. Totally absorbed in the kiss, Simone didn't realized that Jackson had returned until she felt a thick fabric slide over her eyes. She assumed it was a scarf as he tied a knot behind her head. And she felt his large hand smooth her hair away from her neck and his firm lips on her neck, at the sensitive spot below her ear.

"I'm blindfolding you to keep you from freaking out based on the bedroom we chose." Jackson said softly, his breath tickling her ear as he flawlessly read her insecurities. "And also because I want to introduce something to you and I don't want you to be nervous about it. So just relax, we'll take care of you. Do you trust us?" Jackson asked.

"Y…yes." Simone whispered hesitantly, her breath coming out in pants of anticipation.

"Good." Jackson said.

He turned her to face him and she felt his arms wrap around her ass a second before he lifted her up. She instinctively circled her legs around his waist and her hands clutched at his shoulders. His mouth found hers and he kissed her deeply, stroking his tongue over hers as he started to walk with her in his arms. He tasted of scotch, like Xander and she felt drunk off of the flavor. He broke the kiss as he started to climb the stairs to one of the bedrooms. Simone was glad that she couldn't see, because she knew she'd be too preoccupied with the meaning behind the room they chose, instead of the passion they were about to unleash upon her.

Once inside a room, Jackson released her ass and let her body slide down his, feeling every hard rippling inch of him. Then he raised her arms up and she felt her shirt glide up her heated flesh and up over her head. Simone could feel her nipples harden from the slight chill in the air. Next, someone grasped the waistband of her flannel pants and slowly pulled them down to her ankles, caressing a path down her smooth legs in the process.

Simone stepped out of the pants, keeping her balance by holding onto the wide shoulders crouched in front of her. She felt them step away from her, leaving her naked, exposed, vulnerable and blind. Her breath came in short little gasps, her skin prickled with gooseflesh and her heart pounded out a beat in her clit.

With her sight taken away from her, her hearing was heightened to the sounds in the room. She could hear the fire crackling in the fireplace and she was sure she heard the whisper of clothing being discarded to the floor. And obviously her sense of touch was elevated as well, because when a sudden fingertip flashed out and retreated with a quick caress across her nipple, she cried out at the feeling.

They unleashed a series of gentle touches on her skin, that were quick but so intense as to feel them minutes later. A knuckle stroking down her throat, a fingertip across the sensitive skin behind her knee, lips and a wet tongue at the base of her spine, warm breath blowing delicately at her nape, a soft tap at her swollen clit, and a flick of a tongue over her erect nipples. At one point she was almost positive she had even felt long eyelashes fluttering against her trembling tummy. They pulled out all the stops, doing everything in their power to leave her a quivering mass of anticipation. No sensitive spot went untouched.

Then something smooth, hard and cool touched her lips and instantly warmed to match her temperature as it slid down her chin, neck and between her breasts. "This is going to get you prepared to take both of us at the same time. I picked it up during lunch today." Jackson explained cryptically.

Simone had absolutely zero knowledge of sex toys, but whatever it was, her gut and behind clenched simultaneously at what was to come. She felt them step up to her and whoever was at her front, she thought it was Jackson, reached around caressing large rough hands down her round globes to firmly spread them apart. With Xander at her back, she felt a cold wet liquid pour over her puckered skin and she shivered in response. His finger smoothed the fluid over her and she tensed.

"Just relax, Si. He's just getting you ready, so that we won't hurt you." Jackson whispered against her lips.

As Xander eased a finger into the tight muscles of her anus, Jackson smoothed a hand from her backside to her front. He stroked a calloused finger over her throbbing clit and Simone gasped, quickly reaching out to grasp his enormous biceps to steady herself.

Xander continued to lubricate her forbidden entrance, as Jackson played at her sensitive nub. Jackson crouched down in front of Simone and his tongue sought out her slick heat, just as she felt the hard object at her back entrance. Jackson must have sensed her trepidation, because he intensified his assault on her clit. Behind her Xander kissed and licked at her neck and back. And wrapping an arm around her chest to hold her still, he slid the object home into her taut muscle. Her rectum stretched and molded around the smooth hardness.

Simone hissed in response to the foreign object inside her. Jackson continued to suck and flick at her clit and her hips pumped into his mouth. Xander placed a hand under her chin and turned her face to him, kissing her deeply from behind. His other hand strummed her nipple gently. The passionate kiss, her sensitive nipple, the plug pressing on an unknown tender spot inside her body and a tongue on her tingling button; sent her over the edge.

Simone's body tensed like a bowstring being pulled back. And with its release, she lost all control of her body's reactions, matching the reverberation of the discharged bow. She released Xander's mouth on a sob. Her body shook violently and she felt wetness running down the insides of her trembling legs. Unable to stand any longer, Simone's legs gave out and Jackson quickly scooped her up into his arms. He held her close to his broad chest, murmuring gentle words to bring her down from the intense orgasm.

Xander unknotted the scarf and pulled it from Simone's face. She squinted at the soft firelight, until her eyes adjusted. Two pairs of eyes looked down at her, one like liquid silver, the other molten sunlight filtered through leaves of green.

"You did so good, Si. And you were so fucking hot! God, I can barely see straight, I want you so bad." Xander groaned before lightly kissing her lips.

"Can you handle one more round?" Jackson asked.

Simone nodded her assent, unable to speak. Xander stepped aside, clearing her obstructed view of the room. *The master suite. Well there's my answer.* Jackson walked over to the massive padded bench at the foot of the bed and placed her on her knees in the middle.

"Now place your hands on the bench for me." Jackson instructed.

They watched as she followed his command. The position presenting them with her already swollen and glistening labia and clit and the base of the purple plug peeking out between her ample round derrière.

"Jesus!" They both exclaimed in unison.

Simone looked back at them and flushed with embarrassment as they stared at her most private place. They were both magnificent examples of the male species. Standing shoulder to shoulder. Tall, broad shouldered, sculpted muscles, beautiful chiseled faces and impressive distended erections, all focused and pointing directly at her. *Dear God, whose fantasy did I wake up in?*

Xander stalked towards her to stand in front of her on one end of the bench and Jackson took up residence behind her. Xander's pulsing manhood stood out only a few inches from her mouth. Taking advantage of his nearness, Simone flicked out her tongue against its swollen head. Xander's breath caught in his throat at the contact.

Jackson placed his knee to one side of Simone's. He grasped his thick cock and rubbed the tip over her slick opening, naturally lubricating himself. His clenched teeth turned to granite as he slowly entered her from behind. The fullness of the plug still inside her, made her already tight passage strangle his throbbing member like a vise grip. He squeezed his eyes shut and his nostrils flared.

"Fuck!" Jackson shouted out as he was finally able to slide to the base. "Shit, shit, shit! That feels *so* fucking good."

Simone cried out at the complete sense of fullness that she felt once he was inside her. Instant tears ran down her face. Xander gently wiped them away with his thumbs. He began to stroke his hard length as he watched Jackson take her from behind.

"Let me." Simone said softly, looking up at him with heavy-lidded dark brown bedroom eyes.

Xander stepped closer to her and held his long cock up to her lips. Opening her full wide mouth for him, he gradually pumped his hips towards her. Simone took him in, inch by long inch. As Jackson started to move within her, forcing Xander further down her throat with each thrust, she thanked whoever was responsible for her lack of gag reflexes.

Her body on sensory overload, her core flooded with moisture, easing the way for Jackson to drive into her with punishing blows. Every thrust and retreat, pushed the plug further in and out of her tight entrance. Once again pressing that hidden button inside her and she moaned deeply around Xander's smooth length.

Xander's hands pulled her hair back away from her face, holding her hair in a loose ponytail at the base of her skull. He watched as his cock emerged and then disappeared between her lush lips. Jackson held on tightly to her ridiculously wide hips, as he too was mesmerized by the pull and suction of her wet heat surrounding him.

Then all was lost as the three merged into one and the tight rein they held on their control slipped. The men looked at each other and nodded in silent understanding as they began to double their efforts. Jackson pummeled Simone's pussy with vigor and she pushed back to meet him, wanting it just as much. And her lips tightened around Xander's steel erection as her moans vibrated over him.

All of their bodies tensed and then shattered a split second later. The men shouted and bellowed out their climaxes and Simone screamed in release. The moment they eased their softening shafts from her body, she melted onto the leather bench. Her only movement was the aftershocks coursing through her limp body.

Gathering up what strength he had left, Xander got up from the bench and walked into the bathroom. He strode out a few minutes later with two warm damp washcloths. Handing one to Jackson, they both eased Simone over onto her back and began to cleanse her of the evidence of their lovemaking.

Jackson gently slid the plug from her body and tenderly wiped away his seed and the remnants of the lube they'd used on her, from her swollen pulsing sex and thick thighs. With equally loving care, Xander wiped at her full mouth and tear stained face. And after cleaning themselves off as well, Jackson tossed the towels into the hamper, while Xander lifted Simone's dead weight off of the leather bench and placed her in the middle of the enormous bed.

They both slid into the bed on either side of her. Lying on her side, they moved in to sandwich her between their warm bodies, tangling their legs with hers. Xander crooked his arm and she rested her head on it like a pillow as he spooned her from behind. Jackson faced her, chest to chest, draping a long arm over Simone and Xander. He gave her plush lips soft kisses as Xander kissed her neck and shoulder gently.

"Are you okay?" Jackson asked her sleepily.

She nodded her head slightly in response. And with exhaustion that can only be had from great sex; they instantly drifted off in a tangle of limbs, sated flesh and beating hearts.

Chapter 10

Jackson's eyes slowly creaked open as his internal alarm clock went off, letting him know it was time to get up and get ready for work. But the vision in front of him, kept him immobile for a little while longer.

Simone and Xander were sharing the same pillow. Her head fit snuggly under Xander's chin and his hand rested limply on the full curve of her hip. And her hair was everywhere; across her face, over the pillow and curling around one dark nipple.

Jackson wished in that moment that he had some kind of artistic ability, because if he could he would paint the image in front of him, so that he could keep it always. Instead, he reached back and grabbed his phone off of the nightstand and took a picture of his two favorite people.

Simone stirred at the sound of the click of the camera. Jackson quickly put the phone back on the table and turning back, he gently brushed a thick strand of ebony hair from Simone's face. She wrinkled her long nose sweetly at the tickle of her hair on her face and burrowed deeper into Xander. Xander's arm that had been resting on her hips steeled around her to cup her breast. And she moaned deeply in the back of her throat, coming awake.

Simone's eyes fluttered open and her already sleepy eyes looked that much more seductive due to real sleepiness. Her dark eyes focused on Jackson and he grinned at her.

"Good morning, beautiful." He said deeply.

"Morning." She replied shyly, realizing he had been watching her.

"So I was wondering if you'd like to come to work with me today. I could give you a tour of the mill and show you what I do." Jackson asked, feeling a little shy himself. He wanted her to know him and vice versa.

"Oh, okay. I was supposed to finally go meet my mom's tribe today, but that could wait I guess." Simone said, grateful that she had an excuse to stall the inevitable for a little while longer.

"Chicken." Xander murmured gravelly as he pulled her tightly against him.

Simone's face flushed with pink. "I'm not chicken! I just want to see where Jackson works. Besides, I was thinking that I'll go when Amber gets here. She helps me loosen up a bit." Simone argued.

"Oh, we can help you loosen up just fine." Xander said as he playfully flexed his hips against Simone's backside.

"*That* is not what I meant." Simone rolled her eyes and tried pulling away from Xander's tight embrace.

"I don't want to take you away from your family, Simone. So if you want to go, I'd be happy to take you." Jackson said thoughtfully.

"No, you're not taking me away from anything. I'd love to see what you do. I still have time to meet them." Simone reassured him.

"You don't have to wait for your friend. We could always go with you." Xander chimed in.

"Ha…uh no. No, thank you. I'm already nervous about how they'll perceive me. I don't need you two coming along making me look like the town hussy." Simone frowned at back at Xander.

"Aw, don't be like that!" Xander exclaimed.

"I'm not saying that you guys can't come with me at some point, but not the first meeting. I need to make a good first impression. And walking up hand and hand with both of you, might start me out on the wrong foot." Simone explained.

"Don't worry about it, Si. I get it. But we just want to be there for you if you need us." Jackson said sweetly.

"Thank you." Simone smiled bashfully at him.

"Now…how about we jump in the shower for a quickie before work. You know. Kill two birds and all that." Xander grinned, adorable dimples framing his radiant smile.

"You've got serious issues, you know that?" Simone looked back at Xander with a small smile.

"Yeah know. I'm totally infatuated with this gorgeous girl and her amazing booty." Xander's smile widened as he smacked the ass in question.

They both jumped out of the bed. Jackson grabbed ahold of Simone's ankles and started to pull her to the edge of the bed. He smiled seductively as he pulled her closer to him, his adorable chestnut curls hanging down on his forehead.

"Hey! You're supposed to be on my side!" Simone cried, trying to put up a front of unwillingness.

"I'm on whatever side that gets this delectable body in my arms." Jackson growled as he lifted her over his shoulder like a ragdoll.

"Well…since you put it that way…" Simone smiled at once again being carried to the shower, but this time looking back at Xander as he followed them.

Simone quickly realized that she enjoyed this particular way of getting ready for a day of work. All slick and soaped up between two hard bodies, with multiple orgasms thrown in for good measure. She hoped it would be a regular occurrence. *No one would be grumpy at work if their day started off like this. Screw* Starbucks*!*

~~~

"Hey, Simone? Would you like some coffee to go?" Xander asked as he poured some of the potent brew into a tall to-go cup.

"Nope. I'm good. Thank you." Simone said with a secretive smile.

They all walked out to the garage, Xander carrying Sampson in his strong arms. He put the beautiful dog into his truck to take to the lodge so he could be babied by the staff, then led Simone to the passenger door of Jackson's truck. He gave her a deep toe-curling goodbye kiss, leaving her a little dizzy as she slid into the truck. He shut the door, waved goodbye and then got into his truck and started the engine.

"Ready?" Jackson asked, pulling her attention away from the blond Adonis as he pulled out of the garage.

"Yep." Simone smiled happily at Jackson.

"You're awfully happy this morning." Jackson noticed.

"It's not often that people get to wake up in such…pleasurable or inventive ways." Simone sighed dreamily, making Jackson chuckle.

"Well then, I guess we better make a habit of giving you similar wakeup calls." He winked at her as he started the truck and backed out of the garage.

"Yes, please." Simone said blushing.

"It amazes me how one minute you can be so shy and quiet and the next, aggressive and *so* very vocal." Jackson commented, deepening Simone's blush at the thought of her passionate cries in the shower not long ago.

"I'm still new to all of this. I was a virgin and completely ignorant to the ways of men not even a full week ago, remember?" Simone looked over at him with raised eyebrows. "I didn't even know all of this was in me. I thought I was asexual, like a plant." Simone finished as Jackson guffawed and started to cough trying to restrain his laughter.

"Go ahead, laugh. Ya big jerk!" Simone tried to hide her smile.

Jackson cleared his throat before speaking. "Sorry. I wasn't trying to make fun." A few more laughs slipped through and he squeezed his lips together in an effort to contain them. "I just wasn't expecting you to say that. Asexual…really? As sexually responsive as you are, how could you not have any interest in sex before us?" Jackson asked incredulous.

"I don't know. It's like you two woke something up inside of me that was buried down deep. I don't even know how I managed to contain all of this for so long." *Or how I'll manage to entomb it once more, if this doesn't work out,* Simone thought sadly, but kept to herself.

"Well, you can't imagine how happy I am that you chose us. I love watching you discover yourself." Jackson said honestly.

"I don't think I had much choice in the matter. You guys are kinda hard to ignore. And you basically coerced me into it." Simone smiled sweetly.

"Hey, we know what we like. And we go for it. And when it comes to you, we had to have you. There was no question. I'm just glad you didn't say no." Jackson clarified, with an unapologetic shrug.

"Oh." Simone said softly, still amazed that she had attracted such gorgeous men.

~~~

They rode the rest of the way in relative silence. Simone gazed out at the dark landscape as they passed the town and drove deeper into thick forest. Finally a large building with industrial looking large conveyor belts sticking out of it like long legs, came into view. Jackson parked near an entrance. He hopped out of the truck and came around to Simone's side and opened the door for her.

"So this is it, J.C. Lumber. My pride and joy." Jackson smirked at her as his arms swept the perimeter of the mill.

"Wow! This is much bigger than I was expecting. How did you come to own all of this?" Simone asked as she took in the area.

"It's been handed down a few generations. My grandfather started it. Much of the work done by hand. Then my dad took over and modernized it for the time. Brought in nice machinery, making the operation thrive. When he passed away my grandfather had to come out of retirement to take care of the business until I was old enough. Then when I took it over, I've been making upgrades to it gradually over the last decade. Making everything more computerized. Come on, I'll show you." Jackson said holding out a hand for Simone to take.

Just inside the entrance hung a few hardhats. Jackson grabbed one and placed it on Simone's head. "Safety first." He said before dropping a quick kiss on her nose and then placing a hat over his own curls.

As he led her around the mill showing her his legacy, Jackson noticed the not so subtle looks his men gave her. He introduced her to a few, but for the most part kept his distance. The blatant looks of appraisal were already pissing him off. And he didn't need his workers making comments that would send their asses straight to the unemployment line unnecessarily, in his anger. *Jesus! They're not just my employees, they're my friends. Fuck...get it together Cole!*

For her part, Simone barely noticed the majority of the looks, but when she did catch one of their eyes, she'd just smile shyly. And as she walked away, the men would practically swoon at the shy woman with the brick house body.

Trying to ignore his raging jealousy he guided her outside where trucks filled with freshly cut logs were parked. A huge bulldozer looking thing with giant claws, that Jackson called a log stacker, picked up the logs and dropped them onto a conveyor belt. Following the belt, they went inside were a colossal angry looking contraption stripped the logs of their rough bark. The logs then made their way to a machine that cut the wood into different sized boards.

"What are the different sized boards made for?" Simone asked loudly over the eardrum shattering noise.

"All sorts of things. Regular two-by-fours for construction, smaller boards for hardwood flooring, furniture, cabinetry, and so on. Even the sawdust and woodchips have a purpose. All of the wood gets shipped out to various woodworking companies and shops across Canada and the States." Jackson bellowed over the noise.

Simone just nodded in awe at the magnitude of the operation and how much responsibility Jackson had, and at such a young age when he started. He took her hand and led her up a flight of metal grated stairs, feeling eyes following them the whole way. He opened the door to a cozy office.

"This is my sanctuary." Jackson said, closing the thick door behind her and all sound instantly went from a loud roar to a low hum. "I had my office sound proofed. Triple paned windows, overlooking the mill." Jackson said as he walked over to the large window that looked down over the operation and closed the blinds. "Sound insulated walls and a thick reinforced door. All to block out the deafening machines so I can concentrate when I'm working or having meetings. And…so they don't hear the screams of a very loud young woman that I'm about to fuck senseless on my desk." Jackson growled as he locked the door behind him and stalked towards Simone with eyes that had turned into melted silver.

"Um…don't…don't you think that that would be a little unprofessional." Simone said nervously, backing up until her butt hit the edge of the desk. "And besides, didn't we just have sex about an hour or so ago? Aren't you tired of me yet?"

"Not even close. And I own the place. I'll decide what's professional or not." Jackson murmured deeply as he placed both arms on either side of her on the desk, caging her in. "I know I'll probably regret this later, but I've always wanted to do this." Jackson whispered against Simone's lips, before reaching back behind her and sweeping his arm across the desk, sending stacks of paperwork fluttering to the floor.

Jackson took off his hardhat and then Simone's and tossed them across the room. They landed with a soft thump on the couch that faced his desk against the opposite wall. Both large work calloused hands grasped her face and pulled her mouth to his. There were no soft kisses that built up to something more. It was a raging inferno the moment his mouth touched hers.

He crushed her lips to his and his tongue plunged in deeply. He held her so tight to him that she could barely breathe. His stubble abraded her face harshly. The kiss was punishing and almost angry in its intensity. Simone pulled back on a gasp to look up at him questioningly.

"What's the matter?" Simone asked softly.

"I want you to understand something. You are mine. Xander's. Ours. No one else. Do you understand?" Jackson asked with a ferocity that scared her.

"What are you talking about?" Simone searched his face nervously. "Who else would I even be interested in? You both overwhelm me as it is, without me adding a third person." Simone assured him, before becoming angry on her own behalf. "Besides, you don't own me Jackson, and neither does Xander. I don't want to be with anyone else, but I sure as hell won't have you bossing me around and talking to me like I'm some slut. I'm not your last girlfriend, so stop treating me that way!" Simone exploded, pushing at his chest, trying to get some distance. But moving Jackson was like trying to move a brick wall.

The anger and jealousy cleared from his silver eyes, replaced by the insecurity he had tried to hide behind. "God! I'm so sorry, Simone. I didn't mean to make you feel like anything less than the phenomenal woman I think you are. I just got so worried when all of my men stared at you like a piece of meat. You don't understand your appeal, but I do. Xander does. And every single one of those fuckers do." Jackson pointed towards the window that looked down at the mill. "And you haven't made your decision yet, on whether you'll stay or not. And just thinking about you leaving and finding someone else rips me apart." Jackson finished sadly.

"Trust me Jackson, I think you both have left an indelible impression on me. Even if I didn't stay, I don't think I could be with anyone else." Simone said honestly.

"Life happens, Simone. It could sneak up on you, without you even realizing it." Jackson said inconsolable.

"Come here." Simone held out her hand to him.

Her hand fit into his like a small child's. Simone knew the power behind his hands, she had felt it. And though he could do anything he wanted to her, she trusted that he would only use his strength to protect her, no matter how angry he got. Wanting to feel that strength, she led him to his desk chair. Once he was seated, she instantly crawled onto his lap.

"I know I haven't decided yet, but I'm gonna need you to calm down and stop acting like a big ol' grumpy bear." Simone smirked at him.

"Harrumph." He grumbled.

Taking his arms, Simone wrapped them around her waist. She placed her hands at his temples, brushing his soft dark curls from his face. Her fingers traced over his thick straight masculine eyebrows and down his slightly crooked nose.

"I broke it playing football with some friends." Jackson answered her silent question.

Undeterred by the interruption, Simone continued to trace his face like a blind person would trace Braille. Jackson closed his eyes and sighed contentedly as her thumbs brushed over his long eyelashes. Next her fingers stroked down his scruffy jawline. The hairs contradicting themselves with their rough but soft scrape. She outlined his lips with her the tip of her index finger and his mouth opened slightly. Taking advantage, she leaned forward a little and took his full bottom lip between her teeth, grazing the tender skin and Jackson shivered in response.

Sliding a hand into the hair at the nape of her neck, Jackson pulled her in for a tender kiss. This time the kiss was easy and loving. Simone's hands found their way into the thick satiny curls at the base of his neck, as she held on for dear life. *God, I want to stay! But can I uproot my life for them…for this. Fuck yeah, you can! Oh, shut up!*

Simone deepened the kiss, trying to shut out the racket going on in her head. Jackson responded in kind and ravished her mouth. He sat up, pulling her off of his lap. He turned her to face away from him and bent her over his desk. Simone's cheek rested against the cool wooden desk. Sitting behind her, Jackson caressed his hands up her legging clad legs, up over her ass to the waistband of her pants. He slowly slid the pants along with her panties, down her legs. He helped her out of her boots and bottoms, till she stood naked from the waist down.

Her gorgeous plump caramel-coated backside and wet pussy beckoned him like a moth to a flame. Burying his face in her heat made her cry out with need. He tormented her this way for a few minutes, before turning her around and lifting her up to sit on the edge of the desk. Pulling the chair closer, Jackson raised her legs to rest her feet on the arms of the chair. Then his head bent down to go to work.

Raised up onto her elbows, Simone's head fell back as she felt his tongue dance across her clit lightly. She moaned deep in her throat at the pleasure he was inflicting upon her. Unable to resist watching, Simone lifted her head that felt weighted and languid to look down at him paying homage to her most intimate place.

She watched his dark head bob and swivel with every lick. His eyes were closed, savoring her taste. And his pink tongue flicked delicately at her swollen nub. She stared as her hips pumped towards his eager mouth. Observing what he was doing to her heightened her awareness and her clit started to tingle in answer. And just as she was cresting over the edge, his molten silver eyes opened to look up at her. The connection and the final flick of his talented tongue, sent her in an upward spiral and her hips bucked furiously against his awaiting tongue. At the last second, she threw back her head and cried out her pleasure.

Before she could come back down from her high, she felt the tip of his cock at the entrance of her fluttering walls. "Look at me." She heard Jackson command from what felt like far above, as if she was submerged in a pool sensations. Slowly she glanced up at him as he stood poised at her threshold. And as she met his gaze, he plunged into her to the hilt. Her eyes widened and she gasped at the fullness of him.

His height put him in an awkward position as he tried to crouch down to her, so grabbing her around the waist he pulled her off the desk onto his lap as he sat in the chair. Her legs draped over the arms of the chair, widening her legs and deepening their connection. She felt him at the top of her womb. Using his hands, hips and powerful arms; he rocked her onto his massive erection.

Simone placed her hands on the back of the chair on either side of Jackson's head. Clutching the chair tightly, she used all of her strength to lift her weight and then released to slide back down his length. They both groaned as they put their foreheads together in deep concentration. Every thought, every move was centered on where their bodies joined. Grasping her ass tightly, Jackson's arms bulged and a thin sheen of sweat broke out across his skin as he increased his speed to a near superhuman pace. He battered at her aching pussy with savagery. Constant cries escaped her lips as he growled deep in his throat.

Simone realized that this was not just sex or lovemaking. This was *possession*. He owned her in that moment. He took from her and then gave back just as much. He held her gaze and she was entranced, unable to look away. His jaw clenched tight, the square angle becoming more sharp and defined. His nostrils flared and the looked of naked love that shown in his eyes as he came hard inside of her, sent Simone over the edge as well.

I am his. Theirs. Fuck...

~~~

After they redressed, Simone helped Jackson pick up all of the papers he had thrown to the floor.

"Nope. Still worth it." Jackson said to himself.

"What?" Simone looked up at him curiously.

"I asked myself if I regretted throwing the papers off the desk. And I just answering." Jackson grinned at her.

"Do you have a habit of talking to yourself?" Simone smiled back.

"Just taking my cue from you. *You* definitely have a habit of accidentally saying what's on your mind often enough." Jackson shot back.

"Ha ha." Simone laughed sarcastically.

An alarm on a loud speaker squawked so loudly that Simone nearly jumped a foot in the air. Her heart pounded as Jackson jumped up and ran to the window, ripping open the blinds to look down on the mill.

"Something's wrong." Jackson said as he ran to the door, swung it open and ran down the stairs.

Simone ran after him, though trying to keep up with his long legs was next to impossible. She saw him round a corner and she ran to catch up, colliding into his solid back when she came around the corner. Peaking around him she saw a man on the floor cradling his hand and rocking back and forth, pain etched on every line of his face.

"Shit Daryl, what happened?!" Jackson exclaimed.

"Something was stuck. And instead of turning off the belt like I was supposed to, like a jackass I reached in to loosen the board. And when the board finally came loose, the belt started up again and the fucking machine crushed my hand." Daryl groaned in pain.

Simone came from behind Jackson and strode over to the injured man with a purpose. "Can I see?" She asked him softly.

Trembling with pain, Daryl held his mangled hand out to her. She took it gently and inspected each digit. "I think you've broken all of them expect your pinky." Simone stated matter-of-factly.

"That's useful." Daryl grumbled.

"How far is the nearest hospital?" Simone asked turning to Jackson.

"About forty-five minutes to an hour. Give or take weather and traffic." Jackson answered, liking her take charge attitude.

"I need you to get me two thin boards and some cloth." Simone order calmly.

"Yes, boss." Jackson grinned at this new side of Simone, as he obeyed her order.

Jackson was back a few minutes later and handed her two thin pieces of plywood and a ripped up t-shirt.

"Thank you, Jax. You're wearing a belt, right?" Simone asked looking up at him from her crouched position next to Daryl.

"Yeah, why?" Jackson asked with a raised eyebrow.

"Can I have it please?" Simone asked, not giving much away.

Jackson just shrugged and undid his belt and handed it to her.

"Okay, Daryl. I'm gonna need you to bite down on this." She said holding the belt up to his mouth. Daryl looked at her with trepidation and Simone explained further. "I'm going to try to set your fingers and then put your hand in a makeshift splint until you can get to the hospital. There's not always a lot that they can do about broken fingers, but in your case I think they might have to surgically put pins in. But anyway, I don't want your fingers to start setting on their own in the shape they're currently in." Simone finished.

Daryl looked up at Jackson, questioningly.

"She's a nurse. You should probably listen to her. Here, you can hold my hand if you need to. Squeeze as hard as you want." Jackson said crouching down on his left side and clutching his good hand.

Simone held the folded belt up to Daryl's mouth and he bit down nervously. Holding his hand out flat, Simone gently grasped his thumb and pulled it into position. Daryl bit down and screamed in agony. Simone made quick work of the other three fingers, placed his hand in between the two pieces of wood and wrapped them together rapidly with the t-shirt.

The belt fell limply from Daryl's mouth and he swayed alarmingly. "Thank you." He whispered before promptly passing out.

Loud applause broke out around them and Simone looked up in surprise. She hadn't noticed the crowd that had gathered around them, too absorbed in helping her patient. She blushed from her roots to the collar of her flannel.

"Alright guys, get back to work. Shows over." Jackson stood up, unfolding to his full six-feet-five inches, instantly commanding the room.

The men scattered immediately.

"Let's get him to the hospital." Jackson sighed, as he gently lifted the unconscious man up and over his shoulder like he weighed next to nothing.

~~~

"You were a rockstar today! I'm so proud of you." Jackson said as they walked out of the hospital.

"Thanks, Jax." Simone blushed, warmth spreading over her at the compliment.

"So…if you stay, you know you've got a job here. You heard what the hospital staff said, they could always use the help and they were definitely impressed with you." Jackson approached cautiously.

"I know. It's definitely something to consider." Simone replied vaguely.

Jackson sighed in resignation. "Since Daryl's wife came to pick him up and we don't have to take him back, I thought we might as well grab a bite to eat. I sent a text to Xander and he said he'd meet up with us for lunch. You hungry?" Jackson asked, getting off of the subject of whether she'd stay or not.

"Yeah. Now that the excitement has died down, I realized I'm starving." Simone said, grateful that he let the subject go.

"Good. I could personally eat a small village." Jackson said, rubbing his flat stomach.

"I bet you could." Simone laughed, looking at the gentle giant who could definitely be mistaken for a bear.

"Let's roll." Jackson said as he opened the truck door for Simone to get in.

As they drove to meet up with the other point in their strange triangle, Simone silently contemplated actually staying. *I have no family back home, unless I consider Amber and her family. But it's not like I won't be able to see her if I wanted to. Besides, she's eventually going to start her own life without me. Knowing Amber, she'll probably meet someone and get serious sooner than later. Then I'd be alone anyway.*

Can I really walk away from all they're offering me? Near constant love and affection that I've been without for far too long? A home that they're offering as my own? To live near my mom's tribe? Not to mention unbelievably mind-blowing sex? I mean panty-dropping, bend over and beg for it sex?! I never even knew I wanted sex. And now that I've had it, could I actually give it up? Amber's always saying how hard it is to find a man that knows what he's doing in bed. And I found TWO! What are they teaching the guys up here in Alaska?!

They pulled up to a quaint little diner named Bacon.

"Well that says it all." Simone chuckled, looking at the word made out of strips of bacon and the O was a sunny-side up egg.

"Yep, you can never go wrong with bacon." Jackson said as he helped her out of the truck.

"I'm assuming this place is pretty popular with the men of Fairbanks." Simone hopped down and held the hand Jackson extended to her.

"Oh we come in droves. They have great food and just like the name, nearly everything on the menu has bacon in it." Jackson held the door open for her.

As Simone walked into the restaurant, she instantly spotted Xander at a curved corner booth. Her heart fluttered at the radiant smile that spread across his beautiful face. His shaggy blond hair brushed his face, his eyes glowed at the sight of her and the stunning muscle defects that were his dimples pulled together the heavenly work of art that was his angelic face.

He slid out from the booth and walked to meet her halfway. Wrapping his strong arms around her waist, he lifted her off her feet and kissed her soundly in front of the whole dining room.

"Xander…everyone is watching." Simone hissed under her breath. Her face turned beet red, not sure how to act with them out in public for the first time.

"Eh. They'll get over it. I missed you." Xander smiled down at her as he placed her back on her feet.

"It's only been a few hours." Simone shook her head with a smile as she walked to the table.

Xander turned to Jackson and clapped him affectionately on the back as they followed Simone. Jackson slid into the curved booth first, then Simone scooched in next to him and Xander finished out the sandwich on Simone's right.

"Is there a reason why more often than not you're on my left side", Simone asked looking at Jackson, "and you're on my right?" She finished looking at Xander.

"Well, I guess it's because I'm left-handed, so I favor the left of a woman and Xander's right-handed, so he favors the right. I never really thought much of it. It's just something we've done from the start." Jackson shrugged, looking over at Xander.

"Huh, you're right, we do. I didn't think much of it either. Does it bother you?" Xander asked.

"Oh no, not at all. Just wondering." Simone smiled at him.

"Okay, good. Maybe one day we'll switch it up to throw you off and spice things up." Xander grinned rakishly and waggled his eyebrows, making Simone giggle. "So I hear that you saved the day today." Xander changed the subject.

"I didn't do anything special. Anyone would have in my position." Simone brushed off the praise.

"I don't buy that. You're a remarkable woman." Xander caressed a finger down her cheek. "You have so many sides. Shy, intelligent, focused, independent, passionate, sexy and brave. That's a whole lot of amazing wrapped up in one gorgeous woman."

Simone hadn't blushed so much in her entire life, as she did in the presence of these two men. "So…what's good here?" Simone dodged as she grabbed the menu. Both men chuckled, but let her off the hook and decided to order instead of embarrassing her with more compliments.

As they ate and interacted with each other, Simone felt the frequent glances that they received. Looks that ranged from innocent curiosity to blatant carnal interest, all the way to downright disgust. And the guys weren't helping the situation either. They touched her affectionately; brushing her hair behind her ears, rubbing her hands or arms with a stroke of a thumb, stealing kisses and even feeding her from their plates, letting her sample their meals.

When they were finally done and walked out to their trucks, Simone breathed a sigh of relief at finally being away from the constant scrutiny. Xander walked with them to Jackson's truck. Xander opened the door for her before turning her into his arms for a warm embrace. Pulling back a little, he brushed her hair away from her face and kissed her softly.

"Are you ready for tonight?" Xander asked after he pulled his full lips away from her.

"No." Simone said honestly.

"It'll be fine, Si. They'll love you." Xander comforted her.

"We'll see. I have absolutely zero experience with meeting a guy's family. I have no idea how to act or what to say." Simone said frantically, working herself up.

"Act like yourself. And just say whatever you would say to anyone you've just met." Xander reasoned.

"I don't do that very well in general. You do remember when I first met you last week. Not so great." *Dear God…it's really only been a week! Not even. It feels like it's been a year. Good Lord, these guys wear me out!*

"So what, you're a little shy. It's no big deal. What would be a problem, was if you talked a mile a minute while cursing like a sailor and belched in between forkfuls of food. You don't do any of that, at least not that I've noticed. So relax." Xander winked at her, kissed her softly and then helped her into the truck. "See you two in a couple of hours at the house. We'll get ready and then head out." Xander said before closing the door.

"Xander's right. You'll do fine, just be yourself." Jackson leaned over and kissed her forehead and then started the truck to head back to the mill. "So I need to go back to the mill for a little bit. Apparently I need to have another safety meeting with my employees. Then I need to make a few calls. But we can head back home a little early, so you can relax and get ready for tonight."

"Alright." Simone responded as she tried to control the butterflies in her stomach at the thought of the night to come.

Chapter 11

Simone braided her hair again for the third time. She had been switching back and forth, unsure if she should wear it down or braid it in her normal side braid that rested against her shoulder and breast. And after the men had insisted that the evening was a casual affair, for her outfit Simone had eventually decided to go with a pair of semi-dark washed skinny jeans, a fitted cream sleeveless sweater with a wide brown belt. She also chose a long-sleeved light brown sweater that draped in lovely folds on either side, and then finished off the ensemble with a pair of brown faux leather knee-high boots and dangling tarnished copper circle earrings.

She took another gulp of the wine that Xander had brought up to her and stared at herself in the mirror or a moment. *Screw it!* Opting to keep the braid, but putting a different spin on it, Simone French braided her hair around one side of her head and braided the rest to lay to the side, in the *Katniss Everdeen* fashion.

Though Amber had loaded her luggage with new clothes, shoes and accessories she hadn't gotten around to makeup. So with nothing else to do to make her reflection look any better, Simone sighed, shrugged and then walked out of the master suite to meet her men. *Huh...my men.* She heard them chatting downstairs and she made her way down and found them in the kitchen.

As usual the sight of them took her breath away. *They're just so...so...male!* Blatant virile, manly, red-blooded, powerful men.

Her mother would have called them hunks and Simone smiled to herself at the memory.

They both wore relaxed fit jeans and boots, their usual. Jackson wore a charcoal gray fitted zip-up sweater that molded over his massive shoulders, tree trunk arms and narrowed waist. The color made his silver eyes glow. And Xander paired his jeans with a winter white sweater with a large collar. His too formed over his sculpted physique; broad shoulders, rippling arms and long tapered waist. The light color matched his personality and bright smile.

One was dark and one was light. One serious. One easy-going. Yin and yang. Two extraordinary men separately in their own right. Together…*magnificent*. And when their eyes lit on her as she walked around the corner, Simone felt like she was the only woman on earth. They did that to her…made her feel like she was the center of the universe. Their universe.

"You look breathtaking." Xander said warmly as Jackson huskily grunted his agreement.

They both strode over to her to take turns greeting her with soft intimate kisses. Overwhelming her, as was their habit. "You both look amazing." Simone said breathlessly as she backed up, needing a little space to think clearly.

"Thanks." Xander said giving her butt a pat.

"Thank you." Jackson said running his index finger and thumb down her braid, inadvertently *-or not*, caressing her breast with the back of his finger.

"Ready to roll?" Xander asked.

"As I'll ever be." Simone sighed in resignation.

~~~

They rode in Xander's truck to his parents' house. Simone sat in between them as they bickered good-naturedly with each other, trying to make her laugh and ease her nerves.

"You know damn well that I got better grades than you!" Jackson taunted Xander.

"Pssh. I was always on honor roll!" Xander shot back.

"What?! That's because you cheated off of me, jackass!" Jackson said incredulous.

"Don't listen to him, Si. He's just jealous 'cause I'm brilliant." Xander took his eyes off the road for a second to smirk down at Simone.

"Ha! He was too busy being the class clown to even pay attention to what the teachers were saying. So he copied my homework and looked over my shoulders during tests. He even got caught once because he was too dumb to change any of the words on a book report. His parents grounded him and stopped us from hanging out 'til the semester was over." Jackson scowled at Xander over Simone's head. "That was the first semester he finally aced his classes on his own." Jackson finished smugly.

"Whatever, Jax. My mom will defend me. Just wait." Xander said confidently as he pulled up to a beautiful three story cedar home, nestled in against a dense forest.

The driveway was U-shaped and Xander parked the truck behind some of the cars that were already there.

"Well, everyone is here already, so you'll at least get to meet them all at once and get it over with." Xander smiled encouragement down at Simone.

"Great." Simone said with half sarcasm and half false bravado.

"Come on, beautiful." Jackson slid out of the truck and held his hand out to help Simone down.

Xander walked around the front of the truck to meet them and they both clasped her hands as they guided her up the icy path to the front door. The red door swung open before they had even reached it and a beautiful older blonde woman stood at the entrance with a big smile.

"Hi, mom." Xander greeted the woman giving her a big bear hug and a kiss on the cheek. "Hey mom, wasn't I smarter than Jax, and got better grades than him?" Xander said after placing her back on her feet.

"You certainly tried, Alexander. But at least you were pretty." His mom said with a straight face, patting his arm affectionately.

Jackson burst out in huge guffaws of laughter and Simone squeezed her lips together in an attempt to hold her giggles in at the look of horror on Xander's face.

"No loyalty." Xander grumbled under his breath as Gail went in to give Jackson a hug.

"Hello, Jackson. I swear you get bigger every time I see you." Gail said fondly.

"You always say that." Jackson said deeply.

"It's no less true. I swear you shot up out of nowhere and you both nearly ate me out of house and home when you were teenagers." Gail patted his chest and then turned her focus on Simone.

"So you must be, Simone. I've already heard so much about you from Delanie." Gail said brushing away Simone's offered hand, and instead pulled her in for a warm hug.

"I bet you have." Xander rolled his eyes.

"Well, it would be nice if my son would call me and let me know what is going on in his life and I didn't have to find out from his sister." Gail scolded as she let go of Simone. She clasped Simone's hands and held them out at her sides to get a better look at her. "Well my my, aren't you lovely. No wonder the boys snatched you up." Gail praised, as Simone blushed and ducked her head bashfully. "Oh my goodness! And shy too?! They probably didn't even know what hit 'em." Gail winked at her.

"T...thank you." Simone finally stuttered out.

"Oh, I'm sorry dear. Where are my manners? I'm Gail. Nice to meet you." Xander's mom greeted Simone more formally, holding out a hand for her to shake.

"Simone Staton. Nice to meet you too, Gail." Simone replied softly.

"Gail, what's taking you so long in here?" A deep voice rumbled as a man that was Xander's twin thirty years in the future came up to the group.

"Oh Frank, calm down. I can be out your sight for a few minutes without you going into a tizzy. I was just greeting the children and meeting the boys' new girlfriend." Gail scolded as he came up to her and placed a kiss on the top of her head.

Xander's dad looked at the trio and when his eyes fell on Simone, they widened and stayed there a moment. "Wow! Well aren't you a looker." Frank exclaimed. "Nice job, boys." Frank held out his hand to fist bump Xander and Jackson, who chuckled at the older man.

Meanwhile, Simone thought she'd die of mortification. Her face had never felt so heated before. She figured she was probably as red as a beet by this point.

"I'm Xander's dad, Frank." The tall older man held out his hand.

"Hello, I'm Simone." She said, barely able to keep eye contact as she took his hand to shake.

"Come on. Get your coats off. Everyone's in the kitchen, hovering over the stove waiting for dinner to be done." Frank said.

As Jackson helped Simone out of her coat, she breathed a sigh of relief that the first meeting with Xander's parents was over. And since she'd already met his sisters, all she had left to meet was Christopher and Ethan. Though she wasn't exactly looking forward to seeing Bethany again after the last disaster.

With two hands at her back, Jackson and Xander led her into the house, towards the kitchen. As they walked in, four blond heads looked up from their conversation. Delanie was sitting on the counter and she jumped down when she saw them. She immediately walked over to Simone and gave her an affectionate embrace.

"Hi, Simone! I'm so glad that you came. Would you like a glass of wine? You're probably so nervous. But don't be, we don't bite. Well maybe Beth does, but don't pay her any attention." Delanie whispered the last part as she rambled on, pulling Simone further into the kitchen and away from the shelter of Jackson and Xander.

The two younger blond men stared at Simone with eyes bugged out of their heads. One even had his mouth agape. Delanie pulled Simone over to the table where both men were sitting.

"This is Christopher. But we call him Chris. He's the middle child. So he's the mediator. Translation: he has to put up with all of our crap. Chris this is Simone." Chris stood up and shook Simone's hand firmly.

"Nice to meet you, Simone." Chris said politely.

"Nice to meet you, Chris." Simone responded quietly.

"I'm the most important one to meet, Simone." The other blond who had been gaping widely, piped in as he shoved his brother out of the way. "I'm Ethan. And now that we've met, you can come to your senses and forget these two and start dating a *real* man." Ethan said, bending dramatically over her hand and kissing it rakishly.

"Simmer down, baby bro." Xander taunted as he pushed Ethan back down into his chair and pulled Simone to him.

Even though Simone couldn't have been any more embarrassed and uncomfortable, she knew she still had to greet Bethany. She looked at the still sour-faced woman leaning on the sill of one of the windows.

"Hello, Bethany. It's nice to see you again." Simone lied.

"Simone." Bethany nodded her acknowledgement, not willing to do much more.

"So what's for dinner, Ma?" Xander asked, diffusing the tense interaction.

"Oh, nothing big. Just some baked Cornish hens, roasted red potatoes in rosemary and olive oil, some mixed veggies and homemade rolls." Gail listed off as if the fancy spread was nothing more than chicken fingers and fries.

"Nice. I'm starving." Xander said, rubbing his flat tummy.

"It smells wonderful." Simone said softly to Gail.

"Thank you, dear. I hope you like it." Gail smiled at her. "Please, sit. Boys, will you help me set the table?" Gail asked Xander and Jackson.

"Of course, Gail." Jackson said, first pulling out a chair for Simone at the huge kitchen table.

Ethan plopped down next to Simone and grinned at her devilishly. "So what brings you to Fairbanks?" He asked curiously.

"Her mother's tribe is here. The Tanana Tribe. She came to meet them for the first time." Delanie answered for her. "Have you went to see them yet?"

"No, I haven't. I'm a little nervous and I've been a little distracted." Simone blushed, ducked her head and glanced briefly at the two men pulling out dinnerware and speaking softly with Gail.

"I bet you have." Delanie giggled.

"Have you dated two men at the same time before?" Ethan asked like it was a normal conversation, like the weather.

"No." Simone continued to look down, her lap all of a sudden becoming the most interesting thing in the room.

"She was a virgin before she met Xan and Jax!" Delanie burst out and Simone wished the ground would open up and swallow her whole.

"LANIE!" Gail shouted out the young woman's name in shock. "You have *got* to learn to keep your thoughts to yourself. That is no one's business but Simone's and the boys'. And that is definitely not an appropriate discussion to have at the dinner table. That goes for you too, Ethan. Now apologize to Simone for your rudeness." Gail scolded at a chagrined Delanie.

"Sorry, Simone." Delanie apologized.

"It's okay." Simone said, barely above a whisper.

"So…what do you do, Simone?" Frank asked, deflecting the awkward situation.

"I just graduated from nursing school. And I have a job at a doctor's office in Seattle when I get back." Simone said before realizing her mistake.

"So you're not staying?" Gail asked, stopping in the middle of placing a platter on the table.

"Um…I…" Simone stammered.

"She's only been here a week, mom. We kinda took her by surprise. And that would be a big move, so she has to take some time to decide." Xander came to her defense across the room as he grabbed some silverware.

"Hmm…well, I guess that's true. Well, I hope you decide to stay. I've never seen these two so happy before." Gail smiled lovingly at Xander and Jackson as they walked up to the table with the rest of the food.

Delanie brought Simone a glass of white wine and sat in the chair across from her. Xander and Jackson finally came over to take their places on either side of her. Jackson gave Ethan a gentle brotherly cuff on the ear, forcing him to get up from the chair on Simone's left. Everyone chuckled as the younger man nearly fell out of the chair.

"Aw, come on Jax! I was just trying to get to know her. You see her all the time." Ethan whined.

"Yeah, right. You were trying to get to know her alright. Find your own girlfriend." Jackson joked good-naturedly.

"Where? I know every girl here!" Ethan exclaimed.

"And dated all of them too." Delanie piped in.

"Shut up, Lanie." Ethan pouted.

"My friend Amber would love you." Simone spoke softly, surprising everyone.

"Really? Where is she? What does she look like?" Ethan said excitedly as he took a chair on the other side of the table.

"As if it matters what she looks like? You'd date a Yeti if you knew it was a female!" Delanie cracked. "Hey!" She screeched as a roll bounced off her head and rolled to the floor.

"Ethan! No throwing food! What does this look like a freakin' zoo?!" Gail yelled.

Simone squeezed her lips together in an attempt to keep from laughing, but looking up at the indignant look on Lanie's face as melted butter ran down her forehead, a snort escaped anyway. And the whole table burst out laughing at the young woman's expense.

"Ha ha, so funny." Lanie scowled as she wiped her forehead with a napkin.

"Anyway, tell me about this Amber girl?" Ethan ignored his sister and focused on Simone.

"Um…" Simone started shyly, as the whole table focused on her. "She's my best friend and she's beautiful. She's tall, with dark red hair and should be a model. But instead she's planning on being a fashion designer. And she's coming to meet up with me tomorrow." Simone told him, but continued at the look of excitement on his face. "But I'm not so sure the wilds of Alaska would be her thing."

"That's okay. I'm down for a fling." Ethan said undeterred. "I vote that we all go out tomorrow night. What time does her flight get in tomorrow?" He asked leaning forward across the table in anticipation.

"In the morning." Simone answered.

"Then it's final. We're all going out. I don't think we've all been out since my twenty-first birthday and plus it'll be a Saturday night." Ethan informed his siblings.

"Yeah, we haven't been out since then because we all still cringe at the memory. No one wants a repeat of you drunk and streaking naked down the street." Chris finally chimed in.

"Hey man, it's been three years! I've matured." Ethan said with self-righteousness.

The table fell silent as they all looked at him and then each other. A split second later the table burst in uncontrollable tear-inducing laughter. Even Ethan chuckled reluctantly.

~~~

As they stood in the doorway putting on their coats and scarves to leave, Jackson thought that the night had went fairly well. Aside from a few mortifying moments for Simone and catching Bethany secretly shooting daggers at Simone whenever he touched her. Seeing the evil looks staggered him, never realizing how deep Beth's feelings apparently ran for him. But he'd never felt anything for her apart from brotherly love.

"Boys? Could I speak with you for a moment?" Gail stopped Xander and Jackson as everyone started walking out to their cars. Delanie and Ethan chatting animatedly with Simone caught in between.

"Yeah, mom. What's up?" Xander asked curiously.

"Now don't get mad at me. I just want to give you both some motherly advice." Gail warned before continuing. "I know you both are intent on having this uncommon relationship. I realized early on, that you two had a different bond than most and that this arrangement worked best for both of you. But that girl is sweet and surprisingly innocent. Just make sure you're both on the same page, so that you don't hurt her. I can tell Jackson is in it for the long haul. But you're still somewhat resistant to committing, because you're a free-spirit." She looked at Xander. "I'm sure she's very confused and uncertain of this unlikely union and she's obviously fallen for both of you, by the way she looks at you. If you both are at odds with the way you're feeling, you'll tear her apart. So figure it out before she uproots her life for you." She laid her hands on each of their arms affectionately. "I've said my piece. Now, have a good-" A loud scream rent the air, cutting Gail off in mid-sentence.

"Simone!" Delanie gasped.

They all instantly turned to see Simone on the ground in a tight ball and standing over her hovered a full grown Black bear standing on its hind legs. It bellowed loudly and took a tentative swipe at her back with a large paw.

Jackson and Xander didn't think, as they sprang into action. With superhuman speed, they ran out the door, jumped down from the porch landing to the ground without missing a beat. Xander ran to Simone, and crouched low as he skid to a stop and immediately draped his body over hers as a shield.

Jackson ran at the bear bellowing back at it like a maniac, as only someone of his size could. Unconcerned for his own safety, only wanting to protect Simone, he stood at his full six-feet-five. Challenging the bear.

"Get back!" Jackson shouted at the animal.

And the bear deciding that it wasn't worth the trouble, bounded back into the dark forest at full speed.

With the threat gone, everyone converged on Simone as Xander lifted his body off of hers. Wide fearful downturned eyes looked around frantically. Once her eyes connected with both Jackson's and Xander's worried faces, tears welled and spilled over. A sob escaped her wide full mouth, her chest rose and fell rapidly to the point of hyperventilation and tremors wracked her entire body.

"Oh my God, Simone! Are you okay?" Delanie exclaimed, kneeling down beside her and smoothing a loose strand of hair from her face.

Jackson could see her throat working, but the words were stuck. Wrapping his strong arms around her, he pulled her to her feet holding her close.

"It's okay. You're okay. The bear's gone." He soothed as he rubbed her back.

"Are you hurt?" Xander asked, stroking a hand down the back of her head.

"No." Simone finally got out around her clogged throat.

"Do you want to come in and sit down for a moment?" Gail asked in concern.

"No…no. I…I'm okay." Simone took a deep breath and blew it out harshly. "What am I, some wild animal magnet?!" She exclaimed in frustration. "First, wolves. And now this! What's next? A moose?!"

They all burst out in relieved laughter.

~~~

When all the commotion had died down and they'd said their goodbyes, the three of them climbed into the truck to head home.

"So what happened, Si?" Xander asked curiously.

"I don't know. I was talking to Delanie and walking towards the truck. And I turned and the bear was crouched down on the side of the truck. For a second I thought it was a person. I tried to stop and slipped on the ice and then the thing stood up over me, growling. So I curled up in a ball like I've heard you're supposed to do. And what the hell! I thought bears were supposed to hibernate in the winter?!" Simone exclaimed.

"It's rare but sometimes they come out to eat a little something before going back to their caves. I bet it was looking for food. You can never leave food in your cars or you'll end up finding some kind of critter in it, around here." Xander cautioned.

"I think you both probably startled each other. But you did good Simone. Curling up in a ball protects all your vital parts and head. That was quick thinking for someone that isn't used to this kind of life. You've done great today. You're quick on your feet. First with the accident earlier today at the mill and then with the bear." Jackson praised. "You'll do great here…if you stay." Jackson finished softly.

Xander spoke up to break the awkward silence from Simone's lack of response to Jackson's last statement. "So what time does your friend's flight get in tomorrow, so we can be there to pick her up?"

"Ten a.m." Simone responded, stifling a yawn.

"You've had a draining day today, you must be tired." Jackson said pulling her closer to him.

Simone laid her head on his solid shoulder and yawned again, not even trying to cover it. Jackson wrapped a burly arm around her, surrounding her with his infallible warmth. Xander's hand found a home on her thigh and rubbed soothingly.

She drifted in and out of sleep as they bumped along down the road. The men murmuring softly, trying not to disturb her.

"We do need to talk, ya know." Jackson finally brought up.

"I know." Xander said reluctantly.

"Your mom was right. We have to be on the same page in order for this to work." Jackson rubbed his free hand down his face. "The last thing I want to do is hurt her."

"Yeah."

"Come on, Xan. I know you've got more to say than that." Jackson prodded.

"What do you want me to say?" Xander practically growled under his voice.

"Something. Anything!" Jackson exclaimed under his voice. "What do you want out of this?"

"I don't know. I care about her alright. A lot. But that doesn't mean that I want to get married tomorrow." Xander admitted, glancing over at Jackson, then the dozing woman on his shoulder. "I didn't want to talk about it, because I'm still trying to figure out things, just like she is. I don't know what to do. I want her to stay. But I also don't want to uproot her life, when I don't know if what I want is permanent."

"What the hell is so difficult to figure out?!" Jackson asked angrily. "You know you're falling for her. I saw the look in your eyes when she was almost attacked by that bear. Why are you being so resistant to it?"

"I don't know, man. I just am." Xander said, squeezing the steering wheel in a death grip.

"Well I know why. You've been spoiled by never having the devastation of losing someone. Oh, you've been broken up with or cheated on. But those were with girls you didn't give two shits about anyway. But to lose someone that you truly love. By breakup or worse. Death. But I have. And I know that when you find something like this and someone like her, you'll do everything in your power to *never* let that shit go." Jackson ran a frustrated hand through his curls. "So do me a favor, if not for yourself than for me."

"What?" Xander said shortly.

"Start acting like you fucking care about losing her." Jackson finished as they turned onto their private driveway.

"Fine."

Simone had heard most of the conversation. When the discussion had started she had been in and out of sleep. But once she realized who the conversation was about, all thought of sleep and exhaustion had escaped her. Though she pretended to still be asleep, not wanting them to know that she had heard everything.

Now her insides were at war. Guilt over coming between the two best friends. Joy over knowing that they cared for her, even if it was grudgingly on Xander's part. Plus, sadness that it wasn't enough for him to want her to stay for good. And now the choice to stay was an even harder one to make.

Stay. Only to risk heartache and disrupt the life they had built. Or go. And be heartbroken anyway and still take a chance at ripping them apart because Jackson would end up resenting Xander for not doing all he could to get her to stay. Any way that she looked at it, it was a lose-lose situation. And her heart sank into the pit of her stomach at the realization.

Xander pulled the truck into the garage and Jackson thinking that she was still asleep, slid her out of the truck and cradled her against his chest as they made their way inside. Not stopping to take off their coats, Jackson carried her into the house and upstairs to their bedroom. *Ours. Not for long it would seem.*

Jackson sat her on the bench in front of the bed, as she pretended to wake up. Xander followed close behind. His normal gregarious nature, sedate with inner turmoil.

"We're home beautiful." Jackson said softly as he caressed a finger down the side of her face. "Let's get you undressed and in bed."

Jackson did the honors of stripping off her coat then her clothing, layer by layer. Xander stood by with his hands in his pockets, unsure of what to do or how to act. Simone could tell that he was fighting a similar battle with his head and his mind that she was. And she knew that there was only one way to bring them all back together again, if even for a little while.

When she was finally stripped down to nothing and Jackson had brought over a night shirt and pants to dress her in, she shook her head no. A blush spread across her face at being naked in front of their fully clothed bodies, but she didn't let it deter her.

Simone stood up and walked over to Xander. She raised up on her tiptoes and kissed him softly on the cheek and proceeded to gradually undress him. She pulled his sweater and undershirt over his head. Her hands caressed a path down his broad shoulders, wide chest and rippling abs to the waist of his pants. She unbuckled the belt, unzipped his jeans and then helped him shimmy out of them, as well as his boxer briefs and boots. His long erection bobbed at his movements and Simone reached out a hand to lightly caress it, making him hiss with need.

Once she was done with Xander, she moved to Jackson that had been watching with hooded silver eyes. She found that raising up on tiptoes to meet Jackson's cheek was a bit harder, but he bent over, obliging her. She smiled slightly as her lips brushed his hair roughened cheek. She then proceeded to strip him down as she had done Xander. Stopping to brush her fingertips across the expanse of his muscular chest and abs and the hair that laid there in swirling patterns. Simone finished out the process with a gentle caress at his thick throbbing member.

Leaving them there naked and wanting, she walked over to the bed and crawled into the middle. Once she was settled in, she laid both hands on either side of her, on their perspective sides.

"Make love to me. At…at the same time." Simone whispered shyly.

"Are you sure you're ready?" Xander asked, hesitating to move towards her and the bed.

"Y…yes." Simone answered nervously.

"You don't have to, if you don't want to." Jackson reassured her, sensing her nerves.

"It's okay. I want to." Simone pressed. "I need to."

Jackson stepped up to her left and Xander to her right as usual. They both slid into the bed, their heated skin making contact with hers. Jackson turned her face to his and kissed her tenderly, so much so that she almost wept from the intimacy of it. As he released her mouth and moved slowly down her neck to her sensitive nipple, Xander turned her face with an index finger, to get a taste of her as well.

Xander's stroking tongue at her mouth and Jackson's at her breast, Simone's hips moved restlessly. The need at the juncture of her thick thighs sought relief. Jackson seeing her agitated movements, caressed his hand down her soft tummy to the landing strip that guided his fingers to where she wanted them most.

One thick finger stroked lightly over her wet slit and her hips shook in response. Simone moaned into Xander's mouth and he deepened the kiss. His tongue flicked over hers, sending electric shocks down to her pulsating clit that Jackson grazed with his thumb. Both in sync with each other and in tune with her body. It was like she was a guitar and they were both playing her perfectly. Xander chose the chord and Jackson strummed the string, making her body sing.

Their song reached its crescendo and the peaceful climax washed over her like lapping waves. Now that she was soft and pliable from her first orgasm, they were ready to take it to the next level.

Xander reached behind him into the nightstand, where they had stored the lubrication from the previous night. Popping the cap up, Simone watched as he drizzled the clear liquid over the bulbous head of his cock and down the long shaft. His hand curled around his length and stroked up and down a couple of times, spreading the slick fluid until it gleamed. Simone's heart rate kicked up a notch at the thought of this long thick erection invading her tight back entrance.

Jackson perceptively took that moment to distract her. Turning Simone towards him, he kissed her deeply as he grabbed her leg at the back of the knee and placed it on his hip, leaving her backside open for Xander's assault. She felt a cold slick finger at her crease and she tensed.

Jackson and Xander felt her hesitation and they both turned up the heat. Jackson plunged his tongue into the deep recesses of Simone's mouth and rubbed the tip of the cock across her labia in time to his kisses. Xander kissed and bit at her neck and shoulders, while his finger stroked in and out of her tight ring, preparing her for what was to come.

Feeling that she was as ready as he could get her, Xander took his throbbing erection in hand and glided the tip over Simone's puckered flesh. Resting his forehead between her shoulder blades, he pressed forward and his slick steel eased passed her tight entrance. Simone freed Jackson's mouth on a gasp and then hissed in mild discomfort.

"Ahh…you're doing so good, Si. Fuck!" Xander groaned.

Xander grimaced at the tightness wrapped around him and he groaned deeply into her back. Jackson grasped his thick steel and slid it over Simone's clit, helping her find her pleasure. And as some of the tension eased from her body, Xander easily slid to the base of his manhood.

Xander grit his teeth as he pulled out to the tip and then slid home gently, getting her accustomed to the feel of him. Simone felt the discomfort dissipate, replaced by a sense of fullness. And as the rest of the tension left her body, Xander gained more confidence and speed. His hips rocked into the lush softness of the large round globes of her ass.

Xander glanced at Jackson and he nodded his head at his friend, and slowed down his pace. Jackson taking the opening, position the head of his erection at her aching core. And as Xander pulled out, Jackson plunged into her weeping pussy. Simone cried out in bliss.

Taking her cry of pleasure as a green light, they unleashed the full power of their assault. Their hips alternated like pistons in an engine. Xander plunged in from the back as Jackson retreated in the front. And as Jackson stroked into her soaking heat, Xander pulled back.

And in the middle, Simone could do nothing but yield to the power of their thrusts. She held onto Jackson's flexing bicep as he gripped her hips pulling her towards him on each turn of his deep strokes. Continual cries escaped her lips as an intense tightness built in her belly.

Jackson's breath fanned harshly against her lips and Xander's at the nape of her neck. Simone felt them everywhere. Inside and out. They consumed her. And she succumbed to them. Her cries turned into screams as they plundered her, stroking so deeply it felt like they touched her soul. Simone's insides fissured like snow atop a cliff and her climax came over her like an avalanche.

Her head thrown back in ecstasy, Simone wailed loudly. Stars and bright colors burst behind her eyelids and a comforting darkness enveloped her.

Her cries and her pulsating sex brought the men to their release seconds later. They both shouted out their pleasure as they spilled their seed deep inside her. They continued to stroke gently as they came down from their high, realizing belatedly that their woman was no longer an active participant.

"Si?"

"Simone?"

Easing out of her limp body, they turned Simone onto her back to get a good look at her. Her eyes were closed and tracks of tears ran down her calm face. And her chest rose and fell softly.

"Holy shit! She passed out!" Xander exclaimed.

Jackson placed his ear to her chest, just to be sure her heart rate and breathing sounded normal. A moment later he looked up at Xander with relieved humor in his eyes.

"Yesterday after you left the lodge, I went down on her and got the process of getting her ready for anal by fingering her and she said that the orgasm was so intense that she thought she was close to passing out. And I told her that when we took her at the same time, she probably would passed out. And she did!" Xander explained in awe.

"I don't think we've ever done that before." Jackson said incredulous, still looking down at her with worry.

"No we haven't. I feel bad, but it's kind of awesome, right?" Xander smiled, dimples deepening at the boost to his sexual self-confidence.

"You're an ass. But yeah…yeah, it kind of is." Jackson grinned back, before getting out of bed to get towels to clean up sleeping beauty.

Chapter 12

As Simone stood with Xander at the baggage claim in the airport waiting for Amber, she blushed to her roots again, thinking about passing out during sex with Jackson and Xander the night before. The guys had messed with her mercilessly since they had woken up that morning. Jackson had stayed behind to move all of their things from the two guest bedrooms to the master suite, making room for Amber. So currently she only had to deal with Xander's jokes.

"No worries, Si. We'll just have to stock up on smelling salts next to the lube." Xander teased, noticing the color that had risen in her cheeks.

"You suck." Simone hissed under her breath.

"Si!" Someone shrieked across the room and they turned to see a blur of red coming at them at an alarming rate of speed.

Simone braced herself as Amber launched her thin frame at her. Amber wrapped her in a tight embrace and jumped up and down in her excitement.

"I missed you, Si!" Amber finally released Simone and wobbled a little. "Whoa, I'm either hungover or still drunk from last night." Amber shook her head gently.

"It's only been a week, Amber. And why are you hungover when you knew you had to get on a plane today?" Simone scolded.

"Well…maybe it's because I found out yesterday that I got the job!" Amber shouted the last four words, drawing attention to them from passersby.

"Oh my God, really?! I'm so happy for you!" Simone exclaimed happily and she hugged Amber tightly.

Amber squeezed Simone back and then opened her eyes to see a gorgeous blond man with heartbreaking dimples, smiling down at them. Amber released her best friend like a hot potato and stared at the guy with her mouth hanging open.

"Oh my. Is this one of *them*?" Amber whispered in awe.

Simone smiled shyly before responding, "Yes, this is Xander Drake. He owns the lodge I was staying at."

"Was?" Amber asked, not taking her eyes off of the blond Adonis.

"I'm staying with them now. And if you like, you can stay in one of their spare bedrooms there. But anyway, Xander this is Amber Holt." Simone finished the introductions.

Xander clasped Amber's hand in a warm handshake. "It's nice to finally meet you, Amber. Simone had told us all about you." Xander said politely.

"Oh, his voice sounds like melted butter." Amber said batting her eyelashes.

"Amber, stop talking like he's not even in the room." Simone said rolling her eyes.

"Oh yeah, sorry. It's nice to meet you too, Xander." Amber finally released the Kung Fu grip she had on his hand.

Xander took her flirtation in stride. Brushing off her comments, he walked over to the baggage carousel, and grabbed the many bags that the tall redhead pointed to. And as Xander managed to carry all of her bags to the truck parked in the parking garage, Amber marveled over his strength.

"You landed a fucking hottie! I can't wait to see the other one." Amber spouted crudely.

"Amber!" Simone shouted at her friend.

"Sorry, sorry." Amber cringed. "I'm just so proud of you. You even look different." Amber stated.

"I do?" Simone asked, surprised as she slid into the truck. She smiled shyly at Xander as he held the door open for her and Amber.

"Yes! You look more relaxed and at ease, less uptight." Amber said and then whispered the next as Xander made his way around the truck to the driver's side. "Like they laid some good pipe. You're even wearing your contacts instead of your glasses! You have to give me all the details." Amber bounced with excitement in her seat.

"We'll talk later." Simone said to her anxious friend.

The ride home made Simone's head spin as Amber asked Xander a bazillion questions. Xander also being a happy upbeat person, answered all of her intrusive questions without pause. And before she realized it they were already pulling into the garage. They got out of the truck and Xander grabbed Amber's bags to carry into the house.

They kicked off their boots and hung their coats and walked into the fragrant kitchen. Jackson stood at the island cutting up potatoes, while sautéing chunks of beef in a skillet on the stove. Amber's eyes nearly popped out of her skull at the sight of the massive bear of a man in a tight black t-shirt, low slung jeans and bare feet. He glanced up as they appeared around the corner and a sexy crooked grin graced his face.

"Holy fucking shit, Simone! Seriously?! You get *both* of them?!" Amber practically screamed in shocked awe, as Jackson failed to keep his composure like Xander did. An adorable blush spread across the burly man's cheeks.

"Jackson, this is my rude friend, Amber Holt. Amber, this is Jackson Cole." Simone introduced with a shake of her head.

Jackson wiped his hands on a towel before holding out an enormous paw to Simone's friend. "Nice to meet you, Amber." Jackson said deeply.

As his hand enveloped Amber's, she tittered like a schoolgirl. "Dear Lord, your voice is sexy enough to make my nipples cut glass." Amber groaned.

Jackson choked and started coughing roughly, as Xander exploded with laughter and Simone moaned in embarrassment.

"Did I say something wrong?" Amber said innocently.

"Excuse me guys, while I remind my friend that she *was* raised with manners." Simone said grabbing Amber's arm and towing her from the room forcibly.

"What?" Amber exclaimed at being manhandled by her best friend.

"What? What?! Amber, do you have to embarrass me? You need to put the whole out of control sex kitten crap on lockdown!" Simone uncharacteristically shouted at her friend.

Amber stepped back a few steps in shock. "Oh. My. God. My big sister from another mister has finally found her voice! You've never yelled at me before. I like it. It's hot. No wonder they're so hot for you. Aside from your smokin' body and exotic face, you now have this feistiness about you." Amber said with a smile and slow nod of her head in affirmation.

Simone rolled her eyes, unable to stay angry at the tall redhead. "Could you just please contain your comments? Please?" Simone pleaded.

"Yeah, sorry. I was just shocked. I know you sent a pic of them, but it just didn't do them justice. They are gorgeous, Si! Are there more like them up here?" Amber asked hopefully.

"Actually, Xander has two younger brothers. Chris and Ethan. Both are around the perfect age for you. And the youngest, Ethan wants us all to go out tonight so that he can meet you." Simone smiled as Amber started to do a little dance.

"Do they look anything like their older brother?" Amber asked.

"Yes, actually. The whole family has that whole tall blond Anglo-Saxon look to them." Simone answered.

"Fantastic. Momma's getting some 'D' later." Amber grinned devilishly. "But after lunch I need a nap. I need to sleep off this hangover so I can rally for tonight."

"I have a feeling that I'm going to need a nap myself, just to prepare my body for the ridiculousness that is going to commence this evening." Simone sighed wondering how she was going to contain the force of nature that was Amber and Ethan combined. Not to mention Delanie.

~~~

Jackson had homemade beef stew on the stove, slowly cooking for dinner. For lunch he had laid out fixings for sandwiches, buffet style. They all chose what they wanted and then sat at the kitchen table for lunch.

Amber watched the dynamic between the two men and her best friend. Granted they were hot, but she wanted to make sure that she didn't have to break out a can of whoop-ass on their tight perfect asses. But all she saw was affection and adoration between the trio. Though Xander was a little more reserved with his affection, choosing to disguise it with humor.

She was surprised and impressed to find that Simone handled both men very well. She juggled showing both of them attention flawlessly. And they doted on her like she was a porcelain doll.

Amber didn't want to lose her friend to these two men, but she couldn't deny that Simone had blossomed under the hands of Jackson and Xander. And it had only been a week. She also couldn't imagine how her virginal friend could handle both huge men. She felt dizzy looking at just one. So she definitely couldn't envision having both of them at the same time.

"So. What are your intentions towards my best friend?" Amber asked both men with a raised brow.

"Amber." Simone warned.

"No. You're my best friend and I want to make sure their intentions are good ones. No one is going to fuck with you, so long as I'm around." She said looking at both men seriously.

"Our intention is to love her…if she'll have us." Jackson spoke up, zero doubt in his voice.

Simone whipped her head to the left to look at him in astonishment. Apparently shocked at the use of the word 'love'.

"And do you feel the same?" Amber asked Xander, singling him out.

"Amber, this is all new to me. And I'm trying to decide whether or not I want to stay. So you can't expect them to commit themselves to me when I haven't decided yet. Just like I need time, they need time." Simone stepped in, pulling Amber's attention to her instead.

"Alright then. I'll back off…for now." She gave them the stink-eye in warning. "Now, if you'll excuse me, I need a nap before tonight." Amber said as she rose from her chair.

The three of them let out breaths of relief, knowing the initial test was over.

~~~

Amber woke up from a deep sleep. So deep that she almost didn't even know where she was at first. She couldn't tell how much time had passed since it was dark all day everyday this time of year. Looking at the clock, she realized that she had slept for quite some time. It was nearly dinnertime.

Getting up, she started out of her temporary room and headed downstairs to find Simone. Stopping once she reached the bottom of the stairs, she heard distant voices from a room nearby. She headed towards the sound.

She reached the doorway and started to open it to what looked like a media room, or the more aptly named "man cave". A large flat screen television, a huge couch that almost looked like a bed, a bar and pool table wasn't what stopped Amber in her tracks at the entrance as she opened the door. It was the trio stripped down to different degrees of undress.

Jackson and Xander were shirtless and they had a very naked Simone stretched out on the pool table. Her skin shone like warm butterscotch under the dim lights above the pool table. Amber's breath caught in her throat. She knew that she should back away from the private moment between her best friend and her men. But like passing by a car wreck, a weird curiosity and the hopes of seeing something she probably shouldn't, kept her rooted to the spot.

She watched as Jackson kissed down Simone's stomach'til he reached the apex of her thighs. Putting her legs on his shoulders, he buried his face there, lapping up her opening and flicking his tongue against her clit. Simone's back arched on a cry and Xander took advantage of her raised breasts, taking a hard little brown nipple into his mouth. Amber clenched her own thighs together as her clit began to ache watching the hot threesome.

Jackson's curly head continued to bob up and down as he pleasured Simone thoroughly. Simone wreathed under their loving ministrations. As her cries became more frequent Xander's mouth took hers in a scorching kiss. Amber could see hints of their tongues dancing together as he absorbed her moans.

Simone's hands that had been clawing at the green felt of the pool table, dove into Jackson's hair and she held onto him as she pumped her hips up to his eager mouth. As Simone's back bowed off the table in release, screaming into Xander's mouth, Amber crossed her legs trying to calm her throbbing sex.

Jackson came up for air on a gasp. Standing up straight, he pulled a small bottle of lube out of his back pocket before unzipping his pants and dropping them to the floor. *Jesus, is he a sex magician or something, pulling random bottles of lube out of his pocket on a moments notice?* But before Amber could dwell on the thought for too long, her eyes focused on the sheer size of the large man's erection. *Holy cannoli! My girl has hit the giant cock jackpot!*

Amber watched with her bottom lip between her teeth as he drizzled the clear gel over his impressive girth. Xander came around to the other two, apparently already having stripped down naked while Amber was mesmerized by what Jackson had to offer. And she realized that Xander too was remarkable in the penis department. He was only somewhat smaller around than his counterpart, but a bit longer. Amber quietly fanned herself in anticipation of what was next.

She was not disappointed. She observed as Xander lifted Simone, her calves draped over his arms and her back rested against Jackson's chest. Slowly, Jackson guided his shaft to Simone's back entrance and gradually they eased her down his lube-slick length. Simone's nails dug into Xander's shoulders and she gasped at the intrusion.

"Fuck! You feel so fucking good." Jackson growled deep in his throat as he stroked in and out of her, his muscles straining as he held her.

Finally on an outward stroke, Xander plunged in. The men started working Simone like a well-oiled machine. They pulled her back and forth between them. Dipping and diving into her deep recesses. Simone's hair spilled over her breast and Jackson's shoulder like a thick black curtain.

"Jax! Xan! Please!" Simone begged.

At her plea, they started to speed up their pace. Their powerful hips, driving into her with relentless abandon. Amber's chest rose and fell rapidly, matching Simone's. And Simone thrashed and clawed at her men as her climax built.

"Aah…God!" Simone screamed as her body tensed and her orgasm ripped through her.

Her feminine come sprayed against her thighs, Xander's tight abs and plunging cock. Xander kissed her fiercely as he came hard inside her rippling core. And Jackson bit her shoulder as his manhood pumped his seed into her.

As the tension eased from the bodies, turning their limbs to liquid, they all collapsed on the floor in a heap of hot sweaty body parts. Amber too, slumped back against the wall after quietly closing the door.

"I need a drink. *And* a hot beef injection." Amber whispered to herself as she tiptoed back upstairs to her room for a cold shower.

Chapter 13

"You're my hero." Amber said to Simone as she applied makeup on her normally bare-faced friend. She had convinced Simone that tonight she needed to knock the guys out. So Simone sat on the counter of the spare bathroom as Amber's guinea pig.

"What are you talking about? Why am I your hero?" Simone asked scrunching up her face. Amber tapped her foot on the tiled floor impatiently. "Oh, sorry." Simone relaxed her face so that Amber could continue.

"Well, first I just wanted to say in my defense that it was by accident." Amber hedged.

"What are you talking about, Amber? Just spit it out." Simone rolled her eyes. "OW!" Simone yelped at being poked in the eye by the eyeliner pencil in Amber's hand.

"I told you to hold still. So anyway…I…I saw you." Amber said hesitantly.

"You saw me?" Simone frowned, not following her friend.

"You know. I saw you…them…together. On the pool table." Amber said bracing herself for Simone's reaction.

"You…WHAT?!" Simone screeched.

"It's not like I meant to. I woke up from my nap and came down looking for you. I heard you guys talking in the man-cave, so I opened the door and…and Jackson was going downtown on you." Amber quickly explained as Simone turned nearly purple in mortification. "And well…it was super hot…*you* were super hot. So I kinda watched 'til you finished." Amber ducked her head in shame.

"AMBER!!!" Simone bellowed, jumping down from the vanity counter, ready to storm out.

"Wait!" Amber exclaimed, grabbing Simone to stop her. "I'm sorry. But I was just so curious to know how you could handle two huge manly-men after holding on to your V-card for far longer than normal. And I was also curious about how this type of relationship works. I wasn't sure if they were into each other as well as you. But anyway, I'm really sorry. I know it was an invasion of your privacy. It was like passing by a car crash…you can't help but look." Amber pleaded with her friend.

"God, this is so embarrassing!" Simone said hiding her red face behind her hands.

"Don't be. It *really* was hot, Si. And you were magnificent! You've blossomed with them. You've turned into this lovely sexual creature and it's beautiful. And if all of your careers don't work out, you guys could definitely make a killing in porn. I'd buy it! God, I got so hot and bothered. I still am! If Xander's brother is as good looking as him with a matching penis, I swear I'm going to fuck his brains out!" Amber proclaimed.

"Jeez Amber, what planet did you come from? I think you should've been born a man." Simone shook her head in frustration as she let Amber guide her back on the counter to finish her makeup.

"I know, right?! I'm always so horny." Amber said with wide golden eyes.

"But I swear to God, Amber…if I ever find out that you've done something like that again, I'll stick my foot so far up your ass that when you smile my toes will show." Simone said with a completely straight face.

"Damn! Yes, ma'am." Amber looked at her friend with genuine apprehension.

~~~

Simone stared at herself in the full length mirror in Amber's temporary bedroom. Her mouth hung open in shock. One thing she had never let Amber do was give her a makeover. She never really had a reason to. But she wanted to look nice for her men, so she had conceded to her friend. And now, looking at her reflection, she was glad that she had.

Amber had straightened her hair to a stick-straight curtain of glossy onyx that reached her tailbone. She lined her downturned eyes with black kohl and gave her lids a seductive smoky eye. She enhanced her skin with a shimmery bronzer that made her caramel skin glow. And she painted her wide full lips a deep blood red.

But her face and hair was just the tip of the iceberg. Amber had designed and sewed a sweater dress for her the moment she told her about Jackson and Xander, hoping she'd have a reason to wear it when she came up to meet her. The dress was a dark charcoal grey with a cowl neck collar. It had long fitted sleeves that hung to her knuckles and had a holes at the ends for her thumbs to go in. The top half of the sweater dress molded to her body like a second skin and the bottom half stopped a few inches above her knees and had a slight flirty flare to it that complimented her wide hips and ass.

But the most dramatic part of the dress was that the cowl neck came all the way up to her long throat in the front and plunged down to the top of her butt-crack in the back. A sparkly delicate chain attached to either side across her shoulders kept the sweater from falling off her body. Another chain hung from the middle of the first and dangled to the middle of her back. And at the very end was a glittering rhinestone that swung daintily when she moved. Amber rounded out the dress with black sheer thigh high stockings with lacey tops and black knee high boots.

Bra and panties were not an option with the dress and Simone blushed with embarrassment and she hadn't even left the room yet.

"Amber, I really don't know about this dress. It's a little over the top for Fairbanks, Alaska. This would be more suitable for L.A. or New York. And *really*...no panties or bra? I'll end up with icicles hanging from my vagina!" Simone whined.

"Simone, you're a woman now, with two gorgeous men that adore you. Every now and again you have to throw them off their game, just so they know what they have and what they'll miss if they lose you. It also doesn't hurt to make them a little jealous too. And trust me, other men will notice you tonight." Amber smiled deviously.

Amber herself was decked out for the evening. She wore skintight low-slung black pleather pants, a sparkly crop top that showed off her flat tummy in the front and hung lower in the back. Bright red high-heeled ankle boots finished off the sexy ensemble. She had curled her hair in big messy sexy curls. She went with a nude shiny lip and dramatically lined eyes.

"Aren't we a pair?" Amber smiled at their reflection. "I've waited years for this moment. My bff has finally come out of her cocoon and has spread her beautiful wings. Oh, I can't wait for them to see you!" Amber squealed and clapped her hands with glee. "Let's go!" She grabbed Simone and started pulling her towards the bedroom door.

They heard the men talking downstairs. Amber stopped Simone at the top step, brushed her hair to hang over one shoulder, exposing her bare back and then turned her and gave her a gentle nudge to descend the stairs. With a shaking hand, Simone clutched the railing and started down.

Jackson and Xander sat in the living room talking and drinking beer, waiting for them to finish getting ready. When they heard her footsteps they turned to look up and they stopped in mid-conversation. They froze in place, only their eyes moved as they tracked her progress down the stairs.

When Simone reached the bottom of the stairs Jackson and Xander slowly rose, as if they were afraid she'd disappear if they moved too fast. Simone walked towards them shyly.

"Jesus Christ, Si!" Xander exclaimed.

"Simone…" Jackson breathed.

"If you think the front is great, wait until you see the back." Amber said proudly as she hopped down from the last step.

She walked over to Simone and gently spun her around to show off the back of the dress. The only sound in the room was a sharp intake of breath and a low hiss.

"Fuck my life!" Xander nearly panted.

"Change of plans. We're staying here. I don't think my heart can take you being in public like this. I mean…I…I have no words." Jackson said deeply.

Simone blushed prettily as Xander stepped closer to her to inspect her close up.

"Um…Si? Are you wearing any underwear?" Xander asked in disbelief.

"Not exactly." Simone answered warily.

"She can't wear a bra or panties because you'd be able to see them. Sexy, right?" Amber beamed.

"That's an understatement." Jackson groaned. "We won't be able to leave your side for one second. I think you're trying to give me a heart attack." Jackson shook his head. "But you are nothing short of breathtaking." He murmured deeply before kissing her softly on the cheek.

"Thank you." Simone responded quietly, a shiver going down her spine as Xander ran a finger down the middle of her exposed back.

The men had her sandwiched in between them. Overwhelming her with their raw masculinity as usual. Simone's pulse jumped in her neck at Jackson ran his fingers down her throat. And Xander's lips found the spot at the base of her neck. Simone closed her eyes on a soft gasp. Wrapped up in each other, they forgot about the pretty redhead.

"Ahem." Amber coughed before the trio could get carried away and she was left with a front row seat to their lovemaking this time around.

Simone's eyes flew open, remembering that they were not alone. "Sorry, Amber." She blushed.

Jackson and Xander reluctantly took a few steps back away from Simone, needing to put some distance between her. Both had no qualms about taking her in front of her best friend, but they figured she'd probably have an issue with it.

As they banked the fire in their eyes, the front door opened suddenly and chaos flowed in from outside.

"The party is here!" Ethan shouted as he burst in the front entrance. He wiped his feet on the rug and tossed his coat and scarf on the bench in the front hall.

Behind him piled in Delanie, Christopher and a pinched face Bethany. They all chattered animatedly as they took off their outside clothes. Ethan walked into the living room first. Not seeing Amber right away he took in Simone's appearance with blatant appreciation and whistled low through his lips.

"Dammit, you fuckers are some lucky son's a bitches!" Ethan said ogling Simone as she blushed at the attention.

Ethan was dressed in nice black boots, dark-washed jeans with a cuff at the bottom, a black button-up dress shirt with the sleeves rolled up to his elbows and his hair was in the current style. It was cut in a fade around the sides and back, slicked over with some type of styling wax with a side part. He definitely had a whole sexy hipster thing going on, which did not escape Amber's notice.

"Uh, Ethan? This is my best friend Amber. Amber this is Xander's youngest brother Ethan." Simone introduced them, so that Ethan could focus his attentions on someone else.

Ethan turned to look at Amber and the look on his face was comical. His eyes bugging out of his head like a cartoon character and he nearly drooled down the front of his shirt. As Amber smiled seductively and held out a slender hand for him to shake, he tried to get control of his shocked expression.

"Youngest, but the most handsome. Nice to meet you, Amber." Ethan boasted as he took her hand and kissed it softly.

"You just might be right." She responded sweetly, beginning to spin her deadly web of temptation Simone had seen her use numerous times on many an unsuspecting man.

"Oh, I like you." Ethan grinned, not realizing that he had already fallen for her trap.

"The feelings mutual…so far." Amber said, golden eyes glowing, knowing she had him.

Simone's attention was quickly pulled away from the interaction of the newly matched couple, by Delanie's squeal of excitement.

"Oh. My. God! Simone, you look sensational! Oh, tonight is going to be so much fun!" Lanie proclaimed.

"That remains to be seen." Jackson said grimly.

"Oh, stop being such a grumpy old bear." Lanie shoved Jackson with sisterly affection.

"You look lovely too, Lanie." Simone smiled at the bubbly woman.

Delanie had went with a pair of bootcut jeans, a pretty green off-the-shoulder sweater that complimented her eyes and her hair up in a messy side bun.

"Thanks, Si." She said hugging Simone and then moving in to greet Xander with a warm hug.

"Hello, Simone. You look stunning. And I'm glad to see that your run in with that bear didn't send you running home screaming." Chris said, giving her a quick embrace and a smile.

"Thanks, Chris. And after dealing with these two fuzzy beasts, I've gotten used to disgruntled animals." Simone joked.

"Hey! We're not that hard to deal with!" Xander said defending them.

Simone gave him a sassy grin before her eyes connected with Bethany's. If looks could kill, Simone would have been on the floor dead with a pool of blood around her. A shiver went down Simone's spine.

"Bethany." Simone said nodding her head in acknowledgement.

"Simone." Bethany responded coldly.

"So are we gonna eat and get outta here? Or are we going to continue standing around shooting the shit?" Ethan asked no one in general.

At Ethan's insistence, they all migrated to the kitchen to help themselves to the delicious beef stew that Jackson had prepared, ready to start the night.

~~~

Jackson, Simone and Xander rode in Jackson's truck toward downtown Fairbanks, while everyone else had piled into Chris's SUV and trailed behind them.

"I feel a little over dressed for Fairbanks. Is there any place that I won't stick out like a sore thumb?" Simone asked nervously.

"Yeah, but it doesn't matter where we go, you'll still stick out." Xander grinned down at her, his dimples charming her as usual.

Jackson grunted in agreement.

"I'm just trying to keep up with the two of you." Simone stated truthfully. "You both look very handsome tonight." Simone praised.

Under their coats Jackson wore a black V-neck sweater that fit his broad muscular frame like a glove and Xander wore a cream tight fitting thermal with a green hooded zip-up sweater that made his hazel eyes glow green and conformed to his lean swimmers physique. And of course they paired them with their usual staples of jeans and boots.

"Mmm…is that so? Just make sure that you stay nearby and don't bend over." Xander murmured low as he moved closer to her, his warm hand stroking a path up her thigh to the naked skin of her quickly moistening labia.

"Xan…don't." Simone tried to protest feebly.

"What?" Xander whispered breathless against her lips.

"Not here, in the truck where we can't finish." Simone pleaded as her hips betrayed her, pumping towards the finger that slipped into her heat.

"Oh, you don't think so?" Xander challenged before unbuckling her seatbelt and pulling her onto his lap.

He made quick work of undoing his pants, releasing his throbbing erection and lifting her up, plunged into the deep recesses of her aching sex. Simone grabbed ahold of the dashboard in front of her as he took her roughly and quickly. Both their climaxes building within seconds. They both shouted out their release as Jackson white knuckled the steering wheel in anticipation, his own erection pressing painfully against his jeans.

Jackson quickly pulled into the parking lot behind the nightclub. Throwing the truck in park, he unbuckled his seatbelt, undid his jeans and grabbed a limp and sated Simone off of Xander's lap like a ragdoll. Pulling her over to straddle his hips, he kissed her red lips as he impaled her with his pulsing cock.

The intrusion hit her sweet spot, instantly revving her body up and immediately sending her into another orgasm. Her quaking muscles rippled around him and he came hard a moment later, after only a handful of deep thrusts.

Her forehead fell on his shoulder in exhaustion. Xander reached into the glove-box for several clean napkins. Lifting her off of Jackson, he gently cleaned her up.

"That should keep the wolves at bay, now that you're completely satisfied and covered in our scent." Xander said softly against her temple.

"Was that what this was all about?" Simone said drowsily. "To mark your territory?"

"Well, that *and* that dress. We wanted to fuck you senseless since the moment we laid eyes on you in it." Jackson admitted.

"You can't even see it right now under my coat." Simone reasoned.

"Doesn't matter. That image will be eternally etched in our minds." Xander smirked, tapping a finger against his temple.

Someone banged on the truck making Simone jump. "Let's go! What are you guys doing in there and why are the windows all foggy?" Ethan shouted from outside.

"Come on, Si. Let's get moving before I have to choke out my baby brother." Xander said, trying to hold onto his patience with his little brother.

They all got out of the truck to meet the others and all of them except Bethany started laughing.

"Well, now we know why the windows were all foggy, if the smeared lipstick all over Jackson's face is any indication. Aside from the fact that the three of you look like the cat that got the cream." Lanie teased them.

Jackson quickly wiped his mouth and face with his coat sleeve, while Amber helped clean up Simone's smeared lipstick and reapplied a fresh layer of color. When they were finally presentable, the eight of them walked briskly into the darkened nightclub.

The pulsing sounds of music reached their ears as they checked their coats. The atmosphere charged their blood with a sense of excitement for the night. Especially for Amber and Ethan who had already disappeared into the dim club. Xander and Jackson flanked either side of Simone, protecting her from any untoward advances, like Norse Gods.

"What do you want to drink, Si?" Lanie shouted to Simone over the music.

"Uh…I don't really drink much. So I have no idea." Simone answered

"How about a Long Island Ice Tea? They make them really good here." Lanie suggested.

"Okay." Simone shrugged not knowing much about the drink.

"Hey boys? Get Simone a Long Island. And I'll take a rum and Coke." She informed them as only a little sister could.

Jackson stood several inches taller and was considerably broader than everyone at the bar, so the bartender spotted him quickly. Within a few minutes Jackson handed them all their drinks.

"So I never got around to asking what all of you do for a living." Simone said to Delanie, curious about the big family.

"Well, I'm a kindergarten teacher." Lanie started and Simone smiled thinking that was the perfect profession for the bubbly woman. "Bethany is a legal aid for a small law firm. And Chris and Ethan are both fishermen like my dad before he retired." Lanie finished.

"I bet your students love you. You have such a happy personality." Simone told the younger woman.

"Yeah, they're a lot of fun." Lanie smiled with a distant look in her eye. Simone assumed she was thinking of her students. "Now drink up. I wanna dance!" Lanie bounced to the music playing as she quickly downed the rest of her drink.

Simone followed her lead and slurped the rest of her drink down. She instantly got a head rush and then a nice fuzzy feeling draped over her like a blanket. Lanie grabbed her empty glass from her hand and placed it on the bar and then grabbed her hand.

We'll be right back." Lanie yelled to the guys as she pulled Simone out onto the dance floor where Amber and Ethan were already grinding against each other.

"Um…Lanie. I don't really dance." Simone said helplessly as Lanie dragged her to the middle of the dancing crowd.

"Just move with the beat and you'll figure it out. Not to stereotype, but both your cultures are known for having great rhythm." Lanie waved off her protests.

Once they had found a relatively empty spot, Lanie started to dance around happily as the song *Bang Bang* started to blare from the speakers. Simone swayed a little to the beat of the song, not exactly sure what to do since she never went dancing. But as the song changed to Usher's *Good Kisser*, the beat turning slower and more seductive, Simone felt someone behind her. Looking back she saw that it was Amber.

"Just roll and sway your hips. Pretend as if their tongues are on your clit. And your body will move accordingly." Amber whispered in her ear, placing her hands on Simone's hips guiding her and nodding her head in the direction of her men.

Simone looked over in their direction. Jackson and Xander's eyes were on her and her alone. As she stood captivated by the weight of their stares; Amber, the crowd and everything else disappeared. All that remained was the throbbing beat of the music, the hazy feeling of alcohol coursing through her veins and her men. It felt as if she was alone on the dance floor and they were her audience. And from someplace buried deep inside, where her body recognized the beat, a pulse spread through her frame that mirrored the rhythm. And her body started to roll, flex and sway seductively to the song.

As the men watched her, their eyes became hooded and they shifted restlessly. Simone rolled her body from her chest to hips. Her ass fitting snugly into Amber's pelvis. Amber slowly moved around to Simone's front. Her hands caressed down the front of Simone's body. She dropped down in front of Simone and slowly slid back up her body.

Simone gazed over at Xander and Jackson, beckoning them. Their mouths were slightly open and their chests rose and fell rapidly. Their gaze so intense, it felt as if everywhere their eyes moved on her she could feel the echo of their hands there.

They quickly swallowed the rest of their drinks and started to make their way onto the dance floor. The song changed to Maroon 5's *Animal* as they reached her. The provocative beat of the song surrounded them as Jackson took her front and Xander her back. They fused into one as they began to dance together.

Simone could feel Jackson's hardened length against her hip and Xander's at the crease of her ass. Jackson's hands ran up and down her sides. His thumbs brushing inconspicuously over her hard nipples. Xander's hands caressed at her bare back. Her clit throbbed with need to the beat of the music. And as if he knew what she needed. What she wanted. Xander's hand secretly snaked between the loose back of her dress and slid down to her naked pussy.

The way they had her sandwiched between them, no one was the wiser as Xander covertly strummed at her clit. Jackson continued to circle her sensitive nipples with his thumbs and Simone wreathed between them in time to the music. And as the song hit its climax, so did she. Simone cried out, but the sounds of the music drowned out any noise from her.

As the song ended, Jackson and Xander guided Simone off of the dance floor for another drink at the bar. Lanie followed close behind, also ready for a break.

"Holy crap! You guys are smokin' hot together!" Lanie declared fanning her flushed face. "I try not to look at my brothers in that way, 'cause that's just gross. But I couldn't help *but* stare at you three together. And neither could the entire club. Literally all eyes were on you guys." Lanie added. "I couldn't tell if my sister wanted to barf, rip your hair out or murder you in your sleep."

This time Xander handed them their fresh drinks. Lanie stopped talking long enough for them to take a much needed sip after dancing up a good sweat. Simone glanced over to where Bethany had been standing on the other side of the bar with another woman. They were talking animatedly and sneaking hateful glances over at her.

"I feel so uncomfortable around her." Simone said as quietly as she could to Lanie without the guys hearing.

"Uncomfortable around who?" Amber said as she bounced up to them. She was the only person Simone knew that could look gorgeous covered in sweat. Instead of looking limp and oily, she glistened.

"Oh, my stupid sister, Beth." Lanie answered for Simone.

"Yeah, what's her deal anyway? I kept noticing her giving you the evil eye all night." Amber asked curiously as she gladly took the drink Ethan handed her.

"She's jealous of Simone because she's in love with Jackson and he only thinks of her as a little sister." Lanie rolled her eyes.

"Well, she'll just have to get over it." Amber shrugged apathetically.

"Don't let her get to you or sway your decision to stay, Si." Lanie comforted.

"Yeah, I know." Simone said thoughtfully.

"By the way, I was wondering what your plans were. Are you coming back with me and starting work at Dr. Roth's office? Or are you going to stay here with them? I know you said you were still deciding, but you have to at least know which way you're leaning towards." Amber asked trying to stay neutral.

"I…I don't know." Simone said hesitantly. Then she took a deep breath and blurted out the next sentence. "I'm in love with them."

Lanie jumped up and down at Simone's admission. "Yes! I knew it!"

"I'm so happy for you! Sad for me, but happy for you." Amber said hugging her.

"Wait. That still doesn't mean I'm staying." Simone cautioned.

"But why not?" Lanie said deflated.

"Well…because I don't know if I can give up everything back home to move here permanently. Especially when Xander doesn't even know if he's in it for the long haul." Simone said sadly.

"What exactly are you giving up? I love you and I'd miss the shit out of you. But you have no family back home, you can get a job as a nurse absolutely anywhere and we can always visit each other. Besides your mother's tribe is here too." Amber said selflessly pushing her best friend in the direction she knew she needed to go.

"I haven't even gotten up the guts to meet them yet. They may not even want me around." Simone tried to reason.

"Well then, let's go tomorrow and get it over with. You'll find out one way or another. And if they want you here, that just might help you decide. Alright?" Amber appealed.

"Alright." Simone gave in.

"Good. Now let's go to the bathroom, before I piss my pants." Amber did a little pee dance, making Simone and Lanie laugh as they followed her.

~~~

"Hey, did you notice that Tracy is here?" Ethan asked Xander and Jackson after swallowing down half his beer.

"What?!" Jackson said, eyes bulging out of his head.

"Yeah, Beth's been over there talking to her." Ethan jerked his head to the side in the direction of the other side of the bar.

Both Jackson and Xander whipped their head in the same direction and saw their ex talking with Xander's sister.

"Fuck! She would be here." Xander groaned.

"And what the hell is Beth doing talking to her? Since when did they become BFFs?" Jackson growled his displeasure.

"Don't ask me, dude." Ethan shrugged.

They both glanced again at where Xander's sister was talking to Tracy, but their ex was no longer there. They quickly turned their heads to scan the room and nearly jumped out of their skin when she popped up right in front of them.

"Hi, boys. It's been a long time." Tracy squeaked with her high pitched voice.

"Not long enough." Jackson said uncharitably, inwardly cringing at her voice. He had never noticed how annoying it was until he'd spent time with Simone and her soft melodic tone.

"Oh, don't be that way, Jax. I really do miss you guys." Tracy pouted.

"Well maybe you should've thought about that before you decided to cheat on us." Jackson said, not backing down.

"Well, what about you Xander? Do you feel the same as Jackson?" Tracy asked Xander with a hopeful look on her face.

Jackson noticed that she kept glancing at the other side of the room, but he thought nothing of it. He just figured she was scoping out the next idiot that would fall for her bullshit.

"I'm not quite as angry as Jackson." Xander started, and Tracy beamed at him before he finished. "But that just means I didn't care enough about you in the first place to be hurt by your infidelity." Xander ended coldly.

Tracy flinched back, shocked. She glanced again across the room and her next move stunned them. She suddenly raised up on her tiptoes and planted her lips fully on Xander's and her hand reached out and caressed Jackson between his legs. They both pushed her away a split second later, but it was a split second too late. Because as she stumbled back and glanced across the room with a devious smile on her face as she wiped her mouth, the men looked in the direction she had glanced and saw as Simone's head turned away and she quickly disappeared onto the crowded dance floor. Lanie looked at them with her mouth hanging open in disapproval and Amber's look of pure disgust cut through them, as they both followed Simone into the sea of people.

Jackson and Xander looked at each other in trepidation. "Fuck!"

~~~

Simone could barely breathe, her heart hurt so badly. She blindly walked through the crowd, not knowing what she was looking for until she spotted them. Two guys stood off to the side of the dance floor, scoping out the perfect girl to pounce on.

Alcohol clouded Simone's judgment as she walked over to them with a purpose. They looked up at her as she came towards them and their eyes sparkled with delight as she pulled them to the floor.

"Simone, what are you doing?" Lanie hissed as she watched Simone being sandwiched between the two strangers.

"She's obviously just trying to get back at them for whatever was going on up at the bar." Amber stated, guessing correctly. "She's not much of a drinker. So she's not thinking clearly." Amber said, watching over the proceedings protectively.

Simone swayed her hips to the music as the guy behind her grinded his erection against her ass. She felt sick at the feel of someone else touching her, but she couldn't seem to come to her senses with the hazy fog of alcohol and heartache still blanketing her. And she realized too late that their hands were getting a little too friendly.

The guy behind her slid his hands into the sweater from the back and quickly wrapped them around to cup her bare breasts. At the same time the guy in front, stroked his hands up her thighs and caressed around to her bare backside, squeezing firmly.

"Damn man, she's not wearing panties!" The man breathed his beer breath on Simone as she tried to twist out of the grasp.

"No bra either." The other one panted.

"Stop." Simone begged.

"Come on, sweetie. You know you want it." The guy in front said before trying to kiss her.

Simone turned her head away. She continued to try to get their hands off of her, but they were latched onto her like an octopus. She finally lost it as the guy behind her trapped her with one arm and stroked his hand down to touch her most intimate place, like Xander had earlier.

"I said, STOP!" Simone screamed.

Amber noticing Simone's struggles and hearing her scream, started to move forward to defend her friend when Jackson and Xander emerged from behind her and Lanie, like avenging angels. Extremely angry angels.

As they moved towards the struggle unfolding before them, Simone ripped away from her tormentors. The move tore the chain holding her sweater together and she clasped the material in front of her, keeping it from falling down around her ankles. The men that were assaulting her threw her down in their anger at being denied.

"Slut!" One spat out, before a massive fist connected with his jaw, instantly knocking him unconscious and he crumpled to the floor.

"What the fuck, man?!" The other yelled as Xander lifted him off his feet by the front of his shirt.

"Don't ever fucking put your hands on her!" Xander roared in the guy's face, before throwing him like a ragdoll across the floor.

Through the chaos, Amber had went to her teary-eyed friend, still huddled on the floor. Jackson crouched down and lifted Simone into his arms and started towards the entrance. Xander, Amber and Delanie followed him. Ethan, Chris and Bethany saw the grim procession and they too started out of the club. Bethany finding it difficult not to grin widely for the first time all night.

Xander grabbed his, Simone's and Jackson's coats while Jackson carried her out to the truck. Everyone followed quietly, feeling the tense storm brewing.

"Jackson, put me down please." Simone hiccuped.

"No." Jackson said the one word firmly, unwilling to argue.

"I said, put me down." Simone grated out.

"And I said, no!" Jackson bellowed, finally losing the tight rein on his anger. "And what the fuck were you doing dancing with those guys like that?" Jackson shouted as she squirmed to get out of his strong arms.

"Me? Me!" Simone shouted back incredulous, finally wiggling out of his arms and she grappled with her dress to keep from exposing herself. "What the fuck were you doing with that woman?! I saw her kissing Xander and her hand on your dick!" Simone said, uncharacteristically crude.

"That was our ex-" Jackson started.

"Oh, that makes it better!" Simone cut him off.

"Si, it was nothing. She tried to come on to us and when we denied her, she caught us off guard by kissing me and grabbing Jackson. If I'm not mistaken, I'd almost bet my life that she did it on purpose for you to see." Xander explained, the only one of the three attempting to stay calm.

"Right." Simone said doubtfully, as she crossed her arms over her chest. A clear sign of trying to stay closed off.

"No, I'm serious. She kept looking towards where the bathrooms were and the minute you came out, she practically jumped us. And when she realized you saw, she smiled and walked away. As if her job was done." Xander continued to defend them.

As the possibility of the truth sunk in, Simone's eyes filled with tears at her stupidity. She realized that she put herself in a potentially dangerous situation in her anger and jealousy. She didn't even recognize herself in that moment. She had never cared enough about men and relationships to experience jealousy and pain. And she didn't like it or herself.

"Can we just go home?" Simone said sadly, her head hanging with shame.

"First, I want to know why you let those guys put their hands all over you." Jackson said in a dangerously low tone.

"Why the hell do you think?! Because I wanted to make you two as jealous and hurt as I felt when I saw her all over you!" Simone yelled up at him.

"And where did that get you? Besides looking like a slut." Jackson said coldly.

"Jackson!" Xander and Delanie gasped.

Before she realized what she was doing, Simone raised her hand and slapped him so hard that the vibrations radiated painfully up her arm. For all her effort, Jackson's head barely moved, but a perfect outline of her handprint glowed red across his cheek.

Simone clutched her aching hand to her chest and stared hard at him. Jackson's jaw flexed in restraint. Her bottom lip started to tremble and a sob escaped her lips.

"I never asked for this." She started softly. "All my life, I had no interest in love and men and relationships. I focused on my studies and my career goals. My life was simple and uncomplicated. I came here to learn about my mom's family. My heritage. You both took me by surprise and gave me little option, other than to say yes. And I gave myself to you freely." Simone's voice quivered, but she continued on. "And all of a sudden you brought passion, pleasure and color into my gray world. I found out what it meant to love someone beyond reason. But I did not ask for this…this jealousy, anger and pain. These ugly feelings that go along with the beautiful ones.

"I wish I could go back and un-see, un-feel and un-love. Because right now…with this disgust I'm feeling for myself, for turning into a person I didn't even know in there-" Simone pointed back at the club. "-and for you, in this moment I actually regret having ever met you. And that rips me in half, because I love you." Simone finally broke down.

Amber and Delanie surrounded her, hugging her and patting her gently on the back. Jackson stepped forward, wanting to go to her. To beg on hands and knees to forgive him. But Xander stopped him with a hand on his chest. Jackson looked up at him and Xander shook his head no. *She needs space.* Jackson nodded his head dejectedly.

Delanie was the only one that noticed the radiant smile that spread across Bethany's face.

Chapter 14

    Simone rode back to the house in Chris' car, getting much needed time away from Jackson and Xander, even if only for the short thirty minute ride. The car was deathly silent. Chris drove and Bethany sat in the passenger seat, quietly delighting in Simone's misery. And Ethan and Amber took up the back seat with Simone.

    Simone rested her hot face against the cold glass of the window. She felt bad for ruining everyone's night, especially Amber and Ethan's. It was obvious that they wanted to flirt and mess around, picking back up where they had left off in the club. But out of respect for Simone, they restrained themselves.

    Simone was sure that Delanie was giving Jackson and Xander an earful in the truck. She hoped their ears bled from the incessant badgering. At the moment she felt as if she was surrounded by an impenetrable cocoon of shame and humiliation. So she held no sympathy for them.

    As Chris pulled up to the house, Simone took a deep breath, dreading being near Jackson and Xander. But knowing she had no choice, she opened the car door and walked into the open garage. Chris and Bethany waited in the running SUV for Delanie as both Amber and Ethan followed Simone inside.

    Simone pulled off her boots in the mudroom, but refused to remove her coat considering her sweater underneath was ready to fall off if she so much as moved wrong. Wrapping her arms protectively around herself, she walked into the kitchen where Jackson, Xander and Delanie were waiting.

    "Hey, Si. You alright?" Lanie asked cautiously.

"I'm fine. Just really tired and need to go to bed." Simone said, looking down at her stocking-clad feet.

"Okay. Well…have a good night. I hope I see you soon." Lanie said as she came up to Simone and gave her a hug.

"Goodbye, Lanie." Simone said hugging her back. The farewell sounding permanent, even to her own ears.

Delanie looked at her sadly and then left through the mudroom.

"Do you need me?" Amber asked thoughtfully.

"No, no. Go enjoy yourself. I'm sorry for ruining your night." Simone said to Amber, who was holding Ethan's hand.

"Okay. But don't hesitate to let me know if you need anything." Amber said before towing Ethan out of the room and upstairs, but not before she gave Jackson and Xander a warning glare.

The kitchen was silent and tense as they stood there, unsure of what to say to each other. Simone refused to look up at them. She wanted to hold onto her anger for as long as she could. And she knew if she looked up at them, she would lose her resolve.

"I'm going to bed." She stated and turned to leave the room.

"Simone-" Jackson started.

"Don't." Simone warned, not looking back.

She bolted out of the kitchen and up the stairs. Once in the master suite she grabbed her pajamas out of the chest of drawers and left the room. She headed to the second guest bedroom and the bathroom it shared with the other that Amber was occupying.

Simone heard the distinct sounds of lovemaking coming from the other room. She quickly turned on the shower, not wanting to hear the passionate sounds. She stripped off her coat, let the ripped sweater fall to the floor and pulled off her stockings. She stepped into the shower, under the hot spray.

All the emotions she had held at bay, came up like vomit and she sank to the shower floor and sobbed. When she finally gained enough composure, she stood up and grabbed a bar of soap. She rubbed the soap between her hands quickly, building up a lather.

Lifting her soapy hands to her face, she scrubbed violently. Trying to remove the makeup and all evidence of the evening from her face. And she continued the rough washing down her body. She tried to scrub away the feel of those men touching her. Saltwater tears mixing in with the spray of the shower.

Once she was done nearly scrubbing her skin raw, she stepped out of the shower and looked at herself in the foggy mirror. Her wavy hair was back to normal and her usual unpainted face stared back at her. Seeing that she was still the same person made her feel a little better.

Simone quickly piled her wet hair on top of her head in a messy bun and pulled on her pajamas. She walked into the spare bedroom, went over to the door and locked it. Satisfied that she wouldn't be bother the rest of the night, she pulled back the covers and crawled into the bed.

She thought that she would have a hard time falling asleep, considering all the turmoil going on inside her. But almost as soon as her head hit the pillow an alcohol induced exhaustion weighed her down and her emotionally drained body drifted off into a dreamless sleep.

~~~

Simone felt weightless. Like she was floating. She briefly opened her eyes and saw silver eyes staring down at her. She tried to hold onto them, but unconsciousness took her again.

She drifted back up to the surface of awareness again, to the feel of strong warm arms wrapping around her.

"I love you." She heard and then fell back into a deep comforting sleep.

~~~

Simone woke up slowly. She began to stretch and stopped. There was a chill in the air that had everything to do with the fact that she didn't have on a stitch of clothing, unlike when she had went to sleep. She also realized that there weren't any blankets covering her. Slowly and curiously she opened her eyes. The room was dark except for the fire blazing in the fireplace.

She recognized the master bedroom instantly and she vaguely recalled the sense of weightlessness she had felt earlier. She gathered that one of them had somehow unlocked the door to the spare bedroom and carried her back to their shared bedroom.

Simone felt someone watching her and she looked up to see that Jackson was sitting in a chair on the side of the bed, gazing at her. He wore his dark blue hooded robe. Part of his handsome face was in shadow, the other half looked worried and pensive in the firelight. His mouth rested against his massive fists that were clutched together in front of him.

"Do you have any idea how beautiful you are?" Jackson finally spoke, lifting his chin to rest on his clasped hands. His deep smooth voice caressing over her like a soothing balm over her bruised heart.

She didn't answer him, just continued to look at him.

"No, I don't suppose you do. I'm sorry if you're cold. I couldn't sleep and I just wanted to look at you for a little while. You can cover yourself back up if you'd like." Jackson offered. But for whatever reason Simone couldn't seem to move under his intense gaze.

Xander sighed heavily behind her in his sleep. He rolled towards her and laid his hand on her naked hip.

"I'm so sorry, Simone. I didn't mean what I said earlier." Jackson continued. "I...I just felt so sick, seeing their hands on you. I was jealous and angry and hurt. So I overreacted. Though that's still not an excuse for hurting you. I love you." Jackson finished, his gray eyes cloudy and heartbreaking.

Simone's glassy eyes brimmed with tears. She slowly rose from the bed and walked over to him. Her skin glowing a deep rich butterscotch in the light of the fire. Reaching down she untied the knot in his robe and pulled it aside, baring his naked glorious colossal physique. She slid onto his hair roughened strong thighs. She raised her hands to push back the hood, exposing his soft chestnut curls. And she stared at his chiseled masculine face with watery eyes.

"I do. I love you so fucking much." He whispered fiercely.

The tears that threatened the corners of her eyes finally spilled over at his words. He caught a few of them with his thumbs and he stroked the salty wetness over her lips and she tasted her tears.

"It's been *so* long since I've heard those words. Eleven years. And I didn't realize how much I missed them…craved them, up until a few moments ago." Simone said softly, and it hit her that maybe it was the same for him. "I love you, Jackson."

Shaky hands shot out and grabbed her face, smashing her mouth to his, catching her off guard with his intensity. Based off of his reaction Simone knew she had done the right thing by telling him how she felt, and this time not following words of anger and hurt.

He kissed her roughly. The hairs of his five o'clock shadow abrading her soft skin. Clasping the large globes of her ass, Jackson lifted and pulled her closer to him. He lowered her over his immense width and her body stretched to accommodate him. His lips moved from her swollen mouth to her wet cheeks. His warm tongue lightly touched her skin, tasting her tears.

Never getting enough of her, his mouth moved down to her jaw and kissed a path down her neck to her pert brown tipped breasts. He leaned her back as he bent forward to get more of her hard nipple in his mouth. All the while he guided her hips with his large hands. Helping her roll her pelvis to him. And Simone cradled his head in her arms, pressing his face against her chest. Her fingers finding their way into his sweet boyish curls.

Her breathing became erratic as he stroked into her again and again. Her breath stirring his hair. Jackson wrapped her in a bear hug, tightly holding her steady as his hips lifted off the chair, bringing them closer to the edge pure pleasure.

Simone's core rupture suddenly. She threw her head back and cried out as stars burst behind her eyes. She collapsed onto his barrel chest and he held her tight as he thrust once more. His entire body shuddered with his release.

Behind them Simone vaguely heard stirring in the bed. She looked back as Xander popped up on one elbow.

"Hey, Si! Does this mean you're not mad at us anymore?" Xander said with a radiant smile and deepening dimples.

Jackson and Simone chuckled at his eager face, blond hair wild around his head, like he'd stuck his finger in a light socket and the tent that his erection was causing under the sheets.

"Yeah, I think so." Simone sighed against Jackson's chest, mentally psyching herself up for round two.

"Sweet!" Xander said as he leapt from the bed.

He practically ran over to them, in his excitement and relief. He grabbed Simone and swept her up into his arms. He kissed her soundly as he walked back towards the bed. They tumbled into the bed amid tangled limbs, sheets and Simone's giggles.

Chapter 15

Simone and Amber bumped along in Jackson's truck down the streets of the Tanana land. Jackson had let Simone borrow his truck, somewhat reluctantly, he and Xander both pouting because she wouldn't allow them to come along for support. She barely knew how to explain herself to her relatives. She definitely didn't know how to explain the two of them.

"Do you know what you're looking for?" Amber asked, as she looked around.

"Yes. When my mom died and I went through all of her belongs, I found some information on her tribe and some addresses." Simone said as she turned a corner.

The little town was old and somewhat bleak in the dark Alaskan afternoon. There was an old two story log building that acted as the Tanana city hall. A few sparse shops here and there. The homes were small and rundown. Some were made of logs and others wood siding. Many of them had skeletons of rusted old cars scattered throughout the yards, tires and other pieces of scrap metal. Giving the look of a massive junkyard, with some houses thrown in for good measure.

"Why did I always think that there would be teepees or something like that?" Amber said, shocked by the reality of it.

"I think it's because that's the image and stereotype we've all put in our heads." Simone said sadly, finally understanding why her mother was so desperate to get away.

Finding what she was looking for, Simone parked the car in front of a house that was a little better organized than the others. The yard had only one rundown car in it and no other nondescript objects sticking out from under the snow. The house itself was painted a pretty blue and looked welcoming. At least Simone hoped so.

"So whose house is this?" Amber asked curiously.

"My grandparents. That is, if they're still alive." Simone said taking a deep breath before opening the truck door.

Amber stopped her with a hand on her arm. "No matter what happens, they deserve to know you exist and that your mom has passed away. And you deserve to know them too." Amber said seriously.

"Thank you, Amber." Simone smiled nervously.

She hopped down from the truck, slipped her hand into Amber's reassuring one, when her friend came around to meet her on the other side and they took tentative steps towards the house. They walked slowly up the porch steps and when Simone stood in front of the door, Amber squeezed her hand tightly in support. She raised her hand and knocked softly, though the sound still rattled her nerves and sounded loud to her ears.

They heard footsteps coming towards the door and Simone took a deep fortifying breath. The open swung open and a little old woman with bright white hair tied back in a bun, a deeply lined reddish brown face weathered from the sun and wind, stared up at them. At first she looked confused, but curious. But as her eyes focused on Simone's face, her eyes widened and she softly gasped.

"You have Halona's eyes. Who are you?" The older woman asked in a strong gravelly voice.

"Simone Dyani Staton. Your granddaughter." Simone said softly.

~~~

However Simone had envisioned the first meeting would go, she couldn't have expected or been more thrilled with the actual reality of it. Her grandmother had instantly embraced her and wept, when Simone introduced herself. She led her and Amber into the cozy and cluttered house.

Currently they were seated at the little kitchen table, drinking her grandmother's apparently famous spiked hot apple cider. As they sipped on the delicious beverage, her grandmother bustled about collecting pictures of family to show Simone.

"This is your grandfather Takoda Hunt, when he was a young man." Her grandmother said, handing her an old framed black and white photograph. "He passed away two years ago, God rest his soul." She said, dabbing at her watery eyes. "My name is Kohana Hunt."

"My mom told me that her name meant 'of happy fortune' and my middle name means 'deer'. What does your name and my grandfather's name mean?" Simone asked shyly.

"Ah, yes. Dyani is a beautiful name. And suitable for you. You are lovely. I see so much of Halona in you." Kohana said stroking a hand down Simone's face. "Anyway, your grandfather's name means 'friend to everyone'. And he was. Everyone loved him and there was a great sadness throughout the village when he past. And my name means 'swift'. I came into this world very quickly." She smiled.

Simone agreed, because even for an older woman, she moved about the house with a swiftness that belied her age.

"So tell me, how did it happen? Halona passing on?" Kohana asked.

"How did you know?" Simone asked surprised.

"I felt her leave this world." Kohana explained. "I have the gift. Some would say I'm a medicine woman."

"Wow!" Amber exclaimed, and Kohana smiled at the redhead.

"So what happened? It felt quick." Simone's grandmother persisted.

"It was an aneurysm. We went to bed one night and the next morning I noticed she wasn't up yet. I went to wake her up and she was cold and wasn't breathing. The doctor said that it happened instantly." Simone said with a wobbly voice.

Kohana wiped at her eyes. "I should have never pushed her away. I missed so much of your life and the remainder of hers. We were just so hurt when she wanted to leave. You have to understand that Fairbanks is as far as any of the tribe move to. And usually high school is as far as any of us go in school. But Halona wanted more for herself. She wanted to see more. I'm surprised that she decided to make her life in Seattle. I would've thought that she would make her way to Los Angeles or New York or someplace like that. Your father must have made a good impression on her." Kohana sighed with regret.

"Yes. I think he did." Simone smiled. "He died when I was five in the Gulf War, but I can still remember how they looked at each other. They were happy."

"Good. I'm glad he found her. Otherwise I wouldn't have part of her sitting before me now." Kohana grinned warmly at Simone. "So how long are you here? I'd love to spend more time with you."

"A week." Simone said, refraining from mentioning to her grandmother that she had already been there for a week.

Now that Simone knew she was more than warmly received by her grandmother, she felt regret at waiting so long to meet her. She'd had a wonderful week with Jackson and Xander, but coming to meet her family was the whole reason she had come and saved up for years for.

"That's not nearly enough time. But I guess we'll make the most of it." Kohana said, clasping Simone's hand tightly. "In the meantime, I have to make some calls. There are a couple of people I want you to meet."

~~~

Simone and Amber blew out mutual breaths of exhaustion as they slammed the truck doors shut. They waved at the crowd of people that stood on the front porch, waving back in farewell. It was nearly dinnertime and looking at the clock, Simone realized that they had been there for six hours.

"Who knew that that little house could hold so many people?" Amber said in wonder.

"Yeah." Simone said, overwhelmed at the events of the day.

Practically the whole Tanana tribe had shown up on Kohana's doorstep. And they had spent the next several hours regaling Simone and Amber on the history of the tribe and stories about her family. It had taken a ton of convincing and a promise to come tomorrow to turn down staying for dinner. Simone had noticed Amber anxiously looking at her phone, and assumed she was waiting with bated breath to see Ethan again. And from the sounds that had come out of her room last night and this morning, Simone knew that Amber had had a great time with Xander's brother.

"So are you happy with the way it all turned out? Was it what you imagined?" Amber asked grinning at Simone.

"Better." Simone sighed contentedly. "Oh my God! I have a grandmother, Amber!" She finally burst out in pure joy.

"I'm so happy for you, Si. So…has this swayed your decision to stay?" Amber asked, solemnly, not wanting to lose her friend, but understanding Simone's need for family.

"I think it just might. Though I don't think I'll tell the guys just yet. I want to be one hundred percent sure before I tell them." Simone said.

"So you guys are alright? Did you kiss and make up? Cause you all looked pretty cozy this morning at breakfast." Amber teased.

"You have no idea. Let's just say that I didn't get much sleep. Makeup sex *is* amazing!" Simone smiled dreamily. "But let's not talk about me. What about you Miss I-brought-the-roof-down-with-my-screams?" Simone teased her best friend.

"Oh God! He was *incredible*! And his cock is just as big as his brother's. Big packages must run in the family." Amber proclaimed, fanning herself.

"You're sick, Amber. I did not need to know that…or to be reminded that you've seen my guys' penises." Simone rolled her eyes.

"I'm just trying to keep up with you, my friend. Maybe I should see if Ethan wouldn't mind if Chris joined in." Amber said, the wheels turning in her head.

"Amber! Don't you dare!" Simone exclaimed.

"I'm just kidding…kind of. You've got me so curious about having the kind of relationship you do. It's hot and I'm totally jealous." Amber admitted.

"Well, I don't know what it's like to be with just one man, but all I can say is this relationship is all-consuming to say the least." Simone sighed, thinking of her men.

They rode the rest of the way home chatting about any and everything. Simone pulled into the garage and they heard the pulsing beats of music pouring from the house before they even opened the door to the mud room. They both looked at each other with frowns of curiosity.

Forgetting to remove their coats wanting to find the source of the music, they peaked around the corner into the kitchen. And there in the middle was Xander in only a pair of long gym shorts singing into a broom stick to the song 'Let's Do It Tonight' by Pitbull. The girls' giggles made him look up. Without missing a beat, Xander dropped the broom, took a running start at the kitchen island. He jumped up and slid across it and landed right in front of Simone. He grabbed her like the singer instructed, spun her out and back, and then dipped her low. Her hair falling in a cascade to the floor. He snapped her back up and kissed her soundly on the lips.

"My goodness! You certainly are happy this evening." Simone said breathless.

"Mmm…" He rumbled in the back of his throat as he continued to dirty dance with her.

"Where's Jackson?" Simone asked trying to ignore the hardness that was becoming noticeably fuller against her thigh.

"Upstairs, cleaning the bathroom. Which he's been sulking and complaining the whole time, because I bitched at him to clean it." Xander smirked happily.

"I see." Simone nodded.

"Wait here. I'll go get him, so you can tell us both at the same time how your day went." Xander said, kissed her on the lips quickly and ran out of the room.

Amber and Simone looked at each other and burst out laughing.

~~~

"So does this mean you'll stay?" Jackson asked, sitting forward anxiously, on the couch in the living room, after Simone told them about her first meeting with her grandmother.

"Well..." Simone decided she couldn't hold it in any longer, against her better judgment. "Yes. Yes, I'm staying." She said softly.

Jackson collapsed back on the couch in frustration and at Simone's expectant expression, he frowned in confusion. "Wait! What did you just say?" Jackson asked cautiously.

"I said, I'll stay." Simone smiled shyly as his face lit up with dawning excitement.

"Really?" He asked, not truly believing her. And at her nod of assent, "Fuck yeah!" He exploded and then grabbed her up in a massive bear hug.

"Uh…Jax? I can't breathe." Simone wheezed out.

"Oh sorry." Jackson said sheepishly, as he released her.

Xander stood up and kissed her on the temple. "I'm glad you're staying." He said quietly, not as exuberant as Simone had hoped.

Just then the front door burst open and the Drake siblings spilled inside the house, like déjà vu of the previous night. Ethan strode in cockily, walking up to Amber and practically sticking his tongue down her throat. And without so much as a backwards glance, grabbed her hand and led her up to her spare bedroom to do God's knows what.

"Alrighty then." Xander said looking up at the loft where the couple had disappeared. "What the hell are all of you doing here? Did we plan something that I don't know about?" Xander asked the rest of his siblings.

"No. But do we really need a reason to stop by to see our big brothers?" Delanie asked walking over to give Simone a kiss on the cheek and a warm hug. "Or our new sister?" She whispered in Simone's ear.

Simone smiled at the thought of having a whole new family as well as her blood relatives a few miles away. *This could be a start to a whole new life for me.*

"I know you, Lanie. You're up to something." Xander said with a raised brow.

"If you must know, Beth and I were at Chris and Ethan's place. Ethan said that he was coming over to see Amber and we all decided to come, just to make sure you guys were doing okay, after last night." Lanie finally explained.

"We're doing great." Jackson beamed with his chest puffed out with pride. "Simone just told us before you so rudely interrupted, that she's going to stay." Jackson burst out, too excited to keep it a secret.

"Oh my God! Really?!" Lanie exclaimed, jumping up and down and quickly hugging the three of them in between bounces.

"Yes." Simone said bashfully, still uncomfortable being the center of attention.

From the looks of disbelief to horror to heartbreak and then finally pure hatred that flashed across Bethany's face, Simone assumed that she had come along for the ride to make sure that there was still trouble in paradise. The look of hate in her eyes made Simone's stomach knot with unease.

"That's fantastic. I'm happy for you guys." Chris congratulated them with pats on the backs for the men and a warm hug for Simone.

"I can't wait to tell mom and dad." Lanie said ready to burst at the seams. "I know they were worried whether you'd stay or-" Lanie continued, before Bethany cut her off.

"Well now that we know everything is just peachy-keen here, I'm ready to go. Besides, don't you have homework to grade, Lanie?" Bethany said with her arms crossed angrily over her chest.

"I teach *kindergarten*. There is no homework." Lanie responded as if her sister had lost her mind. Bethany gave her younger sister a look that spoke volumes. "But I *am* tired." Lanie said with a fake yawn. "Yeah, let's let them celebrate in private." Lanie winked at Simone.

Lanie and Chris gave them final hugs before leaving. Bethany remained at a distance, unwilling to speak further or even look at them.

"I guess, I'll be seeing you soon." Lanie said to Simone in farewell.

"Yep. I think so." Simone smiled, trying not to let Bethany ruin one of the best days of her life.

The front door shut and the room was drenched in silence, aside from the cries of pleasure from above in Amber's room. Simone looked up at her two men and smiled. Feeling that for the first time in eleven years that there was hope for her future.

Chapter 16

Amber spent the next couple of afternoons holed up at Ethan and Chris' place. She said she was getting as much 'sweet lovin', as she could before it was time for her to leave and time for Ethan to go back out to sea for work. While Simone spent the afternoons with her grandmother.

Simone had already called Dr. Roth's office to let them know that she would unfortunately not be starting her nursing job with them, because she was relocating. And she had an interview at the local hospital tomorrow, and the day after that Xander's parents wanted to have another Friday dinner with the family to celebrate her staying. And then on Sunday she was heading back with Amber to Seattle to pack up her things, sell her car, since it was not equipped to handle the treacherous Alaskan weather and ship her belongs up to her new home.

She nearly bubbled over with excitement as she sat in her Grandma K's kitchen, drinking her famous cider.

"I am so happy you're staying. I can barely contain myself." Her grandma said happily, grabbing Simone's hand across the table. "You'll have to bring your men over soon, for me to meet."

"Men?" Simone said hesitantly, knowing that she had never told her grandmother about Jackson and Xander.

"Mmhmm, unless you have only one with a split personality, because I definitely sense two people." Kohana smiled knowingly. "I might be old, but I see more than most."

"Apparently so." Simone said bashfully.

"So tell me about them." Her grandmother coaxed.

"Well, their names are Xander Drake and Jackson Cole. And…and…I don't know where to begin." Simone shrugged.

"I know of them. It's not a very big town, especially with two strapping young men like them. They've done good for themselves and so have you for finding them." Kohana said, seeing the blush spread across Simone's cheeks. "And don't be embarrassed. If I was a younger woman, I'd jump on that train myself."

"Grandma K!" Simone gasped, holding back her laughter.

"I'm not blind or dead, child. A woman is always a woman, no matter how old she gets. It's just more often than not, when you get older you find a man more for security than passion. But you still never forget what it's like." Her grandmother smiled wistfully.

"Anyway, they love you. But there may be some trouble ahead. Just keep your head up and everything will work itself out." Kohana cautioned.

"What do you mean, Grandma K?" Simone asked with trepidation.

"Don't worry about it, honey. That's all I can tell you though. I don't know specifics. I just get a sense of things." Kohana finished, patting Simone's hand in comfort.

"Okay." Simone said unsure.

~~~

Simone had woken up nervous for her interview, but Jackson and Xander had relaxed her in the best sort of way before sending her off in Jackson's truck. Xander was dropping Jackson off at the mill before heading to the lodge, so that she could have free rein without worrying about rushing around town dropping off and picking up either of them.

Their way of relaxing her must have worked, because she nailed the interview. Her once tense nerves, calm and her normally shy demeanor was pumped full of endorphins, making her more bubbly. Now she drove home feeling pumped. She turned on the radio and blasted 'All About that Bass'. She uncharacteristically danced and sang at the top of her lungs to the song as she maneuvered the truck down the street toward home.

Pulling the truck up the drive, she noticed a car that she didn't recognize. She drove into the garage and looked at the car again, wondering who it could be, before closing the garage door. She entered into the mudroom and removed her coat and shoes. She slipped her feet into Jackson's slippers and walked into the kitchen. No one was there, so she walked further into the house.

"Hello?" She called out, but there was no answer.

Checking the living room and the man cave, she found that no one was there. She made her way slowly upstairs and checked Amber's bedroom, but it too as empty. As well as the other guest room. Finally she walked back to their shared bedroom and upon opening the door she found someone in their bed. *What the fuck?!*

"Oh, hello." Said the brunette from the bar, Simone recognized as the guys' ex.

She sat up in the bed with the sheet clutched to her obviously naked body underneath.

"What are you doing here? And in our bed?" Simone said still in shock.

"Xander told me I could relax afterwards, if I wanted to for a little while." She said flippantly, as if they were chitchatting during brunch.

"After what?" Simone tried to keep a tight rein on her emotions.

"Why, sex of course." Tracy said, lifting an eyebrow at her.

"That's bullshit! He would never." Simone was starting to lose her control.

"Wouldn't he? Think about it. Jackson might be hook-line-and-sinker for you, but Xander isn't. You know just as well as I

259

do that he isn't ready to commit. And he just proved it by fucking me senseless…in your bed." Tracy said, snidely. "Look for yourself." She said as she tossed her cellphone to the foot of the bed.

Simone glanced down at the phone and sure enough, she could see a text message from Xander.

God I missed u. Tasting u. Fucking u. I'll meet up with u again as soon as I can get away.

"Fuck you!" Simone screamed, clenching her fists at her sides. She had never wanted to hit someone so badly in all her life.

"See you can't even deny it, because you know it's true." Tracy said as she got out of the bed, not even trying to cover her slender naked body. "Besides he'd never settle down with some half-breed bitch anyway."

Simone wasn't one for fighting, but she was suddenly blinded by rage. And before she knew what was happening, she walked up to the petite woman and punched her so hard in the face that she sprawled flat on her back, naked and spread eagle.

"Get the fuck out of my house!" Simone screeched at the top of her lungs.

"You bitch! You fucking hit me!" Tracy shrieked, holding a hand up to her face.

"I'll do more than that, if you don't get the hell out." Simone growled.

"Fuck you!" Tracy wailed.

Simone had had enough. She quickly squatted down, picking up all of Tracy's clothes. She then walked up to the woman, grabbed her by her hair and started pulling her out of the room. Tracy kicked and screamed as Simone dragged her roughly down the hall, down the stairs and to the front door. At this point, Simone had several scratches down her arms and hands, but she didn't feel them as the woman tried to fight her off. With superhuman strength that she didn't know she had, Simone tossed the screaming woman out into the snow and then threw her clothes out after her and shut the door with a slam.

As quickly as the adrenaline had come, it swept out of her blood just as rapidly and she slid down the door with a heartbreaking sob. She didn't want to believe the nasty woman, but she knew that Xander was resistant to fully committing to her. And her heart broke further, knowing that this relationship didn't work without him. She loved him just as much as she loved Jackson. They both brought something to the relationship that would be left empty, if one of them was not there. So in the process, she'd have to lose both of them. *Fuck you, Xander!*

Taking deep breaths past the erratic hiccups and tears, Simone got up and walked to the kitchen. She found her purse and pulled out her cell.

"Am…Amber. I need your help." Simone sobbed into the phone.

~~~

Jackson and Xander walked into the house that evening, hoping to hear good news. They didn't care one way or another if Simone got the job or not, but they hoped she got it on her behalf. They knew it was what she wanted.

"Do you think she got the job?" Xander asked.

"Oh, for sure. They were pretty impressed with her when we came in with Daryl last week. And I think they need the help, anyway." Jackson said with confidence. "Simone?" Jackson bellowed, but there was no response.

"Maybe she's upstairs. I'll go get her." Xander said, making his way upstairs.

A few moments later, he walked back to the loft and looked down at Jackson with an expression mixed with fear and worry.

"What's wrong?" Jackson said, sensing something wasn't right.

"I…I think she's gone." Xander barely said above a whisper.

"What? What the fuck are you talking about, Xan? What do you mean she's gone?" Jackson said incredulous.

"Her things. Clothes, bags…everything is gone." Xander said gripping the banister.

Jackson didn't hesitate. He took the stairs three at a time. At the top, he ran into the bedroom and then through the closet and into the bathroom. He realized that Xander was right. Everything was gone. He ran back out to the loft in a panic.

"Check Amber's room!" Jackson said, but didn't wait for Xander to move and ran straight to the spare bedroom that Amber had been using.

Her room was also completely empty. Jackson whipped around to look at Xander's somber face. Jackson walked up to him and snatched him up by his collar.

"What did you do? What the fuck did you do?!" Jackson roared.

"I didn't do anything. And maybe that's the problem. I didn't show enough that I cared…that I love her. And maybe that's why she left." Xander said, blinking rapidly, eyes glassy with regret.

"But she was staying. She said she was going to stay! What could have happened between her going to an interview this morning and now leaving without a trace?" Jackson said frantically, finally letting go of Xander's shirt front.

"I don't know." Xander said, just as perplexed.

Jackson stopped to think for a moment, then he grabbed his phone from his back pocket and pulled up Lanie's number.

"Lanie! Do you have any idea where Simone is?" Jackson said briskly into the phone.

"No. Why?" Lanie asked, confused.

"She's gone. We just got home and she's gone. All of her things and Amber's are gone." Jackson voiced started to rise a few octaves.

"Oh my God! I don't know. Have you called Ethan? Maybe Amber told him." Lanie suggested.

"Oh, yeah. Good idea. Call me if you hear anything." Jackson said before hanging up. "She doesn't know. I'm calling Ethan to see if he does." Jackson told Xander as he pulled up Ethan's number.

"Ethan. Do you know where Simone and Amber are?" Jackson asked.

"No. But Amber was with me when she got a call from Simone. I guess she was crying and freaking out over something and Amber left. I haven't heard from her since." Ethan said.

"Shit!" Jackson spat out. "Call me if you hear from Amber." Jackson said and then hung up.

They stood there a moment, unsure of what to do next. Then in the distance they could hear the vague sounds of a phone ringing. Both men looked at each other and started towards the noise. They followed it into the master bedroom. The noise got louder as the came closer to the bed. And as it rang once more, Jackson saw an illuminated cellphone screen under the sheets. Quickly pulling back the sheet, he grabbed the unfamiliar phone. He tapped the main button and the screen lit up with a picture of Tracy on it.

Jackson looked up in shock at Xander and Xander just shook his head in confusion. Luckily the phone didn't have a code to get into it, so he swiped it open. He hit the back button a few times to clear the screen of missed calls. The last screen sent instant rage through his blood stream. Before Xander could say a word of defense, Jackson slammed his fist into his jaw, knocking his best friend to the floor.

"How could you fucking do it?! With Tracy?! Are you fucking kidding me?!" Jackson roared over him.

"Fuck, Jax! I didn't send that text. I swear to God! I would never fuck with that girl again." Xander said rubbing his tender jaw.

Jackson knew his best friend almost better than he knew himself. So he knew that Xander was telling the truth.

"Then how did this text get on her phone?" Jackson asked anyway.

"I don't…FUCK!" Xander shouted as realization hit. "I can't believe that she'd do it, but…that's the only possibility." Xander shook his head angrily.

"Start making sense, Xan. Before I crack one of your ribs." Jackson warned.

"Beth. She came to see me today at the lodge. We ended up having lunch there. There was an issue in the kitchen and I got up to fix the situation and I left my phone on the table. She must have sent that text while I was gone. My own fucking sister, man!" Xander cried out, feeling the stab to his heart as if she sunk a knife through him.

Jackson held out his hand to help Xander up, feeling just as betrayed at Xander. And Jackson felt the guilt pour over him, because it was Beth's feelings for him that had caused the mess that they were in.

"I think it's time for an emergency family meeting." Xander said in a deadly calm voice.

~~~

The Drake family, plus Jackson sat at the kitchen table, in the heart of the house. Everyone but Bethany was there, and they grimly awaited her arrival.

"Are you sure that it was Beth, Alexander?" Gail asked again.

"Yes, mom." Xander said again, frowning in frustration.

"I knew she was upset over your relationship with Simone, but this is just over the top!" Lanie shook her head in disbelief.

Frank rubbed his face roughly, also finding it hard to believe that one of his children could be so deceitful. All of their ears perked up at the sound of the front door opening and closing. A few moments later Bethany walked into the kitchen. Her eyes quickly scanned the table.

"Hey, guys! Where's Simone?" Beth asked in a sugary sweet voice, with an equally sickening smile.

"Why don't you tell us?" Xander asked.

"How should I know?" Beth asked with a nervous frown.

Without a word, Xander slid Tracy's cellphone onto the table.

"Do you know whose phone this is?" Xander asked quietly.

"No." Beth said, then turned away to grab a bottle of water out of the fridge.

"It's Tracy's." Xander said to her back that stiffened at the woman's name. "She told us everything." Xander lied, waiting for her to call his bluff.

"I don't know what you're talking about." Beth said turning to face them, her face carefully devoid of any expression.

"Don't you? You and Tracy both masterminded this whole scheme to get rid of Simone. My only question is why use her to break us up? Weren't you worried that if your plan worked that we'd go back to her, and then you still wouldn't have Jackson?" Xander said calmly, but to anyone paying attention, rage laid just beneath the surface.

"I don't know what you're talking about!" Beth gritted out.

"Don't give me that bullshit, Beth! I know you took my phone and texted Tracy with that garbage so that she could show it to Simone!" Xander exploded, jumping out of his chair and cornering Beth against the fridge, almost nose to nose. "You were never this jealous before with our other girlfriends. But you knew this time it was serious, that Jackson was head over heels for Simone. And that scared you. So you cooked up this whole fucking lie to make her run. Now admit it!" Xander roared in her face.

"He's *mine*!" Beth screamed back into his face. "Yes, I did it!" Everyone at the table gasped at her confession. "What does it matter? You weren't ready to commit to her anyway." Beth tried to justify her actions.

"You don't know my mind! And you definitely have no right to decide for me. I am in love with her. And your stupid selfish actions just pushed me to realize it! So it backfired. And now what? You'd hurt you own flesh and blood to have something that's never going to happen!" Xander exclaimed, driving a fist into the refrigerator next to her head.

"Alexander! Calm down!" Frank spoke up.

"Seriously, dad!? She just tried to ruin my life. And possibly succeeded." Xander said in exasperation.

"I know, son. But you can't beat her to a pulp either." Frank reasoned.

Xander shoved away from Bethany, raking a hand through his already disheveled blond locks.

"I didn't think I was hurting you, Xan. I thought you'd be happy and then I could have a chance with Jackson." Beth pleaded.

Jackson's fist came down on the table and it creaked alarmingly under to blow. He stood up to make sure that what he had to say was heard.

"It. Will. *Never*. Happen." Jackson said each word individually to put emphasis on his meaning. "Do you understand? Never!" He bellowed and everyone shrunk back. He had never truly raised his voice at any of them in anger before.

"But Jackson-" Beth started.

"What did I say?!" Jackson interrupted, slowly walking towards her. "If we're lucky enough to get her back, you will never speak to her in anything but a polite and cordial manner. You will smile in front and behind her back. You will not plot to do any harm to her. And you will go and find your own FUCKING BOYFRIEND!" Jackson's voice raised to the rafters and Bethany cowered in fear. "Now, do I make myself clear?" He said quietly.

"Yes." Bethany's voiced quivered and tears threatened to spill down her face.

Xander walked over and grabbed the cellphone off of the table and walked it back over to her. "Now take this back to your new BFF and let her know your little ploy failed. And that we had better not see her anytime soon." Xander shoved the offensive device in her hand.

"Bethany?" Gail said quietly and Beth turned to look at her. "When you're done, I'd like you to come back here. We need to talk." Gail finished.

Beth hung her head and walked out of the house.

"Now…how do we get her back?" Xander said anxiously.

"Does anyone know where she lives?" Delanie asked the room at large.

"No." Jackson and Xander said dejectedly at the same time.

"Great." Lanie said deflated.

"Yeah." They both said.

Everyone looked around at each other, unsure of what to do.

"Can you call her?" Lanie piped up hopeful.

"She wouldn't answer." Xander said despondently.

"But I know who would." Ethan smiled, puffing out his chest. "And guess who's got her number? This guy!" Ethan pointed at his chest with his thumbs. "Now who's the annoying baby brother?"

"You're a pain in my ass sometimes, but you just saved our lives, little bro." Xander said, grabbing Ethan around the neck, putting him in a headlock and rubbing his knuckles roughly through his hair.

"Just make me the godfather of your first kid." Ethan said pulling his head away from Xander's assault.

"Done." Xander said.

"Now call her." Jackson order, not wanting to wait a moment longer.

Ethan brought out his phone and pulled up his favorite redhead's number.

Chapter 17

Simone felt awful. She went from feeling nothing, like a zombie, to feeling everything. She prayed for the zombie moments, because at least it was a break from the crushing feeling of heartache. And when the crushing came it felt as if she could crawl out of her skin. Her body felt like it wanted to splinter into a thousand pieces.

And the tears, dear God the tears. When she thought there were none left to shed, more would come out of nowhere. Her eyes were constantly rimmed with red and puffy. Amber had finally went to one of the giant wholesale clubs to buy her tissues in bulk. And it had only been three days. She had no idea why people put themselves through this particular brand of torture.

Now, she had to go through the torture of an impromptu party that Amber was throwing. She said it was a belated party for Simone's graduation and her new job. But Simone knew better. She also knew that Amber meant well, but she was in no shape to party or be around other human beings.

Simone currently sat in a corner at Amber's parents' house, trying to remain unseen. But it was like whatever Pandora's Box that Jackson and Xander had opened, continued its affects back in Washington as well. Guys kept coming up to Simone trying to talk to her or get her to dance. Amber had her parents hire a D.J. and it seemed as if she had invited every available guy in a hundred mile radius. *I think some of these guys are her ex-boyfriends. Jeez, she must be really desperate for me to snap out of it.*

Amber had practically dragged her out of their apartment for the party. But not before forcing her into the shower, which she hadn't taken one since before her interview. After her shower, where she had basically just cried on the shower floor, Amber had brushed out all of the tangles in her hair and then flat ironed her hair again. She painted her face with a natural copper and gold eye and shiny nude lips.

She dressed Simone in a two piece outfit. The skirt and top were made out of a pretty winter white embroidered mesh with a modesty lining of the same color, to cover up her private bits. The skirt was a tight fitting high-waisted pencil skirt that came to right below the knees, and the top was a crop top with three-quarter length sleeves. The ensemble showing off an inch of her midriff. To finish off the outfit, Amber forced her into strappy white heels. The whole time Simone complained that her ass was too big for the outfit, but Amber just ignored her and practically shoved her into her car and sped off towards her parents' house.

As Simone sat there watching people mingling, a vision of Jackson and Xander's faces flashed in her memory. A wave of that crushing feeling hit her and her heart squeezed. Instantly tears clouded her vision and she felt like she was going to have a nervous breakdown in front of the whole party.

"Oh no you don't." Amber said appearing in front of Simone with a drink in hand. "Don't you dare ruin your face. Weepy Simone is *not* making an appearance tonight. Drink up." Amber scolded and the tears instantly dried up as she drew strength from her friend.

"Okay." She said taking a fortifying drink. "I'm good. I'm good." She reassured her friend.

"Alright. Now let's move around and mingle. Sitting here wallowing in misery is only going to make it worse." Amber said taking Simone's hand and pulling her up from the security of her chair. Amber guided Simone over to where her parents were, using them as a distraction.

"Oh, Simone! I didn't even know you were here. Where have you been hiding?" Amber's mom exclaimed in surprise. "This party is as much for you as it is for Amber."

"I know, Vivian. Sorry, I've been anti-social." Simone apologized.

"So how was your trip? Did you find your tribe?" Vivian asked.

"Yes, it was won…wonderful." Simone faltered, her voice going wobbly and then she took a deep breath, sucking it up. "I met my grandmother and most of the tribe. She was lovely." Simone smiled sadly. Feeling sorrow over how everything had fallen apart when she had thought she was going to get the life she hadn't dared to dream of.

"Do you have any plans to go back soon?" Bill, Amber's father asked.

"No." Simone said gloomily.

"You will, if I have anything to say about it." A deep voice commanded, sending a shiver down Simone's spine as she realized that the room had gone completely still.

"I second that." Another familiar masculine voice stated.

Simone slowly turned. She saw Amber's beaming face before she saw a sight that nearly made her collapse. Before her stood Jackson and Xander, unlike she'd ever seen them. Jackson was in a slate gray three piece suit, white shirt and dark charcoal gray tie. And Xander was in a pretty dark blue three piece suit with a white shirt and electric blue tie.

Even their hair was combed to perfection. Xander's was slicked back, reminding her a little of David Beckham. And Jackson's curls were combed and smoothed back with some sort of styling wax, into luxurious shiny waves.

"Wha…what are you doing here?" Simone asked, not exactly sure what to feel.

"We're here to bring you back." Xander started.

"But…" Simone trailed off, not knowing what to say and not wanting to cause a scene.

"But nothing. I love you, Si. And I'm so sorry that I didn't tell you that before. I was being so stupid. Please forgive me." Xander pleaded.

"But what about Tracy?" Simone asked with a lifted eyebrow.

"What about her? Beth and Tracy plotted that whole messed up scene to get you to leave us. Beth sent that text to Tracy's phone from mine when she came to visit me at the lodge." Xander explained. "I'm so sorry that you had to go through that. If I'd have made my feelings for you know, maybe you would've at least stayed long enough to hear us out. You can't imagine how torn up we were when we came home and all of your stuff was gone." Xander continued, eyes glassy with unshed tears. "Say you'll forgive us?"

Simone looked to Jackson and he nodded his head. "It's true, Simone."

"I…I don't know." Simone said shakily.

"We figured you'd need more convincing." They stepped aside, revealing the entourage behind them. "So we brought reinforcements.

Behind them stood the whole Drake family and at the center was her Grandma K. Simone's eyes widened in disbelief. Beth who stood off to the side, stepped forward.

"It's true, Simone. And I'm so sorry for hurting you. All of you. Don't be mad at them when it was my fault." Beth said and then stepped back.

Simone nodded acknowledgement. Then she looked back at her two men and a tentative smile touched her lips.

"Okay. Forgiven." Simone said letting out a deep healing breath.

Lanie peeked around Xander and beamed at Simone and gave her a thumbs up. Simone laughed to herself at the bubbly woman.

"Good. We were hoping you'd say that." Jackson said grinning ear to ear.

They both dropped to their knees and the crowd as well as Simone took in a collective gasp.

"Simone Dyani Staton, we know this is a little sudden, but we know that there is no other woman that can complete our trio better than you. I knew you'd change our lives the moment we saw you." Jackson started.

"We love you, Si. More than anything in this world. We would move heaven and earth for you. We'd protect you from a pack of ravenous wolves, bears and the occasional moose, if need be." Xander continued, always finding a way to make a joke. And Simone burst out in a watery laugh.

"Simone, will you marry us?" They both asked in unison as Jackson held up a stunning radiant round cut diamond ring, in a vintage style with little diamonds running down the sides.

Simone was sure that everyone that didn't know the story behind their unorthodox relationship, were probably shocked beyond belief and would tell this story until they're were old and gray. But she looked up at the faces she knew and they all beamed at her.

"Do it!" Ethan shouted out, cupping his hands over his mouth to make his voice carry further. "They promised I'd be the godfather of your first kid. Don't take that away from me." He persisted.

Simone laughed and looked back down at her gorgeous men. She could barely see them her eyes were so filled with tears.

"Yes." She whispered, unable to get much else around her tightening throat.

Jackson slid the ring on the ring finger of her left hand. They stood up and Xander grabbed her face and kissed her deeply. And as soon as he came up for air, Jackson stepped in and kissed her just as deeply. Simone could hear the women in the room murmur appreciatively.

"Good. We were hoping you'd say that as well." Xander grinned down at her, his dimples charming her as usual.

"Who gives this woman away?" A man spoke behind her and Simone whipped around to see a man standing before her with a bible in his hands.

"I do." Kohana said loudly.

"Wha…?" Simone looked around in confusion.

"You didn't know?" Jackson asked taking her left side.

"This is your wedding party." Xander informed her, taking her right.

"Do you Jackson Mitchell Cole and you Alexander Philip Drake take Simone Dyani Staton to be your spiritually wedded wife?" The supposed pastor began.

"We do." Both men answered proudly and deeply.

"Do you Simone Dyani Staton take Jackson Mitchell Cole and Alexander Philip Drake to be your spiritually wedded husbands?" He asked expectantly.

"I…I do." Simone answered disoriented, making it almost sound like a question.

"Alright, may we have the rings please?" The pastor asked the room. Ethan and Chris stepped forward with two diamond eternity bands, handing one to Jackson and one to Xander. And Amber gave Simone two matching masculine titanium bands. "Gentlemen, repeat after me…"

~~~

"Can someone explain to me what just happened?" Simone asked after the pastor had given them permission to kiss the bride and they'd kissed her senseless amid deafening cheers and applause.

"You just got married!" Lanie screeched happily. "Congratulations, sister!" She said, pulling Simone into a tight embrace.

"Oh my God! I'm so happy for you!" Amber came up and pulled Simone out of Lanie's embrace and wrapped her in a hug. "Happy Simone is *so* much better than Weepy Simone." She whispered in Simone's ear.

"You were in on all of this? You let me mope around for three days?!" Simone grounded out through her teeth.

"Surprise!" Amber said brightly.

"You're a dead woman." Simone grinned back at Amber, deceptively sweet.

"Oh you love me. This was the best surprise ever. Admit it." Amber brushed off Simone's evil eye.

"And I'll *weep*, after I choke you to death." Simone kissed Amber on the cheek, before being pulled into another affectionate hug.

"See I told you everything would work itself out." Grandma K said embracing Simone.

"Yeah, I guess you were right. Though it didn't feel so hot forty-five minutes ago." Simone grimaced thinking of the painful squeeze on her heart, now just a distant memory.

"You have to understand the pain of love lost, in order to appreciate what you've got." Kohana grinned at her.

"You're just full of words of wisdom, aren't you?" Simone teased.

"You don't get to be my age and not learn some things along the way." Kohana winked at her.

Simone was suddenly swept up into the arms of one of her favorite people.

"Xander." She said breathless, as he spun her around.

"I need to speak with you…in private." He whispered against her temple.

"Alright." Simone said nervously, glancing over at Jackson, who nodded in support.

Xander carried her outside into the quiet chill night. He strode over to a private bench under a giant maple tree. He sat down keeping Simone firmly in his lap.

"I just wanted to take a moment to talk to you, away from all the commotion." Xander started, and Simone nodded. "I'm sorry that we bamboozled you into a surprise wedding. But we wanted you to know just how serious we are about wanting you in our life for good.

"I truly am sorry I was so resistant at first. It absolutely does not mean that I love you any less than Jackson. I've just lived a charmed life, never really losing anyone. So I didn't understand what loss felt like. You and Jackson have, so you both give yourselves freely and up front when you're in love. I held back thinking that maybe something was better around the corner. I was a fucking knuckle head for even thinking that it was possible to find something or someone as miraculous and life-altering than you. And when you left, you ripped my heart out and did a little dance on top of it." Xander cleared his throat trying to dislodge the lump that had formed there. "And now that I know what it feels like, I never want to go through that again. You're mine. And Jackson's. And I'm yours…if you'll have me?" Xander finished solemnly.

"Oh, Xan! Of course I'll have you." Simone exclaimed kissing him softly on his beautiful full lips. "I haven't told you this myself, but I love you…so much." Simone said looking at his tear filled eyes.

At the same time they both started clumsily planting rapid kissing over the others face. Simone burst out giggling and Xander chuckled deeply.

"Is there room for one more?" Jackson said walking up to them, coming to check on them.

"Always." Simone said sweetly.

~~~

The whirlwind that was Jackson and Xander had all of her things packed and shipped, her car sold and back in Alaska within a handful of days. As they finally pulled up to the house, Simone's heart filled with so much joy that she could barely sit still between them.

Once inside the garage, Simone started to walk into the house when they stopped her.

"Not so fast." Xander said with a hand on her shoulder.

They stood face to face with her in the middle and they lifted her in their arms cradling her close to their chests and then they squeezed through the door, carrying her over the threshold.

"We have to keep things traditional." Jackson smiled down at her as they let her down.

"As if anything we do is traditional. Our marriage isn't even legal." Simone rolled her eyes at them.

"It's as legal in my eyes as anyone else's marriage." Xander said seriously.

"Agreed." Jackson said, equally serious.

Simone's eyes welled with tears of happiness for the millionth time since they came barreling back into her life, like bulls in a china shop.

"What's wrong, Si." Xander asked stroking a finger down her face.

"I'm just so incredibly happy. I came here looking for my family and found so much more. Now my heart is so…so *full*." The tears finally slipped down her face.

Xander picked her up and walked through the house and up the stairs to their bedroom as Jackson followed. Inside their room the men slowly undressed Simone. Kissing paths down her body. Simone's skin tingled with pleasure.

"We have a surprise for you." Jackson said after they had undressed.

Simone admired as his enormous body bunched and flexed as he walked to the chest of drawers. He grabbed something out of the top drawer and walked back over to her, handing her a box.

She unwrapped the box and her eyebrows bunched together in confusion.

"What is it?" She asked perplexed.

"We'll show you." Xander said taking the box out of her hand and pulling out the object.

Xander unhooked one of the straps that was attached to what looked like a purple butterfly. He placed the butterfly against her heated sex and then wrapped the strap around her thigh and reattached it to the butterfly. Jackson did the same on the other side. The butterfly was now firmly against her clit. She looked up at them with curiosity. Jackson took a matching little purple box with buttons out of the packaging. And pressing the button, the butterfly came alive against her sensitive nub.

Simone cried out and her knees gave out on her. Both men reached out to steady her. Jackson pressed another button and the vibrations stopped. He picked her up and placed her gently in bed. Jackson laid back on the bed and he pulled her over him. Her hair cascaded down around his face and he wrapped a hand around her neck pulling her closer to flick his tongue over her lips.

Simone gasped and he took advantage of her opening to him and his tongue dipped into her mouth. His warm tongue stroking against hers. He positioned his throbbing erection at her opening and Simone willingly lowered her wet cleft over him.

Xander poured lube over his hardened length and positioned himself behind Simone, at her back entrance. He teased and stroked against her puckered flesh. Slowly he entered her and she threw her head back, adjusting to the fullness of having both men inside of her.

Jackson pressed the button for the lowest setting on the remote and the butterfly once again came to life and Simone bucked reflexively. Gently they began to move. Jackson stroked up and Xander out, then back again. Xander kissed and bit at her neck and shoulder. Jackson reached up to caress at her erect nipples.

Simone leaned forward, wanting Jackson's mouth on her. He obliged her. He flicked his tongue over her chocolate kiss nipples in time to each thrust of his powerful hips. As they both increased their speed, Jackson pressed the button for the medium setting for the butterfly.

"Aah, fuck!" Simone cried.

Her body started to tremble as they built up her climax. At her reaction, the men took it as their green light to pick up the pace. Their hips worked liked pistons, pumping in and out. Simone's body tensed and Jackson delivered the final explosion by pressing the last button to high.

Simone bucked wildly between them. Her inner muscles flexed and squeezed around their cocks and they roared with their release.

"Fuck!"

"Shit!"

They all collapsed, sprawling together. They fell in a pile of twitching limbs, pounding hearts and sweat soaked skin. Once they caught their breath, Jackson weakly got out of bed to grab a damp towel to clean them up. He removed the butterfly and Simone twitched at the movement against her sensitive nub. Then he gently wiped her clean.

Jackson laid back down after they were clean, and they snuggled close together. The three of them sighed deeply and then chuckled at each other.

"You're mine." Simone said sleepily.

"And you're ours." They replied.

Simone wrapped snugly in their warm embrace, thought of two words before she slipped into oblivion, *I'm home*.

The End

Acknowledgements

Thank you to my parents for your continual support for my career and putting a roof over my head while I get my writing off the ground. One day I'll be able get my own place again and maybe another for you too, if I'm lucky.

And a special thanks to my Dad for helping me try to come up with a title for the book. Thanks to you, in my head THREE will forever be known as "From Unda Tundra".

Thank you to Nadia, Sam and Randi for reading, editing and/or giving me precious feedback on this novel. You can't imagine how helpful you've been. Your feedback gives me the reassurance and confidence that my books are good enough to show the world.

Thank you so much to Patrice, Marcia and Bee's Books! The word that you ladies are spreading have given my books a boost that I couldn't be more grateful for. I love your reviews and your words of praise and encouragement. You ladies remind me why I started writing to begin with- to touch people's lives and make them just a little brighter…and maybe steamier. ;)

About the Author

Twyla Turner currently resides in Arizona. She was born and raised in Joliet, Illinois, a Midwest girl at heart, though constantly moving from place to place and always thinking of where she wants to go next. Having been an avid romance novel reader since junior high and minoring in Creative Writing, she felt that it was finally time to start combining her love of travel and writing, as well as her life experiences and putting them down on "paper". Which experiences, she'll never tell…well maybe, if you ask nicely.

Connect with Me

https://twylaturner11.wix.com/novelswithcurves

Follow me:

https://www.facebook.com/twylaturner11

Twitter: @TwylaTurner11

CPSIA information can be obtained
at www.ICGtesting.com
Printed in the USA
FFOW02n2054020118
44327174-43968FF